# PAGAN'S VEIL

## Matt Eaton

# PREFACE

This novel is a work of fiction. Many of the characters contained within were prominent figures in US history.

Some are entirely fictional.

The events in the skies above Washington D.C. and across the Eastern Seaboard of the United States in 1952 — and the official response to these events — are matters of public record.

However, the full extent of government knowledge related to these events has never been made public.

This is a story about what might have occurred behind the scenes.

Moments such as these — if and when they occurred — were played out amongst small unacknowledged cabals and classified Top Secret. In these instances, the words and actions of all characters are entirely my invention.

However, they are drawn from extensive research in the field of ufology, conducted over many decades by dedicated investigative writers and the US Government's own Project Blue Book.

In July 2022, the US Department of Defense created AARO — the All-domain Anomaly Resolution Office — to once more examine credible sightings of objects in our skies and oceans that defy explanation. Whether this will bring new truths to light remains to be seen.

**Matt Eaton**

# ONE

June 30, 1952

Helen Barber sucked on her cigarette like it was the only thing keeping her alive. She kept throwing furtive glances around the diner and out the window, to the bustle of black faces moving up and down M Street.

She didn't want anybody to know she was meeting with a reporter — Barber's job and her liberty depended on keeping that a secret. She was feeling very much like a fish out of water. Edna Drake had, for reasons known only to herself, chosen to meet Barber in a colored eatery in Southwest D.C., a part of town Barber normally avoided like the plague.

The place itself seemed familiar enough. The booths were a clean, cheerful mix of white vinyl cushioned seats and baby blue Formica tabletops. On the surface, it could have been any normal whites-only diner. Except that they were the only two white faces in the joint, and Barber thought the two of them were too conspicuous. An oily odor coming from the kitchen was not at all to her liking.

Edna, on the other hand, felt right at home. "Relax Helen, nobody around here knows you."

"Easy for you to say."

"If anybody followed you, we'd see them a mile away."

With a gun to her head, Barber might have grudgingly admitted this made sense; this only served to intensify her frustration. She pulled out a copy of *The Times-Herald* from her purse and slapped it down on the table. "I stuck my neck out for page three?"

"I don't know what to say, Helen. I mean, it wasn't a big news day and I'd had high hopes too, but I don't get to decide where the paper runs my stories."

Mamma Rey delivered their coffees and pulled out her notepad. "What'll it be? Breakfast or lunch? We in between. I can do eggs or chitlins. Or both. Both is goo-ood, m'hm."

"I'll have some eggs, Mamma," Edna said. "And some of that fried chicken I can smell."

Mamma Rey's café was a local institution.

"Nothing for me," said Barber, without bothering to meet Mamma's gaze. "I'm not staying."

Mamma threw Barber a none-too-subtle "screw you sister" with her eyebrow — to which Barber was oblivious. She smiled at Edna. "Eggs and fried chicken comin' right up, sugar."

"I take it you live around here," said Barber.

"Next door. Above the tailor shop. I'm not sure for how much longer. The Government wants to put a wrecking ball through Southwest D.C."

"Can't happen soon enough if you ask me," said Barber, drawing back hard on her cigarette until it burnt to the edge of her fingers.

Barber and Drake had met through a mutual friend. As two women working deep inside a man's world, they'd struck up a connection. Barber was managing editor of the Air Intelligence Digest, a collation of works of interest for officers in the Pentagon with proper clearance. Barber herself was Eyes Only; she didn't see the most sensitive material, but plenty crossed her desk to make a reporter's mouth water.

Barber's position might have been a testament to equal opportunity in the military, if not for the fact that she had gotten her job because no man had wanted it.

"Will you for the love of God tell me why you had to share the credit with Joe Eldridge?" Barber asked. "This was your story."

"That was my editor's idea. Having Joe's byline there with mine is protection for you. This way, it looks like the leak came from one of his Capitol sources."

Eldridge had a long list of contacts on Capitol Hill, but Helen Barber wasn't one of them.

"You did all the work."

"You're right," Edna agreed. "But I don't mind sharing the heat on this one."

"Yet the name Joseph Eldridge was not enough to elevate the story to a more deserving position of prominence in the paper."

"This story is being seen by the people who count, don't you worry about that."

Helen Barber was good at her job. She had to be; she wouldn't have gotten anywhere on looks alone.

Edna was well aware that women at the *Times-Herald* were ranked on appearance more than ability, and knew how to grease that wheel. Barber however looked like she had given up that fight a long time ago. She was probably ten years older than Edna, but looked like she was pushing fifty. A career spinster, Barber kept her hair dourly pulled back into a bun, with pronounced crow's feet from years of chain smoking and a perpetual scowl of disapproval to match. She'd given up all pretense of needing the approval of any man.

Edna had been a wall flower in high school. Back then, she would never have called herself good looking.

Before the war, the Rockaway Boardwalk had been her entire universe. Edna often wondered whether she'd still be there now, if not for Hitler's Germany and the date which would "live in infamy" that had compelled America to join the fight. Against her father's advice, she'd signed up for the Army Nursing Corps.

In her months of following the Allied advance through Europe, Edna and the other nurses had enjoyed the attention lavished on them by all those lonely, battle-weary boys. It had been a crash course in the mindset of the opposite sex — not that there was a whole lot to understand.

She'd learned a lot from other women too. Particularly from going on leave in northern Italy, where she had found herself fascinated by the allure and bravado of courtship. She had returned to New York with jet-black hair like Sophia Loren and had begun dressing to accentuate her ample curves.

Two months back at home with her folks in Rockaway after the war was enough to know she couldn't stay.

Had it been this way after the First World War? Had years of self-reliance and gritty survival all just fallen away when the men returned from the battle fields? It was beyond her why so many women seemed happy to settle for being an adornment. Maybe she knew too much. They were, after all, simple creatures. Stroke them just right and they purred like pussycats. But Edna had no time for men who needed to feel they were in charge.

Edna suspected the only pussycat in Helen Barber's life was a four-legged Tom, spraying the rugs and scratching up the furniture in her smokey one-bedder.

She'd leaked Edna an application from a Georgetown University researcher, chasing government funding to study the flying saucer phenomenon in Europe. Political scientist Dr Stephan Possony had argued that the recent rash of sightings across the US presented a security risk, if these craft proved to be Russian-built.

But it got better. Dr Possony was also a security consultant to the US Air Force. He was proposing to visit Europe in the company of Lt. Colonel Edwin Sterling from US Air Force Intelligence. In other words, a well-connected academic with USAF intelligence connections was acknowledging the reality of a phenomenon the Air Force had been trying hard to deny publicly.

"I went out on a limb here, Edna. Do you have any idea of the risk I've taken?" Barber hissed.

"I do. Trust me, I do. We're the same, you and me."

Barber laughed. "Cut the crap, sister."

"I don't mean we look the same. Clearly that's not..." Edna pulled herself up just in time. Barber lit another cigarette and sucked hard. Edna persisted. "What I mean is, you and I both believe the public has a right to know the truth about the men running this country."

"Is that right?"

"They can't just do as they please behind closed doors with no accountability and expect our unswerving faith."

"I see where this is going and I'll stop you there," said Barber. "You're right. I see stuff all the time that makes me want to throw my typewriter across the room. Or leak it to the media. Mostly I don't dare — because I know it'll trace back to my desk. They watch me as closely as I watch them."

"Then why come to me at all?" Edna asked.

"This one was different," said Barber. "Like you say, your source could have been inside the Capitol or the university — it didn't have to come from the Pentagon. This was a one-off, kid. If I leak to you again and they find out, they'll lock me up and throw away the key."

"But come on, Helen, we've only just started," Edna persisted. "What you gave me is signs of the light under the door. I want to kick that door wide open."

Barber smiled wearily. "Don't be in too much of a hurry."

Edna stared out the window at the passersby. "The only reason I'm in a hurry is everyone else is moving too slow."

# TWO

July 1, 1952

Edna kept her eyes on the telephone, willing it to ring. She'd spent an entire afternoon fruitlessly chasing comments for a follow-up story on Dr Possony. Everyone had clammed up. Neither Possony nor Colonel Sterling were available for comment. She'd overheard Sterling yelling at his secretary that Edna could go to hell, but she assumed that was off the record.

Everyone else in Washington was pleading ignorance. Her limited list of Pentagon contacts had turned up a big fat zero, and now, she was hoping that Joe Eldridge would have better luck.

"Yeah, well thanks anyway," Eldridge muttered dejectedly, hanging up the phone. He shrugged his shoulders without bothering to turn around. "I've got nothing for you. Everyone's crawled under a rock."

"Well... Fuck," she muttered, a little louder than intended. It earned a stern glare from features editor Theodore Mankiewicz inside his glass-paneled office. Edna pretended not to notice. Mankiewicz was one of the men in this place who terrified her the most; nothing she ever did was good enough for him. He thought you needed a pair of balls to swear in the newsroom. Which was ironic because, in her opinion, many of the rusting old codgers on this paper lacked a decent set of their own.

"This was a good story, Joe. It deserves a follow-up."

Joe turned around and smiled. "I could always manufacture a few remarks from an unnamed Capitol source."

Edna stared back at him in horror. "You wouldn't."

Joe shrugged. "No, you're right. I wouldn't. But it's tempting sometimes. Ever since the war ended, everyone in D.C. is more concerned with covering their asses than doing the right thing by the American people."

"The right thing in this case being?

"Talking to the *Times-Herald,* of course." It sounded hokey, but he was serious. "Democracy is no better than dictatorship if the people in power aren't held accountable."

"Couldn't have said it better myself."

"I've had enough of this," Joe said. "Fancy a drink?"

"Aren't you supposed to be taking your wife out to dinner?"

"That's hours away. Come on, I'm buying."

Edna liked Joe Eldridge. He wasn't especially tall and he'd been better looking before he'd lost all his hair, but he was smart, confident, funny, and a mighty fine reporter. He was also her only friend at the *Times-Herald*, which was a poor showing considering she had spent more than two years in the news pool. Trouble was, he was always hitting on her. She didn't hold it against him — she was flattered and more than a little interested — but it made the friendship side of things complicated. She knew very well that offering to buy her a drink was his way of broadening their relationship, and that one night soon he'd come knocking on her door in the wee small hours with a bottle in hand, hoping to wet his whistle at both ends.

"I'm here late, Joe, remember? You can get away with drinking on the job, but it's not the done thing for a lady."

Eldridge chuckled. He opened his mouth to speak, then closed it again. She figured he'd been about to assure her she was no lady, but he'd held his tongue at the last moment. Pity; she hated when a man pulled his punch lines.

"Drinking is how I get all my best story leads," he said.

"Figures. Now if you could just find a way to stop writing like an old drunk, you'd have a future in this business."

Eldridge clutched his heart. "Ow, she got me. A cruel blow. Now I really need a drink. Last chance…"

"Get out of here, ya bum."

"Suit yourself. Just tell me you'll miss me."

"Are you kidding? From this distance, I could get you right between the eyes."

He laughed. "You're on fire tonight, Drake." Joe Eldridge threw on his coat and hat, then straightened his tie. "Later, sister."

Edna watched him cross paths with Danny the mail boy, who was holding out an envelope. Eldridge took it, looked it over, then threw it at Edna. "Fan mail," he said, walking away.

The envelope was addressed to both of them. She tore it open with low expectations; Eldridge had fobbed it off because he thought the contents wouldn't be worth their attention.

One glance at the document inside told Edna he couldn't have been more wrong.

# THREE

J uly 2, 1952

Jimmy's Diner was right across the street from the paper, but Eldridge was late. Edna was on her second coffee and couldn't stop herself from compulsively reading the letter over and over.

It was stamped Top Secret Majestic, supposedly written by Admiral Roscoe Hillenkoetter and marked for the urgent consideration of three men — CIA Director General Walter Smith, and Air Force Chief of Staff General Hoyt Vandenberg. The third was President Truman himself. The letter was a brief request for permission to conduct a test flight of an aircraft codenamed FS-1. On its own, this would seem neither unusual nor newsworthy. But the letter included a strange remark about the craft itself:

*"...progress limited in determining composition of outer hull. Project engineers yet to confirm method of propulsion."*

Hillenkoetter said they had made advances in "understanding the method of craft's operation" and hence was requesting permission to conduct a flight test.

Since when did such tests require presidential approval? And what sort of plane could be beyond the understanding of aeronautical engineers?

Then there was the fact that Hillenkoetter referred to himself as "FS-1 LIAISON." Truman had unceremoniously sacked Hillenkoetter as CIA Director in 1950, after two massive intelligence blunders. The agency had failed to predict the first Soviet nuclear test in 1949, then the following year America's spooks didn't see it coming when the communists had invaded South Korea. So why would Hillenkoetter be Truman's liaison on a top-secret research program? Was this some sort of captured Russian experimental plane, or something even more interesting? FS-1. As in Flying Saucer? Surely it couldn't be that obvious.

The letter had been mailed from the City Post Office; the reporters' names and the newspaper's street address were typed on a label affixed to the front of the envelope. No return address, no note with the letter — Edna had no idea who had sent it or where it had come from.

Which was a problem.

She had left a note on Eldridge's desk, asking him to meet her at 7.30am. He always started early on the political round, and she didn't want to talk about it in the middle of the newsroom.

He finally showed his face around eight o'clock. "Sorry," Joe said breathlessly, sliding into the booth. He mouthed "black coffee" at the approaching waitress, who nodded and headed off to pour him a cup. "I've been on the phone with Senator Margaret Smith. She wouldn't shut up."

Edna frowned. "She always has a lot to say." Edna felt he wasn't showing America's first and only female senator the respect she deserved.

"Don't I know it. She's certainly no fan of Joe McCarthy."

"I've heard."

Senator Smith's 1950 'Declaration of Conscience' against what she'd called 'McCarthyism' was already Washington legend.

"She could run for president one day, you know," Edna added.

"A woman president," said Eldridge, "that'll be the day."

The coffee came and he gulped half of it down in one go. He looked rough. Another day, another hangover. "What's up? Why the cloak and dagger?"

Edna showed him the letter. "I'm not due back in the office until this afternoon, but I didn't think this could wait."

Eldridge placed it down on the table and looked up at her without any obvious sign of enthusiasm. "Well, it's a great story — if it's true."

"Doesn't it strike you as authentic?"

"Not for me to say. We need to verify it. Go to the sources."

"Assuming it is genuine, why would Hillenkoetter be involved? Doesn't that seem odd? He's persona non grata at the White House."

Eldridge shrugged. "Maybe not so strange. Roscoe fell on his sword because that's what happens to men in charge of political institutions when something goes wrong. But it's not like he was personally to blame for the CIA's shortcomings. Truman sacked him reluctantly. In an odd kind of a way, seeing Hillenkoetter's name on this lends it credibility. It's unlikely you'd put his name on a hoax if you wanted people to believe it."

Edna smiled. "You have a devious mind, Mr Eldridge. I like it."

He waved at the waitress for a refill. "Roscoe Hillenkoetter is a good place to start. I can start making some discreet inquiries about how we can get to him."

"Actually," she said, "I'd rather you didn't. Will you let me have this one?"

He looked surprised. "Then what am I doing here?"

"You're helping a colleague. I trust you, which is more than I can say for half the people in that newsroom. But this was my story to begin with. Your name was mostly there for political cover."

Eldridge had the temerity to look put out. "I did more than that, Edna." He stopped talking while the waitress topped up his coffee, staring at Edna like they were two prize fighters pulled out of a clinch.

Alone again he said, "We got that story over the line together — my name is on that envelope too."

She reached across the table and put her hand on his. "Please, Joe. I need this more than you. Will you leave it with me? Just for a few days?"

Eldridge sat back in his chair petulantly, placated by the touch of her hand, but aware he was being manipulated. "Just do me a favor," he said. "Don't take it to Bazy. Not yet. She'll want to run it straight away, but you'll get a better story if you dig around a bit more. You want to be sure this is genuine, or you'll have egg on your face."

Edna nodded and smiled demurely. *Times-Herald* publisher Ruth 'Bazy' McCormick Miller was only thirty-one, and had shown no hesitation in printing sensationalist flights of fancy to sell papers. She'd been handed control of the paper by its owner and her uncle, Colonel Robert McCormick, who also owned the *Chicago Tribune*. Edna was five years younger than Bazy, but she'd seen a lot more of the world. While Bazy was breeding Arabian horses and frocking up to live the high life, Edna had been up to her neck in blood and guts in a field hospital in Western Europe.

"Be discreet," said Eldridge. "Take it slowly. This could be an attempt to discredit the paper; we've made plenty of enemies in Washington. Powerful forces at work and all that. You don't want to be throwing yourself under the tank treads."

"Yes, good advice. Thank you, Joe."

Eldridge got up to leave. "Coffee's on you today." It was a subtle slap-down, but she got the message. She almost threw the salt shaker at him.

No way in hell was Joe Eldridge getting his name on this story.

# FOUR

J uly 2, 1952

Edna's taxicab had pulled up in front of a very unattractive two-story duplex in Ridgecrest, one of Washington's more forgettable suburbs. The street was quiet enough, but the houses were all depressingly identical. The timid street lights revealed a line of houses in varying states of disrepair. It was only nine o'clock at night, but lights were out already in half the houses. It was so quiet it gave her the willies.

She paid her driver what she owed him, plus an extra fifty cents. "I can't afford to have you waiting here with the meter running, but if you come back for me in half an hour, I'll be more generous on the return trip."

He looked her up and down. "I got nowhere else to be, toots. I can wait a while."

"Suit yourself. But turn that meter off or I'm walking home."

Helen Barber's front door was painted blue, the only sign of cheerfulness in what otherwise looked like a brown brick mausoleum. Edna knocked loudly three times. After a few seconds, she heard movement. The door opened and a wall of smoke hit Edna like a German mustard gas attack. Edna coughed.

"What are you doing here?" Barber asked angrily.

"You wouldn't take my calls."

"Most people take that as a hint."

"Look, calm down, will you? I need to talk."

Barber's cat scuttled through Edna's legs and disappeared into the night. "Now look what you've done — Harry come back here!"

"I don't think Harry likes you as much as you think."

"Go to hell," said Barber.

"Look, I'm sorry Helen, but it's important. I need your help."

Barber stared at her, shaking her head.

An old man appeared on a stoop across the street. "Everything all right, Helen?"

"Fine, Jack. It's a friend of mine. She's been drinking."

Edna turned and gave him a wave. Seeing it was another woman, Jack waved back and went inside.

"For Christ's sake, get inside before someone else sees you."

Edna stepped through the door without hesitation, immediately wondering if the whole excursion was a mistake. By the time she reached the lounge room, the smoke was so thick her eyes were stinging.

"Jesus Helen, how about opening a window?"

"Whenever I do that, Harry Truman jumps out and I don't see him for days."

Edna looked at her curiously. "You named your cat after the President?"

"I found him going through my bins the day after Truman's inauguration. It seemed like a good idea at the time. Are you going to tell me what you're doing here?"

Edna stared at her a moment, trying to get a read on Barber's reaction. Did she really have no idea what it was about? "I got something very interesting in the post yesterday. Sent anonymously. A letter, stamped Top Secret. Don't suppose you'd know anything about that?"

Barber said nothing for a moment. "You think I sent it to you."

"Did you?"

Barber sat down on her well-worn green two-seater and pulled a cigarette loose from the pack lying on the arm. She lit it up and sucked back the smoke like it had healing properties. "Why would I do something stupid like that?"

"Because despite all your bluster, I think you want to help me."

"It wasn't me, Drake."

"I have it with me. Wanna see it?"

"No," said Barber emphatically, blowing out a wall of smoke. "OK, yes. Show it to me."

Edna pulled a small envelope out of her purse, removed the letter, and handed it over. As Barber read it in silence, Edna noticed the brown tar stains on the wallpaper. A shelf of tiny collectables in the corner was the only other personal touch in the room. There was no radio, no television. Books were stacked beside the couch at the foot of a standing ashtray, overflowing with butts.

"I'm sorry Helen, but Harry Truman has already flown the coop and I'm dying in here." She pulled back the curtains and pushed open a window as far as it would go. Fresh air invaded the room like a thief in the night.

"I have no idea what this is," said Barber, handing back the letter.

Edna took it and looked at it for the umpteenth time. "You've never heard of Project FS-1?"

"I don't have Top Secret clearance."

"Does it look to you like the sort of thing that might be genuine?"

"You're worried someone's trying to feed you disinformation?"

Edna said, "The thought had crossed my mind, yes."

"It's possible. Seeing Hillenkoetter's name there is odd. I didn't think he and the President got on so well."

"Is there any chance you could ask around?"

Barber laughed. "Can you hear yourself? If this letter is genuine, just having it in your possession is enough to have you tossed in jail."

"Who's going to find out?"

"You write a story, they'll find out soon enough."

"That's not going to happen until I can find someone to authenticate this."

"Well, don't look at me."

"Come on, Helen. Us gals need to stick together," Edna insisted. "Don't you want to help stick it to the man?"

"Sorry, I can't help you, kid. You need someone higher up the food chain. If this is the real deal, you're going to need a team of reporters working on it."

"Joe Eldridge has offered to help."

"There you go."

"He's good," said Edna, "but like most people in that newsroom, he's only looking out for himself. I'd lay short odds on him tossing me aside once he thinks it's genuine. But it's my story, and you're my contact. I like you, Helen. Your motives are pure."

Barber shook her head. "Nobody's motives are pure, kid. Sometimes you just need to love the one you're with. If Eldridge is offering to help, let him. Because if this is the genuine article, I don't wanna know about it."

"But you want to do what's right."

Barber stubbed out her cigarette. "I'm not going to jail for you or anyone else."

Edna sighed. She threw herself down on the lounge beside Barber. "I have issues, OK? It's fair to say my dad is the only man I've ever fully trusted."

"Take a look around," Barber beckoned with a wave of her cigarette. "This is what you get when you lock men out of your life. Is this what you want for yourself?"

It was an utterly depressing thought. "You'll always have Harry Truman."

"That damn cat will be tearing the flesh from my bones the minute I show signs of weakness," Barber said. "Now you need to get the hell out of here, I want to go to bed."

Edna started for the door.

"There is one thing you could do," said Barber. "Try giving Project Blue Book a call. I hear those guys take this stuff pretty seriously."

"Aren't they based at Wright-Patterson in Ohio?"

Barber tried to smile. She didn't quite pull it off, but Edna gave her points for effort. "They have an office at the Pentagon. Major Dewey Fournet is your man. Blue Book are doing solid work. It's ruffling feathers in Air Force intelligence, but they've got some serious brass behind them."

"General Garland?" said Edna. Barber nodded conspiratorially. Garland was high up in the Air Force directorate of intelligence; Edna knew he was Barber's source for the juiciest flying saucer info.

"Garland told me he saw a flying saucer himself," said Barber. "Ever since then, he's been hell-bent on finding out what's going on. But he won't talk to you. Give Dewey a call. If he opens up, maybe you can work your way up the food chain."

"I'm not sure I'd trust a General to give it to me straight," said Edna.

"That's your problem, not mine. Like I said, Eldridge is in a position to open doors for you — think long and hard before you say no to that. You won't make any friends asking these questions. You need all the help you can get."

As the door closed behind her, Edna was left with the strongest suspicion that Barber knew more about the letter than she was letting on. Whoever had sent it had done it within hours of seeing Edna's flying saucer story in the paper. Had Barber leaked the FS-1 letter, then had second thoughts? It would explain why she'd denied it.

# FIVE

J uly 3, 1952

"You're late." The night editor, Bob Steele, wasn't happy as Edna arrived in the newsroom floor.

"I told you, Bob. I was out chasing up a lead. I said I'd be late, remember?"

Sure, he remembered. But he was still going to hold it against her.

"There's a fire in an apartment block up near Eighteenth and Florida Avenue. Two floors burning. Get up there and check it out, but I need you back here before one o'clock."

Chasing cops and fire engines — typical night shift. Most of the city's inhabitants were safely tucked up in bed. In the wee small hours, it was drunks, desperadoes, and dipshits who made the morning news.

The crime and grime round didn't let up all night. Steele kept Edna bouncing in and out of the office like a yo-yo. By the time the sun was creeping in through the newsroom blinds, she'd written four stories — the fire (two injured, four apartments gutted), a mugging, a burst sewage pipe that sent a river of shit cascading through Downtown, followed by a restaurant robbery in Chinatown. It was the second time in a week the restaurant had been done over at gunpoint; someone had forgotten to pay the police for protection. Detectives from the newly formed D.C. internal affairs unit were all over it.

The early edition of the paper soaked all of this up like the proverbial sponge. With ten editions a day to print, they needed every word Edna wrote.

She was utterly exhausted and ready for bed, but it was only with all of that out of the way that Edna could turn her mind to what Helen Barber had suggested — tracking down Major Dewey Fournet at Project Blue Book.

She ventured into the clippings library and learned Blue Book was an Air Force project, based at Wright-Patterson and created from the ashes of something called Project Grudge. The former had been shut down by General Charles Cabell and reformed into Blue Book, ostensibly with a view of treating the saucer topic with rational objectivity.

Among the stacks, Edna located the *Life* magazine story on flying saucers that had caused such a stir when it hit the newsstands in April. The explosive quote from aerodynamicist and physicist Dr Maurice Biot was already highlighted in the clipping file:

*"The least improbable explanation is that these things are artificial and controlled ... My opinion for some time has been that they have an extraterrestrial origin."*

But there was another quote that caught her eye:

*"The higher you go in the Air Force," conceded one Intelligence officer, "the more seriously they take the flying saucers."*

Edna believed that to be the case, although finding somebody in the Air Force who was willing to talk about it was another matter entirely.

Telephoning the Pentagon proved an exercise in futility. The switchboard operators, she strongly suspected, had been instructed to act as a roadblock to unknown callers. It took her nearly fifteen minutes of persistence while she was misdirected through three wrong departments, before her call finally ended up in the office of Major Dewey Fournet.

"I'm sorry, Major Fournet is not available to take your call," his secretary declared.

Oh, for God's sake. She could hear a man's voice in the background. Edna took a deep breath. "Can you tell me when he will be available?"

"He has meetings for the rest of today and he's flying to Ohio this evening."

She was getting the kiss-off. She left her name and number, making sure to identify herself as a *Times-Herald* reporter, so Fournet didn't simply write her off as a lunatic with a bee in her bonnet about little green men.

But as she hung up the phone, Edna realized she'd gone about it all wrong. Fournet had probably dodged the call precisely because she was a reporter. She remembered Helen Barber saying something about how *Life* magazine had rubbed the defense brass the wrong way. Blue Book's officers might have been instructed not to speak to reporters.

Fournet wouldn't be calling back.

There was no misunderstanding at the switchboard when she rang back and asked to be put through to the Office of the Chief of Naval Operations. But she was kept on the line for nearly five minutes, before she heard the voice of Admiral William Fechteler's secretary.

This time, she had a cover story ready. "My name is Edna Quinlivan. I'm hoping you can help me. I'm trying to find Admiral Roscoe Hillenkoetter. He's a friend of the family, you see."

"I'm afraid we don't give out that kind of detail over the telephone, my dear."

As expected.

"Oh no." Edna let out a couple of short, sharp sobs. One of her better efforts. "I'm sorry. It's just that both my parents have been killed in a car accident. I know they'd want Roscoe to hear the news from me."

There was silence at the other end of the phone, and for a moment Edna thought she'd blown it.

"You poor thing. Let me see what I can do."

Edna heard a filing cabinet being pulled open, urgent whispering, the words inaudible. Finally the filing cabinet slammed shut again.

"I'm sorry dear — all I can tell you is that Admiral Hillenkoetter is on leave. He was serving with the Pacific Fleet in South Korea, but his posting there concluded last September. I simply don't have any more information."

Meaning none she was at liberty to divulge.

"You don't have a current address for him and his wife?"

"No dear, I'm afraid not. Which is unusual, now you come to mention it. I'm sorry I can't be of any more help. All the best to you now. God bless. Goodbye."

The phone went dead.

Edna Drake was still staring at the back of the empty chair in front of her when Joe Eldridge threw his suit jacket over the back of it. "Morning Drake."

"Oh, hey Joe."

"You look like you've seen a ghost."

It took her a moment to register what he'd said. "I just had the strangest phone conversation. Apparently, Roscoe Hillenkoetter is missing. The Chief of Naval Operations has no record for him since he returned from South Korea, last September."

Eldridge smiled. "Is that what they told you?"

"Yep. Just then."

"They're giving you the run-around."

"Yeah maybe," she conceded. "But I just delivered an Academy Award-winning performance as an orphaned daughter seeking the solace of a family friend. The woman I spoke to bought it hook, line and sinker. She was trying to help me, but had no home address for him in their files."

"Sounds like the Admiral is working off the books."

Edna nodded. "Which is all very interesting." She glanced around and lowered her voice. "But it doesn't get me any closer to verifying that letter."

"You need to broaden your horizons."

"Care to be more specific?"

Eldridge grinned. "What's the best way to loosen lips?"

"Alcohol."

"Give that woman a cigar."

"I'm not with you."

"You will be. Tomorrow night. Big Independence Day party in Georgetown. You're invited."

"Am I?"

"You are now."

# SIX

July 4, 1952

Edna was feeling like an imposter as Joe's car reached the long driveway of Lady Norma Lewis's Georgetown mansion. She had always been intimidated by gregarious wealth; it was responsible for the world's greatest ills.

Not that the communists were any better. In Berlin, she'd witnessed the black heart at the core of the Soviet ideal. Russian soldiers there had preyed on the weak with a brutality she wouldn't have believed possible, if she hadn't seen it for herself. She had no problem with anyone turning a buck, but entering Lady Lewis's wrought-iron front gates still felt like an act of moral compromise.

Edna Drake told herself the world would turn regardless of her misgivings. Besides, she was here for a reason.

At the top of the drive, an immaculately dressed negro valet was waiting for them, his white-gloved hand extended for Eldridge to hand over his car keys. Resplendent but reassuringly uncomfortable in his rented tux, Joe was reluctant to hand them over. "You'll take good care of this car won't you, boy?"

"Yes sir," the valet replied confidently.

Edna detected a twist of irony in the man's smile. Joe's '48 Studebaker would undoubtedly be the cheapest car in this parking lot.

Her mouth fell open as she looked up the stairs to the mansion's open foyer. "Wowee, this is quite the slum." The two-story Georgian pile reminded her of the buildings in France they'd used as army hospitals. She took a deep breath. Her little black dress revealed plenty of cleavage, and an abundance of leg. She felt Joe's eyes upon her, looking her up and down.

"You are gorgeous tonight, Edna Drake."

"Thank you, suh," she replied, giving him her best southern belle.

The heels may yet prove to be a mistake. They were already rubbing, and they left her a couple of inches taller than her companion. Eldridge smiled, offered the crook of his arm, and together they made their way to the mansion's double-doored entrance.

"You'll like Norma Lewis," Joe assured her. "You've got a lot in common."

Edna laughed. "Yeah, I can see we have a bunch to talk about."

Lady Lewis was renowned for her Washington soirees. A party woman in every sense of the word, she had not let the death of her third husband in 1950 dampen her social life. Parties in the wealthy suburbs of D.C. regularly brimmed with intrigue and backroom deals. Lady Lewis went out of her way to encourage such affairs, ensuring her events were always very well attended.

Edna knew Bazy Miller would be somewhere here in the crowd, along with her former mentor, the paper's social columnist Martha Blair. Edna planned to walk quickly in the opposite direction the moment she spotted Mrs Blair in the crowd; it would mean being regaled with biographies on all of the most eligible bachelors. The fact that Edna Drake was in her late twenties and still single was a matter of no small concern among the women of the *Times-Herald*.

From the vast foyer, a staircase rose majestically to the second floor. The ballroom was an annex, opening off the foyer to their right. Here, two negro footmen took their coats and waved them inside. The ballroom took up an entire wing of the house; its walls were lined with glass doors and windows overlooking an immaculate garden. High above them, a line of chandeliers illuminated the vast space, already packed with guests; everyone who was anyone. She spotted Democrat Senate Majority Leader 'Mac' McFarland talking to Barry Goldwater, the Phoenix Republican who was likely to challenge him in the November election.

Edna pointed the pair out to Joe. "They're being downright civil to one another."

"These parties are treated as neutral territory. Everyone takes the night off from politics," he explained.

A string quartet hidden somewhere in the crowd was playing a Strauss waltz. Nobody was dancing. It felt like she'd stepped back in time to pre-Civil War days; Lady Lewis clearly had a fondness for colored help. There wasn't a white face among the wait staff, who moved seamlessly through the crowd sporting trays of drinks and hors d'oeuvres.

The guests themselves were all tuxedos and cocktail gowns with not a hair out of place. Edna quickly checked herself in a nearby mirror, hoping she didn't look as uncomfortable as she felt.

Eldridge was still talking. "...in France with the Red Cross in the Great War" — he meant Lady Lewis — "I'm sure she'll regale you with gory stories if you let her."

"I served in the other one, remember? The second world war?"

"Same shit, different year," said Eldridge, who seemed to enjoy getting under her skin. He'd served in the Navy and fought as a gunner in the Pacific. Eldridge was one of the last men to make it off the USS Yorktown alive after it was hit by Japanese torpedoes, during the Battle of Midway. She knew he'd seen his own share of horror, yet sometimes he seemed almost casually dismissive of his own service. Eldridge never talked about it; they had that in common. The chaos and hell she'd seen with her own eyes would remain with Edna until the day she died. Words had never gone close to setting the scene, or explaining the myriad of ways in which their lives had been tipped upside down and torn apart.

"Just so we're clear, I was a photographer as well as a nurse," she said. "I worked with Martha Gellhorn."

Another Martha.

Eldridge managed to look both surprised and impressed. "The war correspondent?"

"In Berlin."

"How come you never mentioned that before?"

"I guess it never came up."

He nodded. "Wasn't Gellhorn one of Hemingway's wives?"

"She was indeed."

"I actually think she was smarter than Hemingway," he said, surprising her.

"Martha thought so too. That's why she divorced him. The bastard did his best to stop her going to Normandy for the Allied invasion. She got there in spite of him — hid in the bathroom of a hospital ship. She was the only woman to land on Omaha Beach on D-Day. She pretended to be a stretcher bearer, for God's sake. But the British found her out and sent her back to London. All because she's not a man."

"Fighting on two fronts at once," Eldridge replied. "Martha's biggest problem might have been her refusal to accept the importance of being Ernest."

"That's good," said Edna, "you should write that one down."

"Some say she slept her way to the top. Not me, but some."

Edna shrugged. "She wasn't averse to using sex to open doors."

"Wasn't she sleeping with General James Gavin?" General Gavin had been the man in charge of the American sector in Berlin, shortly after the war. "That's gotta open some few doors."

"Martha was never going to let herself be defined by a man. We roamed Berlin together for weeks. God, what an eye-opener. The squalor, the desperation. Humanity reduced to its horrible essence. I've never seen anything like it." Even now, the scenes flooded back into her thoughts like it had all been yesterday. "She was in love with Jim Gavin. At least, that's what she told me," Edna continued. "Wouldn't marry him because she didn't want to be an Army wife."

Eldridge spotted a whiskey on a passing tray and moved in for the kill, grabbing a champagne at the same motion and passing it to Edna. They clinked glasses. Joe's most alluring feature was his self-confidence. She admired it particularly because it was something she had always lacked. He could be a bit tedious at times with his one-track mind, but he valued her mind as well as her body, which set him apart from almost every other man Edna knew. "So tell me how a couple of grubby *Times-Herald* reporters get themselves invited here?" she asked.

"Lady Lewis is a press sympathizer," said Eldridge, "and an avowed Republican. She loves us."

Edna groaned.

"Her dearly departed Sir Willmott was the Washington correspondent for the *London Times*. He was also Great Britain's so-called 'Ambassador Incognito'."

"Doesn't being incognito defeat the purpose of an ambassador?"

"It's so very British, right? A role assigned by *The Times* to serve as an unofficial agent of British foreign policy. Old Willmott was the perfect man for the job. He used to hold court once a week with diplomats and journalists. Liquid lunches where they'd pick apart foreign policy and share each another's mistresses."

"Blimey," said Edna in her best mock cockney. "Lady Lewis put up with all that?"

"I'm sure she knew. He did love her, but it's true to say he loved many women. And all of this" — he waved his hand around the room — "it's all Norma's money. The product of *two* divorces and canny investment of the proceeds. Willmott had money, but he was lazy. Norma worked out how to get rich and stay that way."

"I'm sure she earnt every penny," said Edna. "And I bet she knows where all the Washington skeletons are hiding."

The string quartet moved on to some cheerful Mozart. Edna twirled on the spot. It wasn't every year the Fourth of July fell on a Friday, and tonight she was letting her hair down. "Who's first?" she asked.

Joe pointed. "There's the Lady herself, talking to Gordon Gray."

"I know that name."

"Let's start there." Eldridge took her hand and gently led her toward their hostess. Lady Lewis was in her mid-sixties, dressed like a woman thirty years younger and somehow managing to pull it off. Not many women her age could manage a red off-the-shoulder V-neck cocktail dress, but her skin was almost flawless, her hair was a jaunty shade of auburn (definitely a dye job), and her diamond necklace was almost as enchanting as her smile.

"Joseph, how wonderful to see you again, my dear," Lady Lewis said, turning to meet their approach with one arm graciously out-stretched.

Eldridge kissed her on the cheek. "I was very pleased to receive the invitation."

"I see you brought a friend."

"Lady Norma Lewis, may I introduce you to my colleague, Miss Edna Drake."

"Delighted," said Lady Lewis. She might even have meant it. "Have either of you met Gordon Gray? He's one of the President's closest friends, don't you know?"

Eldridge shook his hand.

Gray nodded politely to Edna. "Our hostess has a tendency to exaggerate."

Lady Lewis looked ready to move on, but Edna touched her on the arm to keep her attention. "Joe was telling me about your work with the Red Cross. I was a nurse with the 24th Evacuation Hospital in Europe."

"My goodness. That was one of those mobile hospitals, wasn't it?"

Edna nodded, smiling. "We started in Normandy and moved through Belgium and Holland. We were the first evac hospital into Germany."

Lady Lewis squeezed her arm earnestly and leant close. "We both know they couldn't have done it without you." She said it with such conviction and Edna knew then they would be friends. Lady Lewis, meanwhile, was still greasing the wheel. "Mr Gray was until recently the Secretary of the Army. Gordon, don't just stand there, thank Miss Drake for her service." Before Gray could even open his mouth to respond, Lady Lewis was fleeing to attend to another of her guests, leaving the President's man alone with the reporters.

Gray smiled politely and raised his glass. "Here's to you, Miss Drake."

Eldridge patted Edna on the shoulder. "Lovely to meet you, Gordon, but you must excuse me; I just saw somebody I've been meaning to speak to."

"Reporters, right?" Edna said apologetically. She hated small talk; she was no good at it. A terrible admission for a reporter to make. Her best efforts came off clumsy, and her worst at times proved to be offensive. But that was why she was here. "I suppose there's a veritable feast of familiar faces here for you tonight. And here you are stuck with me."

Gordon Gray shrugged, reading her shyness and taking pity on her. "I don't often make it out to social events. Life has a habit of getting in the way."

"I guess you'll have a keen eye on Chicago next week." She meant the Republican National Convention, due to start on Monday. Gray pouted pensively, and Edna couldn't get a read on what he was thinking. "Have you picked a horse in that race?" she asked. "The owner of our paper is raising objections to General Eisenhower. Thinks he's too liberal."

She was talking too much. Being indiscrete. But Gray seemed to enjoy her candor. "There's been some persistent speculation about General MacArthur," said Gray, "though Taft still has his nose in front coming into the final turn."

Edna said, "I'm guessing Mr Truman isn't so happy about MacArthur."

"No," Gray agreed avidly.

"But with two generals to choose from, I can't help thinking one of them must surely get the nod."

"A bold call, but you may be right. America does love a general in the White House."

"Although it'd be the first time this century," she said. "How would you feel, working for a Republican president?"

"It's always an honor to serve one's country, Miss Drake."

"I hear you're regarded as one of the more brilliant men in Washington."

"I don't know whether to be feel flattered or frightened by that."

She smiled. "Maybe you should be both."

Gray laughed. "You are a breath of fresh air."

"My window is always wide open," she said. "I'd been hoping I might catch a glimpse of the Commander in Chief."

"Not exactly his crowd. He's at the baseball game. He and Bess love the Senators, though I hear the Yankees are all over them tonight."

"You do know him well, don't you?" Edna asked.

"As well as anyone else in the White House, I suppose."

"Am I right in thinking you're a newspaper man as well as a political heavyweight, Mr Gray?"

"That's right. I'm the publisher of the *Winston-Salem Journal*."

"You don't find that's a conflict of interest?"

He gazed long and hard into her eyes before he responded. "I keep myself at arm's length from the day-to-day operations. I have more than enough going on elsewhere to keep me busy."

"Anything I might not already know about?" Edna asked.

"Well, I'm the president of the University of North Carolina. That tends to consume most of my time these days, for better or worse."

"Yet here you are in Washington."

"I still have a toe in government waters," Gray admitted.

"Care to elaborate?" she asked.

"I'm afraid I really can't say any more than that."

"Well, now I am intrigued," she said, flashing her most winsome smile. "You're not a spook, are you?"

"Careful with that word." Gray nodded toward a passing waiter. "Someone could take it the wrong way."

Edna smiled and blushed; she knew he was only needling her. Gordon Gray was unexpectedly witty. And deliciously mysterious.

"No, I'm not a spook, Miss Drake. Just a bureaucrat."

"I'm not sure I believe you, but I won't labor the point. And it's Edna, by the way." A white man across the room caught her attention. He was quietly but firmly directing the catering staff. Norma Lewis stopped in her tracks when he waved at her. "That man with our hostess — do you know him?"

"He helps Norma out with staffing for her big events."

"Does he run some sort of colored employment agency?"

"Something along those lines, yes. I'm told he pays well above the minimum. Black or white, it's no difference to him. But this crowd loves seeing colored help. It lets them feel superior and munificent all at once."

"And Lady Lewis is happy to pay extra?"

Gray nodded, eyebrow raised. "For which I hold her in the highest estimation." He finished off his scotch and readied himself to beat a polite retreat. "You might want to watch yourself with Joe Eldridge. He's notorious."

"I've heard. But when he told me where we were going, what's a gal to do?"

"You must excuse me, Edna. I believe there are going to be fireworks."

"I'd expect nothing less."

"It was lovely to meet you. Maybe we'll run into one another again some time."

"Maybe you'll let me buy you a drink," she said.

"You are a modern girl, aren't you?"

"A pearl among swine."

Gordon Gray walked away laughing.

# SEVEN

J uly 4, 1952

The party had spilled onto the rear lawn for the light show. Edna hadn't seen Eldridge in almost half an hour, and found herself staring up at the fireworks alone. A tight scrum of men had formed around Senator Robert Taft, frontrunner for the Republican presidential nomination. They were laughing and pointing at the fireworks as if this was their own private celebration, glad-handing each other like they'd already won the election.

The only familiar face Edna had seen in the past fifteen minutes had been her boss. Bazy Miller was every inch the patrician in her gorgeous black Dior cocktail dress and elbow-length gloves. She'd nodded at Edna and rolled her eyes quickly, before promptly turning back to her conversation with a knot of senatorial wives. Edna felt certain it was an act of mercy that she hadn't been drawn into that group.

People were leaving her alone. Edna had grown weary of finding excuses to break away from tiresome conversations and lewd offers, and suspected she was starting to come across as rude and aloof.

"You look a bit lost, my dear." Lady Lewis caught her completely by surprise.

"I'm just taking it all in. Observing."

Norma Lewis patted her fondly on the arm. "These old codgers must be boring you to tears. Which is why I always have fireworks at my parties. Nothing quite like staring up at the heavens to put the dark corners of Washington into perspective."

Edna smiled, and for several moments they stared at the fireworks together. "Why do men and women always stick together at social gatherings?" she asked. "What are we so afraid of?"

"Missteps," said Lady Lewis. "Scandal. All the things that make life interesting. That stuff we love to hide behind our pretense."

"Your parties are famous, though. I'm glad I came. I know everyone wants to be on your guest list."

Lady Lewis laughed, pleased by the compliment. "You're sweet. It's true, I love beauty and glamour. I find it so enjoyable to see people at their best. I've seen more than enough of them at their worst."

"Do you ever talk about it? The war?"

"Not really."

"Don't you wish you could simply forget it all?" Edna asked.

Lady Lewis smiled sympathetically and touched her on the cheek. "In the end, I think it's better to know what men are capable of."

A cheer erupted as a large red mushroom erupted in the sky above. Edna flinched at the noise of it. For a moment, she was back in France with the night set on fire by anti-aircraft guns. "This is not my world," Edna said, "but I'm glad I got to see it. If I'm being honest though, I did come here with an ulterior motive."

"A good reporter is always working," said Lady Lewis. "That's what my husband used to say. Joe has been singing your praises around the room, you know. Who else would you like to meet? Senator Taft perhaps?"

Edna laughed nervously; it was the moment she'd been waiting for. "I've been trying to shed some light on some sensitive information that came my way. But I'm a bit light on introductions to the intelligence world."

Lady Lewis scanned her guests. "Well, you've met Gordon. Let's see, who else? Ah yes, of course, there he is. Back against the wall, sipping his whiskey, see the fellow? The one watching and not talking?"

Edna nodded, recognizing the man immediately. She couldn't believe she had failed to do so sooner. Blame it on the champagne. But he did seem to be doing his best to cling to the shadows.

"I'll wander over for a chat," said Lady Lewis. "You give it a minute then come and join us, and I'll do the introductions."

Which was how Edna found herself face-to-face with none other than the master of America's wartime intelligence service, 'Wild' Bill Donovan.

By the time Lady Lewis had finished telling Donovan how much he and Edna had in common, Edna could have kissed her. Lady Lewis quickly vanished, muttering something about the dessert tray.

Donovan, while charming, seemed distracted. He also appeared to be stone cold sober. Edna found herself taking another sip of champagne. She tried her best to sound witty and urbane. "There are such a lot of generals in Washington, don't you find, General?"

"You're right," said Donovan. "Wars do tend to boost the general population."

"General population. I like that. And what would a spymaster make of this crowd?"

His eyes flickered ever so briefly in her direction. "That depends upon the nature of your interest. Political, financial, romantic... What are you asking me, Miss Drake? I assume you arranged our meeting for a reason."

He was wily.

"I'd heard it was good legal practice to know the answer to questions before you ask them," Edna offered.

"Well, we've only just met, you see. Is it business or pleasure that brings you here tonight?" He was looking around. Watching. For what?

"A little of both."

"If it's inside information you're after, I'm afraid I don't move in those circles anymore." A wistful expression flickered briefly in his eyes. His face turned bright pink from one final burst of fireworks above them.

"Is that a note of bitterness I detect, General?"

Donovan turned toward her. "A touch of regret, maybe. I've reached that age where one tends to look back fondly on the old days. But c'est la vie, as they say in Saigon." His guard was up, and she was too drunk to charm anything out of him.

"There is something I'd very much like to talk over with you at a later date," Edna tested, "if that's at all possible."

Donovan smiled. She could see he must have been a rake in his younger days. "If it's reminiscing, then by all means. Otherwise, I doubt I'm of much use."

"Would you mind if we had a talk anyway? Somewhere quieter, when I'm a little more sober?"

"I don't have anything to say to the readers of the *Times-Herald*, other than to note that Lady Lewis has once more thrown a wonderful party."

She was losing him; Edna Drake decided to go for broke. "I wonder if you have anything to say on the topic of flying saucers?"

Donovan was momentarily taken aback, but then tried to laugh. "I don't believe in little green men. Or women. It's all hot air."

"Yet I have it from reliable sources the Government is taking the matter very seriously."

"Is that so?"

"For instance, I wonder if you've heard of something called FS-1?"

Donovan kept a straight face, but she saw his jaw tense. A brief downward glance revealed he had squeezed his hand into a fist. "It doesn't ring a bell."

Something in his tone had stiffened. He was lying. Strangely, he wasn't terribly good at it. She took a punt. "Not to worry. My source has already laid it out for me. I just thought it wouldn't hurt to seek a second opinion. It was an honor to meet you sir, but if you don't mind, I'm going to call it a night."

She was taking a risk. It would complicate matters if Edna was forced to admit the truth. Or he could simply choose not to take the bait.

But a moment later, Edna felt her fishing line pull tight.

"Tell you what," said Donovan, tapping her on the shoulder. She turned around to face him. "Let me ask around." He pulled out a business card. "Give my secretary a call in the morning."

"Tomorrow is Saturday," said Edna.

"Are you Jewish?"

She raised an eyebrow and shook her head slowly. "Is eight o'clock too early?"

"I never talk to anyone before ten on Saturdays." Donovan nodded his head gently and walked away.

Edna was still trying to get her head around what had just happened by the time she spotted Eldridge leaning against the bar. She was aching to tell him about Donovan, but decided at that moment he didn't need to know. She'd also made her mind up about something else.

"Put down the whiskey, Joe."

"Why?"

She moved in close and stared deep into his eyes. "This is your one shot. Don't blow it."

His eyes flared. Joe Eldridge put the glass down and stood up. She took him by the hand and headed for the door. By the time they had retrieved hats and coats, his car was waiting for them in the driveway.

Edna snatched up the keys from the valet. "My turn to drive."

"Fine," he said. He pulled open the passenger side door and fell into the front seat. "I'll navigate."

"Do you have anywhere in particular in mind?"

"Friend of mine's a lobbyist for the Atlantic Refining Company," Eldridge said. "He has an apartment."

"I take it he's not home."

"He's in Philadelphia for the weekend. But I know where he hides the key."

Edna started the engine. "The perfect crime." She pointed the car at the gate. "Just so we're clear Joe, from now on we're off the record."

"Roger," said Eldridge. "Deep background." He pulled an imaginary zip across his lips.

She knew all too well that suited him as much as her.

Part of Edna knew she should drive Joe home to his wife and catch a taxi home. It was a source of endless amazement that her worst ideas always made perfect sense around midnight.

# EIGHT

June 30, 1952

Even as he held the glass to his lips, Bill Donovan knew the third tumbler of scotch was a mistake. He'd never been a drinker. Tonight he was savoring the buzz, though he knew he'd pay the price in the morning.

Test pilot Tony LeVier held up a packet of Chesterfields — "You mind?"

"I'd prefer it if you didn't."

LeVier shrugged and threw the pack down on the table between them. He looked around at the dusty, wood-paneled room. It was like a cheap motel, minus the charm. "They spared no expense for you, General."

War hero, spymaster, and unofficial presidential enforcer, Donovan was no stranger to rough sleeping quarters. The cabin at White Sands wasn't exactly the trenches. "Just like summer camp," he said.

LeVier chuckled. Lockheed's chief test pilot was billeted in Las Cruces, opting to drive back and forth each day to avoid the camp-out.

Normally, the company turned on better facilities — as head of security for both Majestic-12 and the Verus Foundation, Donovan normally insisted on it.

Verus was a Truman initiative; funded privately and entirely off the books, it was tasked with collating all of America's secrets for future posterity. Truman figured America had begun to gather so many secrets, some of them could get lost along the way. Verus was a way to prevent that, and an attempt to keep people honest.

The FS-1 project was being run out of Lockheed's classified Skunkworks division. It had been hastily assembled at the behest of the Majestic-12 group: a committee of military men, technical experts, and the greatest minds in science who, on Truman's behalf, oversaw all matters involving extraterrestrial contact. Lockheed had been called in on this one because they had a more proprietary sense of confidentiality than government researchers. Verus was recording their progress.

"Who started calling you people Skunkworks anyway?" Donovan asked.

"I dunno, but I hate it," said LeVier. "I don't wanna go down in history as Lockheed's head skunk."

"Oh, I'd say you're more of a flying fox. Garrick Stamford's head skunk, right?"

LeVier was smart enough to let that one slide. "Flying fox. I like that. Listen, something I've been wanting to ask... The story about your ghost, is it true?"

Donovan never liked to talk about that, and LeVier wasn't even supposed to know. Somebody had loose lips.

What the hell. "Sometimes it feels like I'm going mad. Hearing a strange voice in your head, it's almost a cliché, right? But that spaceship out there is proof — it's the world that's gone mad, not me." It felt good to get that off his chest. A burden lifted.

"Why won't he help us, your ghost?" LeVier asked.

"His name's Paolo. He won't help because we made that deal with the Russians."

"What do you mean?"

"Mastering this craft too quickly would make the United States unstoppable. No other military force in the world could touch us."

"Sounds like a pretty good outcome to me," said LeVier.

"Except it would probably trigger a nuclear war."

LeVier didn't know how to respond to that. Donovan stared at him, the memories of their trip to the Russian frontier still fresh in his mind. "Have you read George Orwell?"

"I know the line — 'Absolute power corrupts'."

"Actually, the line is, 'Absolute power corrupts absolutely'."

"But this is America," said LeVier. "We're not the Nazis or the Russians."

"You think we'd be any different, armed with the certainty nobody could stand in our way?"

LeVier sighed. "I don't know. We've got the A-bomb and we're not using it."

"Because other people have it too. That's called mutually assured destruction. The risk of Russian retaliation is the only reason we haven't blown China or North Korea off the face of the Earth already. God knows MacArthur would have done so given half the chance. It's one of the reasons Truman fired him."

LeVier shook his head in disbelief. "Who knew the little farmer had a set of gonads that big? But that also proves my point. Nuclear weapons are only deployed by the Commander in Chief."

"And now MacArthur's seeking the Republican nomination for president," said Donovan.

Outside, a cold wind blew across the desert sands, whistling beneath the wooden floorboards of the cabin like Mother Nature's warning. For a long while, neither man said a word. They were both men who found solace in silence.

Finally, LeVier stood up. "I need a smoke, General. I'll just stand over here by the door." He swung it open and the desert chill turned the room into an icebox.

"The point is," Donovan said, "if Russia thought we'd unlocked the secrets of this ship, they'd be the ones dropping bombs to stop us."

"But the Russians *know* we have it. They saw you flying it."

"The topic of numerous back channel discussions, believe me. I shouldn't be telling you any of this."

"We're researching a flying craft that is not of this world. It's a bit late to worry about me keeping my mouth shut."

Donovan was already half lost in the recollection. "I guess so." He wasn't about to stop now. "Paolo is a ghost, but he's also flesh and blood. I took him in person to the Diomede Islands."

"Where's that?"

"Two hunks of rock in the middle of the Bering Strait. Little Diomede is in Alaskan waters. A few miles west, Big Diomede is Russian territory. The international border runs between the two islands. We sailed there in a decommissioned Navy ship, the USS Alaska, and met on the Russian side. They call the big one Tomorrow Island because the border is also the international date line. We crossed the line into tomorrow and met with Joe Stalin himself."

"Are you shitting me?"

"He was there with his Chief of General Staff Sergei Shtemenko, the man in charge of Russian armed forces, as well as the Minister of State Security Semyon Ignatyev and a platoon of crack Russian troops, no doubt liberally sprinkled with members of Ignatyev's secret police."

"Who was with you?"

"It was just me, Paolo, and our Russian translator. We flew there by helicopter. I'd made it clear that if our chopper pilot didn't radio the all-clear every five minutes on my signal, the Alaska would open fire on our location."

"Christ."

"I visited the Russian secret service in Moscow back in '43," said Donovan, "when I was running the OSS. Back then I had a decent rapport with Stalin's intelligence service. Anyway, the meeting went smoothly."

"Why the remote location?" LeVier asked.

"It was the closest thing to neutral territory," Donovan explained. "Big Diomede is uninhabited. The Russians evacuated the native inhabitants to the mainland after the war."

"Still, it was risky. You never know what those bastards are up to."

"The saucer incident had inflamed tensions," Donovan disclosed. "We got into a fire fight with a platoon of Russian soldiers shortly after we retrieved the saucer in Lebanon. We needed to calm things down."

"What did Ivan the Horrible make of your guy?"

"Paolo is more than eleven feet tall in the flesh." LeVier's eyes widened in disbelief. "He's enough to stop any man in his tracks. Even Stalin."

"What happened?"

"Paolo assured them he would not divulge the secrets of the saucer to America."

"Did Stalin believe him?"

Donovan shook his head. "Stalin told us the moment the Soviet Union saw evidence to the contrary, our two countries would be on a war footing. We agreed that Paolo would remain in Rome as a 'guest' of the Vatican, and that once a month a Russian agent would be allowed to pay him a visit."

LeVier lit his cigarette and blew the smoke out the door. "That's a hell of a concession to our sworn enemies."

"I hear every word that's said," Donovan pointed out. "Paolo isn't giving anything away."

LeVier shook his head; he didn't like it one bit.

Donovan could have kicked himself. He knew he'd said too much. "That information absolutely does not leave this room."

"No. Of course," said LeVier. But..."

"What's the matter?"

"I can't believe we're sharing secrets with the Russians."

"I wouldn't share a cigarette with those bastards," Donovan said.

"You don't smoke."

"I'm saying it's not as simple as that."

"But it casts tomorrow in a whole new light," said LeVier.

"Stalin doesn't have eyes on us out here."

LeVier flicked his butt out the door. "Tell me something — do you still hear Paolo's voice in your head?" Donovan nodded. "What does he think about this test flight of ours?"

"He knew it would happen eventually."

"But here's what I don't get. You've flown it once, why not try again? Why me?"

Donovan drained the last of his whiskey. "Flying that space ship nearly killed me." LeVier was visibly shocked. "But listen Tony, I'm old. Too old to learn new tricks. We didn't have a choice out there. If we didn't fly that day, the Russians would have killed us and they'd have the saucer now."

It had been more than a year since Donovan's great adventure: an improbable search mission in the company of a rogue priest, a corrupt Lebanese Army captain, and a platoon of clueless soldiers. "I'd thought our trip would be a waste of time. But there it was, hermetically sealed beneath layers of Roman and Sumerian ruins. An alien spacecraft, fully operable despite the fact that it's six thousand years old."

Donovan explained how the technology belonged to an interplanetary race known as the Ryl. "They lived openly on Earth in the days of ancient Sumer. Back then, they were called the Anunnaki. They vanished from human view sometime around 2000BC. But they didn't leave Earth. They'd decided it was easier to live in secret so they didn't have to deal with us. Can't say I blame them."

The saucer Donovan had discovered was stolen from the Ryl by a Sumerian king — half Ryl, half human — known to the world as Utnapishtim. He'd ruled Sumer circa 4000BC, at the time a flood of biblical proportions wiped out most of the Middle East.

The flood was no accident; it was population control. Utnapishtim had found out ahead of time. He'd decided the ship would be his means of escape. But the Ryl were too clever for him. They'd caught him, and trapped him in a living death: a sarcophagus life-support unit. Vowed to keep him there until he gave up the location of the stolen ship.

He never did.

Thousands of years later, Utnapishtim, still alive, had set Donovan upon the quest of spaceship retrieval.

"Except these days he calls himself Paolo Favaloro. He likes to think of himself as a new man."

"How did he get inside your head?"

Donovan grabbed the whiskey bottle and poured himself a double. "No idea. But as you know, the ship's operating system is thought-controlled. It takes time to master, particularly given the system was designed for nonhuman minds way more advanced than us. There was no time to configure my thoughts to the ship while Russians were shooting at us. So Paolo's ghost climbed inside my head. Even now, my heart is pounding just thinking about it. It was the most invasive thing I've ever experienced. It felt like demonic possession. I mean, I've never been possessed by a demon, but I don't know how else to describe it."

"Glad I won't be doing that then," said LeVier.

"I've been permanently connected with Paolo since then. All I do is think about him and he's here with me. I'm like his spirit familiar, except he's the only voice I hear. Don't you dare repeat that to anybody..."

LeVier held his hands up in surrender. "Who would I tell?"

Donovan looked past him into the night. "You gonna shut that door so we don't freeze to death?"

"I'm going to leave you in peace, General. Maybe we can get a couple of hours sleep."

"Yeah. Maybe."

"Any last minute tips?"

Donovan thought about it, then waited for the words to come. "Paolo says focus is the key. Don't doubt yourself or let your mind wander. Focus on where you wish to go."

# NINE

July 1, 1952

The early morning sun was still low on the desert horizon as the saucer rose slowly into the air, a hot metal bastard child gleaming in the daylight against the eternal backdrop of the Organ Mountains.

Donovan pulled the rim of his hat down further, wishing he'd remembered to bring sunglasses. He had a hangover that could kill a horse. It felt like he was still exhaling whiskey fumes as he watched his breath condense in the cold air. Alongside him were Verus Foundation colleague and astrophysicist, Donald Menzel, Garrick Stamford from Lockheed, and Roscoe Hillenkoetter from MJ-12.

Half a dozen engineers were huddled in tight formation directly in front of them. A couple chattered in German, and Donovan noted a rather persistent urge to pull out his pistol and shoot them. Everyone stared with grim fascination as the craft's leading edge dipped ever so slightly toward the desert, then began moving sideways in the direction of the mountains.

Something didn't seem right, but nobody dared speak. Despite the best efforts of some of the finest minds in science, after more than a year of analysis, they had no more than a rudimentary understanding of the flight control system, and no idea about how to replicate its power plant and propulsion system. All they had worked out was that it generated its own gravity.

Paolo had remained tight-lipped about the Ryl technology; he insisted they decipher it for themselves. He said the knowledge would come when they were ready. Donovan knew he meant it in more of a spiritual sense.

It was not the only alien technology available to their scientists. Wreckage from the Roswell crash in '47 was still being combed over diligently, and there had been a number of crash retrievals in the years afterwards. These didn't make the press because the debacle of the Roswell Army Air Force press release — and the subsequent cover-up — meant USAF officers now knew to keep their goddamn mouths shut if they valued their careers.

But those retrievals had only given them fragments and dead bodies. No living beings with whom to communicate, and no way of knowing how the recovered pieces might fit together. It was like trying to decipher Egyptian hieroglyphics without a Rosetta stone, in reverse.

They had much higher hopes for this saucer. To the best of anyone's knowledge, it was the only intact alien craft in human possession anywhere in the world. Its value was beyond measure. Donovan had been hailed as a hero for bringing it home, though the effort had taken a heavy toll on him. He'd made it abundantly clear he was no good to them as a test pilot.

Tony LeVier was a much better choice. His expertise had been vital in Lockheed's development of the P-38 Lightning fighter for the Army Air Corps during the war. More importantly, LeVier had helped develop the T-33 jet for the US Navy. He knew airplanes back to front, and as a test pilot he had the perfect combination of fearlessness and skill that ensured he kept himself alive when things got hairy.

"Powering up."

It was LeVier's voice in their headsets. The ship picked up speed quickly. In a fraction of a second, it shot a thousand feet into the air then dipped on its side, where it hung frozen at an odd angle. LeVier muttered an obscenity under his breath. An engineer in front of them gasped.

"That's not a good sign," Hillenkoetter muttered.

Stamford said, "Give him a moment, he'll come good."

The saucer began to correct itself to the proper attitude, but it retained a disturbing wobble. A moment later, its leading edge dipped again, and it began to spin around and around in a circle. Within seconds, it was spinning so fast it was the fuzzy blur of a propeller. No pilot could maintain consciousness for long in those G-forces.

Donovan swallowed the desire to look away, knowing what came next.

The ship began plummeting toward the desert. There was no explosion; just a sickening thud. A cloud of sand and dust pulsed into the air like a tiny mushroom cloud.

An engineer was calling on the radio, and getting no response. "Tony? You there? LeVier, respond, over."

Nothing. Just static.

# TEN

July 2, 1952

They took off from White Sands in one of Lockheed's new Super Constellations, fitted out for Garrick Stamford's personal use. Donovan had never seen such an overt display of wealth in an airplane interior. This didn't particularly impress Donovan, who'd had his own C-54 Skymaster to traverse the globe during the war. It occurred to him this was Stamford's way of reminding himself those days were long gone.

"This company is the future of aviation, Bill. We are in lockstep with the Air Force. If anyone can get that saucer in the air, it's us."

"I admire your spirit of enterprise, Garrick. But today was nothing to smile about."

"One thing I've learned in the aviation business is the need for patience. And deep pockets. Our research is just beginning. It could take years. We're going to need a lot more money."

Donovan sighed and looked out the window.

"Do you have any pressing engagements in New York tonight?" Stamford asked him.

"Not really. Why?"

"Someone I'd like you to meet in Atlantic City."

Donovan frowned. "I'm not sure that's the sort of money you should be chasing."

Stamford laughed. "This man is one of my main financial advisors. I've got to tell you, from the moment I met this man, amazing things started to happen."

"You and I might have a different threshold for amazement."

Stamford was untroubled by Donovan's lassitude. "It's hard to explain. His name's Lee Tavon, have you heard of him?"

The name didn't ring a bell, which on its own was enough to make Donovan wary of the man. Donovan's business, personal, and political connections constituted a vast global network. He was a voracious reader and had a prodigious memory. People with genuine financial acumen were also rare, and thus generally well-known among the financial and political elite of Washington and New York.

It was dark by the time they had taxied to the terminal of the Atlantic City Naval Air Station. "How'd you get permission to land here?" Donovan asked.

The naval air station wasn't normally open to civil aviation. Another sign of the high regard for Skunkworks within the Defense Department.

"Rank hath its privileges." said Stamford.

The marquee above the 500 Club declared "He's Back". Sinatra was such a regular onstage at The Five that they didn't need a name on the banner. Their cab pulled up amidst a crowd of people queuing to get inside.

"Looks like quite a wait," said Donovan.

"Tonight, you're a VIP," said Stamford. On cue, two elegantly dressed men emerged from the crowd to meet them. Stamford shook the hand of one — it had to be Tavon — who in turn introduced Stamford to the man beside him. Donovan nearly got back in the taxi when he heard the name Enoch Johnson. Tavon stepped forward, holding out his hand. "General Donovan, I presume. Lee Tavon. It's an absolute pleasure to make your acquaintance."

Donovan was surprised by the firmness and enthusiasm of the man's grip. Tavon put his arm around Donovan's shoulder and nudged him closer to his criminal associate. "I think you and Nucky Johnson might have already met."

Donovan curtly shook Johnson's hand. Of the two men, Johnson was better dressed. His hair was greased back immaculately, a handkerchief was arranged stylishly in his suit pocket, and his black Italian loafers gleamed. He looked older in the flesh than the mug shot they'd used in the papers.

"You've shed your prison greys I see, Mr Johnson," Donovan said.

"Yes indeed. And I'm welcomed warmly at the Saturn Club. Have they let you back in yet?" Johnson asked.

"Reluctantly," said Donovan.

As a US attorney back in '23, Donovan had been a vigorous enforcer of Prohibition and had infamously arranged a raid on the Saturn Club in Buffalo — where Donovan and his wife were themselves members. Ruth had never forgiven him. She'd called it an act of gross hypocrisy. Maybe she was right. But Donovan was no fan of having his nose rubbed in his own foibles by a gangster; he hoped nobody from the press was hanging around. When had Garrick started consorting with criminals?

Perhaps reading Donovan's uneasiness, Stamford leaned in close. "Sorry, I had no idea he was bringing Nucky tonight."

"It really is an honor to meet you, General," said Tavon. "I've been looking forward to this."

"Lead on, Lee," said Stamford, trying to put on a brave face.

Tavon made no effort to join the queue. "Please," said Johnson, "allow me." He pushed casually through the milling crowd to speak to the doorman.

"Hey Nucky!" the bouncer yelled.

"Walter! Good to see you again." As they shook hands, Donovan was fairly sure he saw a sly exchange of currency. Johnson said, "A table for four would be brilliant, Walter."

The doorman nodded reassuringly. "All sorted. The boss is expecting you." He waved his hands, and the crowd parted like the Red Sea to let them through. Enoch Johnson might not have been the big wheel he once was, but in Atlantic City they still treated him like a king.

They made their way past an expansive bar with more curves than Rita Hayworth. The walls were black and white zebra stripes. People were three-deep, clamoring for service from a team of busy barmen. In one corner, an indoor waterfall added to the jungle vibe. A little way further in, they found the entrance to the Vermilion Room.

Paul D'Amato, owner of the 500, was waiting at the door, smiling. "Nucky! It's been too long." The gleam in D'Amato's eyes suggested he held the former Atlantic City prohibition kingpin in genuine affection.

"Hello Paul," said Johnson, "good to see you again."

Through the 1920s and for much of the '30s, Nucky Johnson had been untouchable. He had deals brokered with all the major mob heavies; Capone, Luciano, Lansky, Siegel, Bernstein and Gambino. He was the boss of the Atlantic County Republican Party. The FBI had tried to bring him down, but there were enough Feds on the take to ensure they never laid a glove on him. In the end, it was Nucky's clash with William Randolph Hearst that had done him in — over a showgirl Hearst didn't want to share. Hearst had lobbied hard for President Roosevelt to have Nucky Johnson tossed in the clink. In the end, it had been tax evasion, the same thing that took down Capone.

The rest, as they say, was history.

Once he was behind bars, Nucky's empire had been split between two men: D'Amato and New Jersey senator Frank Farley. Donovan knew of D'Amato as a Johnson acolyte. After Nucky went to prison, D'Amato also became Atlantic County treasurer. Since Nucky Johnson's release following a four-year stretch, the Feds had been sticking to Nucky like glue. He'd taken a pauper's oath to avoid paying a $20,000 fine. Now everyone was watching closely to see if D'Amato offered Nucky any obvious sign of support. The two men were clearly still friendly; who said there was no honor among thieves?

The Vermilion Room was lined in burgundy velvet wallpaper and red carpet, lending the space a boudoir ambiance. It was a big room, and it was packed to overflowing. Dozens of people were on their feet at the back, left with standing room only, but D'Amato led them to an open table right in front of the stage. A comic was midway through his routine; he saw them coming. "Welcome ladies. Powdering our noses, were we?"

The crowd roared with laughter.

"Sinatra's running late," D'Amato explained, a little too loudly. "But I've heard this guy's pretty good." He gave them a wink.

A light ripple of knowing laughter came from a table beside them. Donovan looked up at the stage and realized it was Jerry Lewis giving them a hard time. His embarrassment melted; he loved this guy.

"You're not Frank," Stamford yelled back at the comedian.

"That's what my mother says. Why can't you be more like Frank?" said Lewis. "I told her, frankly my dear, I blame you and Dad. There's a reason cousins don't marry."

More laughs.

Donovan could have punched Garrick in the ribs for making their entrance even more of a spectacle, but if Jerry Lewis recognized Nucky Johnson, he knew better than to mention it.

"I hope to see you afterwards," D'Amato told them.

"You will," said Nucky, shaking his hand. When the club owner was out of earshot, Nucky added, "I bet Sinatra's out back playing craps. He's a demon of the dice."

Tavon raised his eyebrows. "He must be on a heck of a roll if he's happy to keep an audience waiting." Donovan thought Tavon looked like a man more at home in a nightclub than a boardroom. He seemed at ease in his own skin and had an aura of confidence. Neither good looking nor ugly, neither tall nor short, he was the everyman you wouldn't even notice on the street.

It could all be a con job. "How do you and Garrick know one another?"

"I'm a major Lockheed investor," said Tavon.

"Lee advised me to increase my holding," explained Stamford. "Best move I ever made."

Tavon pointed at the ceiling. "The future is in the heavens."

Jerry Lewis was wrapping up with a clumsy bow as an attractive waitress arrived to take their drink orders. The applause was still booming in Donovan's ears as he screamed "whiskey neat" in her direction, but failed to catch her response. Tavon called her over and whispered in her ear, sliding a twenty-dollar note onto her tray. She immediately brightened and departed in haste.

"My, how times have changed," said Nucky, lifting his glass to his lips.

Donovan wasn't a drinker during prohibition. Back then, he'd had no problem with abstaining, and not just because of the law. Drinking wasn't particularly his thing. He'd come to it later in life with a greater degree of interest. But in truth, he was just as happy with a good hot cup of tea or coffee.

"Tell me, General," said Tavon, "am I right in thinking you're an Eisenhower man?"

"Correct," said Donovan. The Republican National Convention was less than a week away.

"He'll make an excellent president," said Tavon.

"Long way to go before that happens," said Donovan.

Tavon tapped his nose and nodded sagely, suggesting he was certain Ike was the man. Donovan couldn't help feeling Tavon was working him.

"Let's hope you're right." Tavon said, "I've been travelling the country for weeks telling everyone to support him."

Stamford leant across the table. "Lee is very well-connected in the Republican Party."

Donovan had his doubts about that. "It seems he's well-connected in many circles."

Their drinks arrived. It took two waiters: one with glasses and an ice bucket, the other carrying a bottle of Jack Daniels and bottle of Jameson's Irish whiskey. Tavon passed the whiskey across the table to Donovan. "I thought it might save time," he said.

The waiters threw ice into four tumblers and started pouring. Donovan swirled the amber liquid in his glass to catch the chill of the ice, then took a mouthful of what might have been the best whiskey he'd ever tasted. Stamford and Johnson opted for bourbon.

Tavon drank nothing but chilled water. "Not a drinker?" Donovan asked him.

"I've never had the taste for it," he said. "I have no problem with other people drinking, though I'd prefer they didn't do it to excess."

"You and me both," Donovan agreed.

"I haven't known many teetotalers," said Nucky. "Never had much time for them. But you're all right, Lee."

"Too kind, Nucky," Tavon praised. Johnson pulled a cigarette from a gold case and was about to light up, but Lee Tavon asked, "Would you mind waiting a while? General Donovan hates the smoke."

The air around them was already a thick fug of tobacco fumes and Donovan was certain Johnson would light up anyway. Instead, Johnson shrugged and stuck the cigarette back inside his case. Donovan nodded at Johnson appreciatively.

"That true, Bill? You don't like cigarette smoke?" said Stamford. "All these years and you never told me."

"Everyone I know is a smoker," said Donovan.

Only when he'd emptied his whiskey tumbler for the second time did Donovan stop to wonder how Tavon had known.

# ELEVEN

July 2, 1952

Sinatra hit the stage like a whirling dervish and his sonorous voice filled the room. He was drunk. Then again, he was always drunk. Donovan had it on good authority Old Blue Eyes self-administered a bottle of Jack a day. He didn't sound any the worse for it, probably because he was so used to singing soused.

To a lesser mortal, his state of inebriation might have resulted in a disconnect with the audience. But for Sinatra, it had the opposite effect. There were moments, in the briefest pauses between notes as he held himself just behind the beat, when you could have heard a pin drop. He held every man and woman in that room in the palm of his hand. Every breath, every note, a thing to cherish.

"Here's one you might have heard before, in a little New York show called *Guys and Dolls*." The crowd let out a cheer. "They're still on Broadway, but I hear they're about to cross the ditch and hit the West End." A lone cheer rose from somewhere at the back of the room. "Anyway," said Sinatra, "we thought we'd take this one out for a spin." The crowd applauded and cheered. Sinatra stood his ground waiting for the room to hush before hitting them with, "They call you Lady Luck." The band went *boom*. A single percussive note. "But there is room for doubt." *Pow*. "At times you have a very unladylike way of running out."

Strings now. Pure schmaltz. "You're on this date with me, the pick-ings have been lush, and yet before the evening is over you might give me the brush, you might forget your manners, you might refuse to stay, and so the best that I can do is praaaay..."

The orchestra kicked into overdrive and Sinatra kicked piety to the curb. "Luck be a lady tonight, luck let a gentleman see, just how nice a dame you can be, I know the way you've treated other guys you've been with, luck be a lady with me..."

When Sinatra finally left the stage, it was like the world became a smaller, darker place. Like all the color had been drained from it.

Nucky said, "I swear that man takes a piece of me with him every time."

There would be no encore; the house lights were up.

"Right," said Tavon, "there's nothing for it now but to hit the tables. And let us pray that luck will indeed be a lady tonight."

Nucky smiled. "I knew we'd get on well the first time we met."

The 500 Club casino wasn't open to the public; you had to be in the know and on the list. It was a big list, but you had to be on it. Nucky Johnson had been on it for twenty years. He led them to the back of the Vermilion Room, where another bouncer guarded a door. The man nodded at Nucky and the door duly swung open. A short corridor led them to a room decked in green velvet, packed with roulette wheels, high-stakes poker games, and craps tables. Attractive male and female waiters were plying the gamblers with alcohol. "Drinks are on the house," said Nucky.

A pretty older woman in a stunning black dress gave Donovan the eye as she leaned against the bar in the corner. Either she was sick of waiting for her man to surface, or trying to find a better one. Maybe both. Donovan smiled and kept walking, determined not to let himself get distracted.

A cashier was tucked away in the corner. There were a few empty tables near the bar. Stamford picked one and took a seat. "I'm happy to sit this one out."

Nucky looked at Stamford like he'd lost his mind. "You sure? Could be your last chance. Paul's ready to shut this place down. The Kefauver Committee has his balls in a vice."

For more than a year, Senator Estes Kefauver's senate special committee had been getting tough on organized crime. Word in Washington was, the good senator had been ramping it up ahead of a bid for the Democratic presidential nomination.

"In my day," said Nucky, "we'd roll a crate of Canadian whiskey through the back door of Congress, and all would be well with the world. It's starting to feel like nobody can be bought anymore."

Donovan's eyes were locked on Garrick Stamford. "Oh, I wouldn't go that far."

Nucky Johnson had fallen on hard times since his release from prison in 1945, though nobody in Atlantic City made him feel any less of a man for it. Donovan wasn't particularly sympathetic to the former bootlegger's fall from grace, but with an arm twisted he might have admitted to liking the man. Nucky was eyeing the nearest craps table, where Sinatra was back on a roll.

"Start with roulette," Tavon told him. "That table there. Wait two throws, then bet on zero."

Nucky raised an eyebrow. "Really?"

Tavon said, "Trust me. One bet on zero, then your winnings on red. Third bet to be advised."

Nucky did as he was told.

"Is this the sort of financial advice you bring to the table?" Donovan asked.

Tavon smiled knowingly. "When in Rome, eh General?" You could have knocked Donovan over with a feather.

"You'd do worse than to follow Nucky's lead, Bill," said Stamford.

Donovan shook his head. "I'm not much of a gambler."

"I'd heard you're quite the risk taker when the occasion arises," said Tavon. "I know being here is unsettling for you, General, but rest assured there'll be no police raids tonight."

Donovan kept a close eye on Nucky, who glanced over and waited for Tavon's nod before he placed a bet. They waited in awkward silence as he laid his money on zero, prompting murmurs of disquiet from the other patrons. Seasoned roulette players regarded betting on zero and double zero as bad luck — you're betting on everyone else to fail. As the croupier sent the ball spinning, nobody else had seen fit to follow Johnson's lead, but the table was notably spare of alternate bets. There were loud cries of anger and amazement as the ball stuck in the green zero slot.

"Not a popular win," said Stamford.

Tavon said, "He won't be spending too long on that table."

"You really expect me to believe your betting tips are little nuggets of gold?" Donovan asked.

"Didn't I just prove it?" Tavon asked.

"It's a con. You and D'Amato are in on it."

Stamford, looking a little embarrassed, rose to his feet. "I'm headed for the bar. First round's on me," he said, trying to lighten the mood. Tavon and Donovan both shook their heads. "Suit yourselves."

"Go on," said Tavon. "Ask me what you want to ask."

"What are your intentions with Garrick? Because if they're less than honorable, and especially if they're illegal, you'll have me to deal with."

Tavon was unruffled. "I've made Garrick a rich man in the past twelve months. He was wealthy before, but now he's stinking rich. One of the untouchables. Nothing illegal. Heck, it wasn't even immoral."

"What's in it for you?"

"Plenty. I wouldn't expect you to understand at this point, nor do I intend to sit here and explain myself, but I have a hand in a lot more than you realize. For instance, I know about that little trip of yours to the Middle East. I know what and who you found, and that it's what Garrick and the Lockheed boys are tinkering with."

"Is that a fact?" Donovan challenged. "I take it you've signed a secrecy agreement?"

"Your secret is safe with me, General."

Nucky Johnson returned with a large wad of chips and a big smile on his face. "I put it all on red, like you said. One or two people followed. They don't hate me so much now."

"Keep three quarters," said Tavon, "that's the golden rule. That way you walk out a winner. But you're on your own now, Nucky. We don't want to ruffle too many feathers."

Johnson poured most of the chips into his coat pocket and shook Tavon's hand. "A pleasure as always, Lee." He nodded at Donovan. "General." Enoch Johnson walked away a happy man.

"To answer your earlier accusation, I'm not conning anybody here, General. It's not magic. It's math and probability. I'm very good at calculating odds and reading the room. They're hard skills to master, but not impossible. I did Enoch Johnson a favor because it suits me to have a man like that in my debt."

"Garrick's in your debt too, isn't he?"

Tavon didn't bite. He changed tack. "I'd been thinking of making a little donation to the Eisenhower campaign, but perhaps it's better if I leave that up to you."

"What exactly did you have in mind?"

"You take fifty dollars of your own money to the roulette wheel and bet on red twenty-three. If you win, you donate the proceeds. Everyone's a winner."

"Then I'd be in your debt."

"Not at all, General, not at all. I hereby relinquish any future claim on a return favor. I'm just playing my part in the democratic process."

Donovan thought about it for a minute. He'd had too much to drink again, despite deliberately leaving the whiskey bottle three-quarters full. A prolonged session at the table would be a quick way to blow a lot of money. On the other hand, one bet probably wouldn't do any harm. Feeling a strong urge to call Tavon's bluff, Donovan pulled out his wallet and headed for the table. The wheel was already spinning.

"Wait for the next turn," Tavon whispered somewhere close behind him.

The ball stuck on red twenty-one. The croupier cleared the losing chips and paid out the winners. Donovan unfolded a note and threw it down, feeling a pang of guilt as he saw the picture of Capitol Hill staring up at him. But the croupier quickly replaced it with a single fifty-dollar chip. He turned around to look at Tavon, who mimed the words 'twenty-three' as confirmation.

Donovan did as instructed, though he thought it unlikely red twenty-three would immediately follow red twenty-one.

The Ike for President campaign picked up a $1700 donation.

# TWELVE

J uly 3, 1952

Harry Truman stepped nimbly from the rear of the limousine, eager to get off the street as quickly as possible. The Mayflower Hotel's stalwart doorman Stanley Coleman smiled as he held open the big brass door of the rear entrance.

"Morning Mr President."

"Good morning, Stanley," said Truman. "You're looking well. I'm afraid I'm running late again."

"They've only just arrived, sir. Ain't nobody mind you keepin' 'em waiting."

Truman smiled and scuttled inside, whispering to his Secret Service detail to impress upon Stanley the need for discretion. Though this was usually a given at the Mayflower, where he was so well-known.

Stanley Coleman had been a Truman man since the President's 1947 address to the NAACP from the steps of the Lincoln Memorial. Stanley still remembered it clear as day: "We must make the Federal Government a friendly, vigilant defender of the rights and equalities of all Americans. When I say all Americans, I mean all Americans. There is no justifiable reason for discrimination because of ancestry or religion or race or color."

Remarkable words from a man who, on becoming vice president in 1945, was hailed by white supremacists as a man who'd keep the niggers in their place.

Stanley came to know Truman personally in '49, when he'd lived at the Mayflower for the first 90 days after his inauguration. The hotel's presidential suite was Truman's home away from home — it was barely half a mile from the White House and Truman had occasionally walked to work. The Mayflower's residential apartments also enjoyed their own separate foyer, allowing for discreet comings and goings.

Stanley felt certain that Truman's awakening to the plight of black people was genuine. He just wished the sentiment extended to his hip pocket; the man was downright stingy. Not once had he slipped Stanley a penny of gratuity. Being generous of soul, Stanley tried hard not to think less of him for this — it must be tough being the President.

While Truman was indeed late, he had thankfully beaten the lunchtime crowd. By using the back entrance, he sought to forestall an awkward encounter with J. Edgar Hoover and Clyde Tolson, who frequented the Mayflower's Town and Country Lounge for lunch.

The Presidential Suite was booked in the name of Dr Vannevar Bush who, among his many other duties, was a director of the American Telephone and Telegraph company.

The suite was as Truman remembered it, spacious and impeccably furnished. His Secret Service advance detail were in the room already. The men who had called the emergency meeting were waiting for him in the dining room, sat around a magnificent walnut dining table. They rose to their feet as he walked in.

Truman shook Vannevar Bush's hand. "You checked this place for listening devices?"

Bush nodded. "All is well, I assure you, sir."

Bill Donovan was next. He grabbed Truman's hand with his usual vice-like grip and the President tried not to wince. Their relationship had been strained ever since Truman had shut down the OSS and made it his business to keep Donovan at arm's length. The CIA was formed in 1947 with little direct input from Donovan. Truman had long been wary of his Republican leaning, and had no faith whatsoever in Donovan's administrative abilities. Despite all of this, General Donovan had done everything Truman had asked of him.

Donald Menzel's handshake was softer by far, as was so often the case with men of science. Truman knew from experience Menzel's mental toughness was his super power. He had an intellect that commanded respect.

Across the table, Air Force Chief of Staff General Hoyt Vandenberg was out of uniform and looking decidedly uncomfortable. He and CIA Director General Walter Smith stood for the Commander in Chief, but didn't bother with handshakes; they were in and out of the Oval Office so frequently those formalities had been dispensed with. Everyone around the table, apart from Donovan, was a member of Majestic-12. Donovan was their unofficial 13th man, being the group's chief of security. He didn't usually attend meetings, but this one had been convened at his request.

"Who's first?" Truman asked.

Hoyt Vandenberg looked at Donovan. "Bill?"

"I woke up in New York this morning and knew this couldn't wait. We have a security problem with FS-1."

"Are you worried about word of your failed test flight getting out?" Truman's implied criticism was clear.

"I'm afraid it's more serious than that," said Donovan. "I spent last night in the company of a man by the name of Lee Tavon. I take it nobody here has heard the name?"

There were murmurs, but heads were shaking.

"Tavon is a major Lockheed investor. He's also, as I discovered, a known associate of gangsters. In my opinion, he's a conman. I'm afraid he's also very well versed on FS-1, despite having no security clearance."

Truman slapped the table. "Who the hell is talking to him?"

"I believe it's Garrick Stamford, the head of Skunkworks," said Donovan.

"Damn it Bill, this project went to Lockheed on your recommendation," said Truman. "Stamford was one of yours, you vouched for him."

"That I did."

"Meaning the mess is of your making. Now you expect us to clean it up, is that it?"

Donovan was lost for words; Truman was being brutally unfair.

Vandenberg came to Donovan's defense. "With respect, Mr President, I don't think we can hold Bill responsible."

"The hell we can't," said Truman, looking squarely at Donovan. "Administration has always been your Achilles heel, Bill."

"Bill alerted me to this last night," said General Smith. "We're checking into Tavon's background."

"The CIA's not supposed to operate domestically," said Truman.

Vannevar Bush weighed in. "We really don't want to be taking this to Hoover."

"Good God, no," Truman agreed. "All right Walter, find out what you can about this man, but for the love of God go easy. Last thing I want so close to November is for any of this to get back to J. Edgar. Tread lightly."

"I can help with that," said Donovan. "I have some new tools at my disposal to aid in covert surveillance."

"You two work together," Truman told them. "We watch this man Tavon and we watch Stamford. And FS-1 is on hold until further notice. Anything else?"

Bush said, "While we're here, I might as well raise the recent rash of unexplained aerial sightings. According to Blue Book, it's a real spike. In January, they had a total of eleven sightings reported. But in the past month, they've logged a hundred forty-nine."

Truman waved his hand dismissively. "It's just yokels staring at the sun. Everyone's all worked up over that story in *Life* magazine."

Vandenberg nodded. "That's what I said."

"I don't think that's it," Menzel challenged. "Sightings are on the rise in Europe and South America too."

"The *Life* factor did cross our minds, sir," said Bush. "But it might also interest you to know that over the past five years, we've consistently recorded the highest volume of unexplained sightings in the month of July."

"Meaning what?" asked Truman.

"Your guess is as good as ours," said Menzel.

"I'd prefer to leave guesswork out of this," said the President.

Menzel shrugged. "Most sightings have rational explanations."

"You play the debunker so convincingly, Donald," said Bush. "I almost believe you myself."

Menzel tried to smile, but it came out more like a grimace. "I said most, not all."

Truman frowned. "Will one of you please get to the point?"

Bush said, "According to Ed Ruppelt from Blue Book, around twenty percent of sightings stay classed as 'unknowns'. That is, they defy all logical and alternate explanation. These are the ones that got *Life* all hot under the collar."

Truman said, "We're seeing more visitor activity?"

"It would appear to be the case, yes," said Bush.

"Why now?"

"All of us are working as hard and as fast as we can to find an answer to that question, sir," said Smith.

"Anyone care to offer up a reasonable hypothesis?"

Smith's eyes widened. He was reluctant to do anything of the sort, knowing he'd be held to it at a later date. Vandenberg was more forthcoming. "Mr President, if I was a betting man, I'd put my money on this being some sort of a message they're sending us."

"Oh, for Christ's sake," Truman yelled. "Why do they have to be so mysterious? Why don't they just land on Pennsylvania Avenue and be done with it?"

The Majestic-12 exchanged startled glances. The idea of it chilled them to the core.

"That is precisely what they won't do," said Menzel. "They know the Army will start shooting at them the moment they do."

Truman sighed. "What was that movie called?"

"*The Day The Earth Stood Still*," said Bush.

"That's the one."

"A window into the American psyche," said Menzel.

Vandenberg continued, "We believe they monitor our television broadcasts. Given the extent that Hollywood influences public opinion, it wouldn't surprise me in the slightest if they'd found a way to watch our movies. I think we can confidently rule out impromptu public appearances."

"Can you imagine it?" asked Menzel. "We'd have panic in the streets."

"What worries me the most about this, Mr President, is the Russians," said Smith. "They could easily stir up some sort of mass flying saucer scare to create a panic."

Vandenberg was likewise concerned.

"I'm not as concerned about Russian interference as I am about finding out what these flying saucers are up to," said Truman.

Vandenberg said, "Don't let Senator McCarthy hear you say that."

Donovan knew Vandenberg hadn't been told about their arrangement with Stalin, and he thought it was a mistake. More circles within circles.

"The junior senator from Wisconsin might be a clown," said Truman, "but he's right about one thing — Stalin cannot be trusted."

On that much, at least, they all agreed.

Smith said, "There might be some merit in reaching out to Russia via back channels, to open up a dialogue on the subject. We've had reports of aerial sightings all over the USSR. It might be useful to compare notes."

"Is there any chance the Russians are colluding with the visitors?" Vannevar Bush asked. "I mean, are we able to definitively rule it out?"

The generals frowned as they pondered the possibility. Donovan could have answered that question, but kept his mouth shut and allowed the President to respond.

"As much as the Kremlin would love to control the world," said Truman, "they've got more chance of writing McCarthy's speeches for him than persuading our alien visitors to side with them over America. I take it you're not suggesting it's the Russians themselves up there in our skies?"

"No sir," said Vandenberg. "We don't believe so."

Truman said, "If the visitors are sending us a message, I want to know what it is. Walt, get back to me soon as you can. My eyes only."

"Yes sir," said Smith.

The President left the room as abruptly as he had arrived. For a moment, the others simply stared at one another. Donovan placed his hand on Wally Smith's shoulder and leant over to have a word in his ear. "You focus on the coded messages and the paper trail. Leave it to me to keep an eye on Tavon."

"That's not what..."

"If he asks, you tell him it was my idea. This way you're not breaking any laws about domestic surveillance."

Smith raised an eyebrow. "That's good of you, Bill, thanks."

"There is one thing you could do for me."

"Name it."

"Lend me Eloise for a few days. She knows all my shortcomings."

# THIRTEEN

July 4, 1952

Donovan slapped the desk. "Goddamn it, Independence Day is too soon. We don't have enough time."

Eloise Page gave him a wistful smile. The same man she knew and loved was much older now, more prone to bad temper and cursing. "We are one step ahead. Our man has no idea he's being watched, and we will have as many sets of eyes on him as we can muster. We will do all we can in the time allowed. So, if you please, Mr Donovan, do not take the Lord's name in vain."

Donovan stared at her fondly. "My humble apologies, Miss Page." He'd forgotten how prim and proper she could be.

Eloise gazed around the book-lined study, and for a moment it was just like old times. She'd spent so many hours in this room, scheming and strategizing. She'd been his executive secretary through the early years of the OSS, though that title hardly did justice to all she'd done to keep the organization running. She'd had a major hand in planning the Allied invasion of North Africa, not that anyone knew.

Donovan himself freely admitted Eloise had been the organizational backbone to many of their earliest successes during the war. It had been no surprise that Eloise Page was one of the first of his people snapped up by the new CIA.

Miss Page was the perfect southern lady: she spent her weekdays planning overseas spy operations, then set aside the world of espionage to teach Sunday school. Part of Donovan wondered if he'd be better off just stepping back to let Eloise run the whole surveillance operation. She'd been here for less than an hour, and had already calmly laid out a clear and sensible plan of attack. Scores of Donovan's people had risen to greatness since the war; it made mustering a trusted crew at short notice a pain in the neck.

"David's not due back in the country for weeks. I couldn't even get through to the embassy in Paris," Donovan admitted.

For his efforts in successfully running OSS European operations, David Bruce had been appointed Ambassador to France in 1949. His posting there was about to run its course, but there was no way to fly him back to Washington for a garden party without questions being asked.

"I think we'll be fine without the Ambassador," Eloise assured him. "We have Barbara Lauwers and Gail Donnalley."

That brightened him up. "Barbara's terrific. But isn't Gail a bureaucrat now?"

"Suffice to say Mr Donnalley is stuck in a basement office at the Bureau of the Budget and bored stiff. He can't wait to join us. There'll be six, including Dr Menzel and General Vandenberg. It's enough, if we spread ourselves out."

Sitting here with him in close quarters, Eloise could see he'd let his guard down; she took that as a sign of his trust. The feeling was distinctly mutual (Eloise had always been a little too fond of the General), but she couldn't help thinking all those years of high pressure had finally caught up with him. It wasn't like Bill Donovan to get this worked up about a straightforward monitoring operation. She wondered if he'd finally lost his notorious appetite for risk.

Donovan's eyes widened at something he'd seen over her shoulder. She turned around. The study was empty. "What is it?"

He said nothing, but his eyes were wide.

"She can't see or hear me," Paolo assured Donovan, even though his sonorous voice seemed to fill the room. How could Eloise not hear that?

"It's nothing," said Donovan. "I thought I saw someone come in. My eyes playing tricks on me."

Paolo moved closer to the desk in a strange half-step, half-glide motion. He had developed the ability to project his apparition to any location on Earth — a remarkable if highly disturbing mental power — refined over thousands of years spent trapped inside a coffin-sized life-support unit. The ghost of Paolo Favaloro had haunted Donovan's thoughts and dreams for more than a year.

Donovan turned his attention to Eloise, ignoring her obvious concern. "I'm afraid I may not be much use tonight. Our man already knows me. And he'll have dozens of his staff there. We'll need to watch all of them."

"What exactly do you think he's up to?" Eloise asked.

"Anything unusual," he said.

"Criminal or political?"

"You don't need this woman," said Paolo. "You only need me."

Donovan gave a quick shake of his head, but didn't dare respond aloud.

"You think neither?" asked Eloise.

"Sorry. Network building, money laundering, drug trafficking, treason." This was why Donovan needed her here — to keep him sharp. Eloise had a knack for putting matters into proper perspective. The ghost was only a distraction. "All I know is, the man associates with criminals and he's privy to highly sensitive information."

"I will watch him for you all night," said Paolo. "I will tell you every word he utters. Do with this woman as you wish, but leave the business to me."

Donovan tried hard to ignore him. "Is there anything I can get you, Eloise? Coffee? Tea?"

She smiled, tilting her head inquisitively as she declined the offer. He was hiding something. "We have the guest list," she said. "I can't see anybody we need to worry about."

"What about the Russians?" asked Paolo.

"There are no Russians... Lucky for us," said Donovan, more forcefully than intended. "But there's always the possibility someone has gone over to the Reds and we don't know about it. We'll need to keep an eye on his staff too."

"It's Tavon we need to watch, not his staff," Eloise argued.

"Unless one of them is a Russian agent."

"Lord, spare me the Joe McCarthy paranoia."

Donovan laughed a little. Paolo was standing right behind her now like the devil on her back. If only she knew. "Paranoia is a spy's best friend, my dear."

"I'm not at all sure that's right, but I agree we need to be prepared for the unexpected."

Eloise Page had come so far since leaving his side. There was no longer fear in her eyes. He used to be the one offering her reassurances. He considered telling her about Paolo, just for the sake of full disclosure. But there was just no time to journey down that rabbit hole.

It was fortuitous that both he and Hoyt Vandenberg were regulars on Lady Lewis's guest list. Donovan had used his invitation as the template to forge copies for the rest of their team. He doubted anybody on the door would question arrivals — nobody in Washington high society would be caught dead at a party to which they weren't invited. But it would be Tavon's people on the door, and he wanted to be ready for anything.

Things began to go wrong the moment they walked through the door. Lee Tavon had been near the entrance to the ballroom; he spotted Donovan on arrival. "We meet again, General Donovan. Good to see you, sir." Tavon glanced at his date.

"Lee Tavon, let me introduce you to my good friend, Eloise Page."

The wicked smile on Tavon's face suggested he thought Donovan was up to no good. He reached out and kissed Miss Page on the hand. "Lovely to meet you, my dear. Now you must both excuse me, I'm working tonight, you see." He directed them into the room. "I'll make sure my boys and girls take good care of you. Enjoy."

Lee Tavon dissolved into the crowd, directing wait staff like he was conducting an orchestra.

"Was that what I think it was?" Eloise whispered.

"Yes, I suspect so."

Tavon might be onto them. Donovan's name was, after all, on the guest list. But he felt certain the operation could still pay off, assuming Tavon didn't know who else they had in the room.

Yet in the hours that followed, they learned next to nothing. Eloise tailed a waiter into the garden and busted him smoking a reefer, but other than that Tavon's operation looked clean as a whistle.

Paolo Favaloro thought so too. "He and his slaves appear to be doing no more than admirably performing the job for which they were hired," Paolo said.

Tavon's operation smelled like a front to Donovan, but he couldn't see any cracks in the façade. If Tavon was up to something tonight, he was a step ahead of everyone. Donovan had just retired to the garden to escape the cigarette smoke and watch the fireworks, when Eloise reappeared with that look in her eye. "Lady Lewis is about to introduce you to a reporter called Edna Drake. Be careful." Then more loudly, "I think I need more champagne." She drifted away and blended seamlessly into the periphery of Robert Taft's entourage, playing the flirty southern belle but observing Donovan all the while.

If he hadn't known it was coming, the introduction might have come off as perfectly spontaneous. But Donovan could see a look of intent in the eyes of Edna Drake. His hackles rose the moment she mentioned flying saucers. When she invoked FS-1, his chest constricted in panic. It took all his self-control not to gasp for air. He felt like he'd been cornered, fearing she must know he was the man who'd acquired the saucer.

Paolo appeared right behind her upon mention of the saucer. "You should have told me about her sooner." Donovan couldn't help but be distracted by his unwanted arrival. Despite Donovan's best effort to ignore him, Paolo had his own stake in the matter. "You must deal with her."

Donovan knew what he meant. And as abhorrent as the notion of killing a fellow American might have been a few minutes ago, he found himself considering it. He got away from her at the first opportunity, his heart pounding as he looked for a place to sit down and catch his breath.

Eloise was at his side. She could read him like a book. "Do we follow her?"

He nodded. "All night if you have to."

Eloise frowned, concerned at what had left him so shocked. "What did she say?"

He shook his head dismissively, taking a moment to catch his breath. Page took him by the hand, fearing Donovan might be having a heart attack. He squeezed her fingers like he was holding on for dear life as the color drained from his face. "She knows, Eloise. She goddamn knows. You need to get after her. Now."

# FOURTEEN

July 5, 1952

Edna woke up early with a sizeable headache, a nagging sense of regret, and no idea where she was. The bedroom was utterly unfamiliar.

Sadly, the man lying on the bed next to her was not. Joe Eldridge was snoring like an air raid siren. It had woken her up. The night's events — good, bad, and ugly — came flooding back. Good was the possibility of a lead from General Donovan. Bad was the pounding in her skull and the stink of stale tobacco smoke and dismal sex. Ugly was the lump asleep beside her. She rose as gingerly as she could manage, hoping not to wake him.

A shower and strong coffee would be a big part of her immediate future, but not before Edna put some distance between her and Eldridge. She could have argued that it seemed like a good idea at the time, but in truth he had been nothing more than a way to avoid another night at home alone. Not a bad thing of itself, except that Joe was the only male colleague Edna had valued as a friend.

Edna Drake picked her clothes up off the floor and dressed quickly, then opened the bedroom door just far enough to slip into the large and well-appointed lounge room. A fully stocked bar was stacked with enough glassware to cater for a wedding. She dimly remembered Joe mentioning it was the Atlantic Oil Company's fuck pad. A place to get congressmen drunk and then bed them down for the night with the hostess of their choice.

Edna looked around for the bathroom, her bladder fit to burst. She made it just in time, sighing with relief and staring at the mosaic tiles like the grout might be a map of the way home. One glance in the mirror confirmed her worst suspicion; makeup was plastered across her face like a Salvador Dali nightmare. She washed off the war paint as best she could and dried her face on a pristine white towel from a stack on a nearby shelf. It was more brown than white by the time she'd finished.

She thought about leaving a note, but decided against it. After arranging her hair into something vaguely forgivable, Edna made a beeline for the lobby.

The building was on Massachusetts Avenue; she had no problem hailing a taxi. The driver huffed when she told him she was headed for the Maine Avenue Fish Markets.

"Nasty part of town. You sure?"

"It's where I live."

She saw his eyes narrow, thinking nice girls didn't go to that part of town.

Southwest Washington might be earmarked for demolition and urban renewal, but until then it remained an enclave of the city's negro population; most white folk steered well clear. The driver had a crucifix hanging from his rearview mirror. Every now and then, he glanced back at Edna darkly like she was a harlot from hell. "Eyes on the road, bub." A harlot she may be, but he could keep his piety to himself while he was on her dime.

Edna didn't believe in any sort of hell that wasn't made by human hands. There had been no room for a god in her life since those horrific weeks in postwar Berlin, treating an endless stream of shamed and shattered women for venereal disease after they were raped by Russian soldiers. Many took their own lives. Others learned quickly to separate themselves from their bodies, and would give freely of themselves for a meal or even a pack of cigarettes. She'd seen the primitive animal within the hearts of men. There was nothing but an utter absence of godliness in their acts of violence.

The air was ripe at the fish markets. She hopped out of the car before handing over the fare. The taxi driver counted the money and didn't look happy with the number.

Edna Drake laughed. "You sit there and judge me and you still want a tip? Here's one: go to hell."

He snarled and spat at her feet. "Nigger whore."

Edna resisted the urge to kick the car door; she saw the atavistic look in his eyes. He wanted her, and he hated himself for it. "Sugar, this nigger whore wouldn't touch you if you were the last drooling slob on Earth."

He looked like he was ready to leap out of the cab and punch her, but the commotion had attracted a crowd and they were assuredly not on his side. He drove away, muttering wild obscenities. Edna sighed, nodding her thanks to the young men standing their ground on her behalf.

Edna walked with as much pride as she could muster toward the unassuming door to her building, wedged between Mamma Rey's and Sheldon's Tailoring. It was like her own secret door; most people never noticed it was there. She closed it behind her, locking the world comfortably outside. The stairwell was dark. The light in the hallway had been out for weeks. When she'd mentioned it to her landlord, he just shrugged like it wasn't his problem. He'd given up spending money on a building everyone expected to take the wrecking ball.

She flipped open her door and gratefully stepped into what was best described as a dirty low-down dive, wondering why she'd been in such a hurry to flee Cathedral Heights. At least it smelled like home. It wasn't much this joint, but it was cheap and private and all hers. No roommate, no man to tell her what to do. She'd furnished the place more with imagination than money, a lively throw rug hiding the holes in her couch, well-worn and wine-stained rugs livening up the threadbare and wine-stained carpet, a kitchen cupboard loaded with stained, cracked crockery liberated from a local restaurant that had shut its doors for good.

Edna didn't exactly do a lot of entertaining; she ate out. A lot.

She opened a window, thrilled to the noise of laughter from the street, the smell of bacon and eggs from Mamma Rey's. She took a deep breath and reminded herself she needed a long, hot bath.

She was feeling much more like herself when she finally picked up her telephone, a recent extravagance that made her feel like a real reporter. Edna loved the feel of the Bakelite receiver in her hand. She'd held guns and knives, but this was her weapon of choice. The rotary dial telephone had to be one of the wonders of the decade, and having one in her home made her feel incredibly modern.

"Chance, Whittle and Spence, good morning." A woman's voice.

"Oh," said Edna, "I was hoping to speak to General Bill Donovan, or his secretary."

"You're speaking to her. Is this Miss Drake?"

"Yes, that's right."

"General Donovan said he would like to see you at eleven o'clock, if that's convenient. Do you know where we are?"

The offices of Chance, Whittle and Spence reflected their high standing in the legal community. They took up four floors of a perfectly terrifying old townhouse in Jefferson Place, a stone's throw from Dupont Circle and the Embassy district.

Just inside the main entrance, a woman in her fifties sat behind the reception desk. She looked up and smiled without meaning it. "Miss Drake?"

"Yes, that's right. I had no idea the General worked here."

"He's a silent partner. Can I get you anything before I take you in?"

"No, I'm fine." In truth, she could do with another coffee, but Edna wasn't going to ask. "What's your name?"

"I am Miss Fisk. Follow me please." She ushered Edna along an elegant wood-lined corridor that smelled like old money. Miss Fisk opened the door to an office where Donovan was planted behind a desk. He rose to his feet, stepped forward to offer her a gentle handshake, then pointed to a chair.

"Thanks for coming in," Donovan began. "I'm glad we crossed paths last night. After you left, I spoke to a few old friends of mine. One of them was Gordon Gray, and it turns out you were talking with him earlier in the night."

"Yes," Edna said, suddenly feeling more nervous. Something in Bill Donovan's tone was off-key.

"Gordon tells me you two did nothing more than pass the time of day." He waved a finger at her. "But I think one of you is lying to me, Miss Drake." Donovan said the words quietly. Almost like he wasn't being serious.

"I never said Mr Gray was my source."

"But you knew I'd assume it was him."

"Honestly, General, I did no such thing. You made that assumption all on your own. Mr Gray is telling you the truth. He gave me nothing but polite party conversation." Edna made a mental note to call Gray back at the first opportunity. "Is this the part where you tell me FS-1 is the real deal?"

Bill Donovan smiled again. It chilled her to the bone. "No, that would be an assumption on *your* part. In my opinion, you're the victim of misinformation. I'm glad I caught it. Neither you nor the US Government needs this splashed across a newspaper."

Edna shook her head, unwilling to let him dismiss it quite so easily. He wouldn't have taken this meeting if he thought it was a waste of time. "General, if the material sent to me has been fabricated, someone's gone to an awful lot of trouble to do so."

Donovan smiled. "That's how this game works, Miss Drake. What sort of material are we talking about? Do you have it with you?"

"I do, as a matter of fact."

"Would you show it to me?"

She realized she'd made a tactical error in not making a copy. Given the simmering threat in Donovan's demeanor, Edna wouldn't put it past him to destroy the letter if he got his hands on it. She pulled it out of her purse and held it up for him to see. "It's a letter. Why don't I read it to you?"

Donovan stood up and reached out his hand. "Please — I'd like to see it."

She pushed her chair back and leapt to her feet. "Take one more step and I'll run out of here as fast as my legs will carry me."

Donovan's face went red and he sat down again. "That won't be necessary."

Edna gave herself a moment to calm down. "It's marked Top Secret Majestic. You may know what that means. There's some sort of code beneath that ... OCS 21367-33. It's dated May fifth, for the urgent consideration of President H. Truman, Director of Central Intelligence General W. Smith, and US Air Force Chief of Staff General H. Vandenberg." She looked down at Donovan for a reaction, but he gave her nothing.

"Go on," he insisted.

"It's headed 'Flight Request'. And it reads: 'Decision required in analysis of FS-1. Since craft acquired April 1951, progress limited in determining composition of outer hull. Engineers yet to confirm method of propulsion. Some advance made in understanding system of operation. Accordingly request approval for test flight at date and location to be determined. Sincerely, R. Hillenkoetter.'"

"Why are you so keen to believe this is genuine?" Donovan asked.

"Frankly sir, the fact that I'm sitting here talking to you already tells me it's genuine."

Bill Donovan laughed, but his feigned amusement was an attempt to hide a more serious concern. "Let me offer you some friendly advice, Miss Drake. Throw that letter away. It's not what I'd call credible intelligence. You'll earn yourself a bad reputation by pursuing it. You don't want that sort of aggravation tainting your journalistic career."

It felt more like a threat than friendly advice. Donovan didn't give a damn about her career.

"Despite what members of the press might want to believe," he continued, "America's flying saucer fascination is nothing more than comic strip make-believe. There isn't a shred of reliable evidence to back it up."

"With respect, General Donovan, you're avoiding the topic at hand. We're talking about a research program apparently being conducted by the Government, or at least on behalf of the Government. So why don't we cut the crap? Why did you really want to meet me this morning?" Edna calmly took her seat again.

Donovan took a deep breath and swallowed the words he so dearly wanted to scream at her. "I'm here as a patriot, Miss Drake. This saucer hysteria is not good. It's damaging the nation's prestige. If enough people start believing the papers, it could become a threat to national security. That is what concerns me."

"How is that possible?"

"If the Russians decide to exploit it."

"Are you telling me it's the Russians up there?" Edna asked.

"No, that's not what I'm saying. But do you see how easily words get twisted? I'm saying the Russians could use our fears against us, say, by staging a mock alien invasion."

"You mean like Orson Wells and *War of the Worlds*?"

An entire nation driven to hysteria by a radio play purporting to be a live news event.

"Precisely," he said. "That was an accident. Imagine what might be possible with malicious intent, all of it powered by our great and powerful free press?"

"You don't want me to publish the story."

"I'm appealing to your conscience. Don't do it. Your reputation is on the line. Who knows, maybe even your entire career."

"Yes, you said that."

"Do you know why we have a free press?" Donovan asked.

Edna pursed her lips and breathed out slowly. He was treating her like a fool, but she didn't want to give him the satisfaction of seeing her lose her cool again. "To defend our rights in a free society, for starters."

"But our world is never truly free, is it? There's always a price paid by someone to defend that freedom."

"I held the hands of dying boys all the way from Normandy to Brandenburg, you don't need to tell me that," Edna bit out.

Donovan nodded sympathetically. "I know you did. So, you must also understand freedom is something we must keep fighting to protect." He leant forward and spoke like the walls had ears. "You've come to the attention of certain people. The sort who would swat you down like an insect the moment they deem you to be a risk to national security. You seem like a smart young woman. I'd hate to see that happen to you."

"That sounds like a threat."

"Well, you're right, that's exactly what it sounds like. But I'm afraid it's rather more of a promise. I'm telling you now, stand down."

Their meeting was over. Edna was starting to feel a little sick. She rose slowly to her feet, feeling giddy. "Thank you for seeing me, General Donovan. I appreciate you taking the time." She tried hard not to let him see her knees were trembling. She didn't want to be here anymore. It didn't feel safe.

"Think about what I said," General Bill Donovan insisted. "Above all else, we are talking about the greater good."

Edna could feel the office walls closing in on her. She turned her back on him to leave the room, half expecting to find the office door locked. But the handle turned. The door opened.

"Needless to say, this is all off the record, Miss Drake." Edna turned to face him with the unshakable certainty that she was staring down a man who was prepared to kill her. "If you try to quote me, I'll deny we've spoken. Then I'll sue you and your paper into the ground."

The offhand certainty hit her more than the words themselves. Edna had stumbled behind the veil — to that place where men of power and renown act without recourse to the law, untroubled by traditional notions of right and wrong. Bill Donovan was making it clear he held Edna Drake's existence in the palm of his hand. She nodded, turning away quickly to step into the corridor and make her escape. Head spinning, she stumbled past Miss Fisk toward the outside world.

It took all her willpower to make it around the corner before throwing up.

# FIFTEEN

July 5, 1952

As he watched Edna Drake pull the office door closed behind her, Donovan wondered whether it was a mistake not to simply force her to hand the letter over. However, doing so would only serve to underline its importance. Besides, he had no way of knowing whether she had made copies, nor whether confiscating it would do anything to deter the reporter from publishing. However he'd put the fear of God into Edna Drake, which was what mattered most at this point.

"She's gone."

A side door opened and Father Clarence Paulson entered the room. His half-grown beard made him look like a bum. Not that Donovan would dare say such a thing to the man — his ego was frail enough as it was.

Flanking Paulson was the apparition of Paolo Favaloro — on this occasion summoned by Paulson, who likewise retained a close connection with the ancient king from their years of close contact in the Vatican archives. Donovan had busted Paulson out of the Vatican to save the father from being committed to a church mental asylum. Now he was part of the Verus Foundation security detail. The priest and Donovan had become a comfort to one another, each assuring the other that Paolo's presence in their lives was the wonder of a long-lost science, and not delusional madness.

For years, the reality of Utnapishtim's existence had been a revelation acknowledged by Clarence Paulson alone. The priest had shared this knowledge with Pope Pius and the Roman Curia. They thought Paulson had lost his mind, because for years Utnapishtim declined to reveal himself to anyone else.

For many years, the Mesopotamian king's sarcophagus was kept cloistered in an underground vault of the Vatican's secret archives, where Paulson had likewise remained. Then Donovan arrived and Paolo saw fit to reveal himself to someone else. Donovan assured the Pope that Father Paulson was not mad, merely misunderstood. For this and for many other reasons, Paulson owed Donovan his life.

Paulson remained on American soil by special arrangement. Officially, he was an Apostolic nuncio to the Verus Foundation, a permanent diplomatic representative of the Holy See. In practice, Paulson was free to perform whatever task Donovan saw fit, so long as he also occasionally played US bagman to the Vatican bank.

"Do you think it worked?" Paulson asked. "Have you scared her off?"

Donovan said, "I scared her half to death. I doubt she'll be a problem. But we'll keep an eye on her, just the same."

Paolo folded his arms. "I told you Gordon Gray was not her source."

Donovan dimly thought it odd that he had almost become accustomed to this translucent specter in his life. "You're right, Paolo. You told me and I didn't listen. But we can, I think, be assured her knowledge is limited to the contents of that letter."

Paulson said, "Edna Drake will try to talk to Gray now, Bill. You'd better warn him." His tone was one of admonishment for Donovan's slipup in mentioning Gordon Gray.

"Perhaps," said Donovan, who was not given to openly admitting his own mistakes. "But I'm sure Gordon will think on his feet. He'll keep his mouth shut. He knows what will happen to Drake if we don't spike this story before it gets any further."

"Speaking of which," said Paulson, "we still need to find the source of the leak, if it's not Tavon."

"I think Roscoe Hillenkoetter might be our man," said Donovan. "That letter can't have had a wide circulation. The names she read out are our prime suspects. We can safely exclude the President, the head of the CIA, and the Air Force Chief of Staff."

"If you say so," said Paolo.

Truman had torn Donovan a new asshole at their last meeting. Donovan had taken it upon himself to investigate the possibility of a leak within FS-1. Donald Menzel was the only other person who knew what Donovan was doing — the fewer people in the loop, the better. "Clarence, I need you to take a close look at Hillenkoetter. But keep your distance. Can you do that for me?"

"Of course," said Paulson. "But if anyone needs to speak to him..."

"It'll have to be me," said Donovan, nodding in agreement. "Paolo. Watch the reporter. See who she's talking to. If we're lucky, she'll lead us straight to our man."

Paolo smiled, pleased he had finally gained admission to Donovan's inner circle.

Paulson asked, "What about you?"

"I'm going to stay on Lee Tavon."

"Edna Drake didn't speak to Tavon at the party," said Paulson.

"Yes, but he's a wild card. I don't understand him, and it troubles me."

Paolo said, "I can help you with Tavon too." Donovan nodded, finally bowing to the inevitable. It was only when he saw the quizzical look on Paulson's face that Donovan realized Paolo had said the words aloud.

# SIXTEEN

J uly 5, 1952

The offices of the *Times-Herald* were pretty quiet on a Saturday. Theo Mankiewicz was his own closed door, putting the Monday feature pages to bed. On the other side of the newsroom, racing reporter Ernie Badmolles was on the sports desk, in the middle of a heated telephone discussion with a bookie. Neither of them gave Edna a second glance, but for once she was glad to see them. After her confrontation with Donovan, she couldn't face being at home on her own. She wanted the comfort of familiar faces around her, while she considered what she was going to do about the fact that her career and future wellbeing might now be in the hands of people who could do what they liked to her and get away with it.

Edna sat at her desk and stared at her typewriter, trying to imagine what might happen if she wrote the story she wanted to write — about a leaked document, and the veiled threats it had evoked from a man who might just be acting on behalf of the President.

But as Edna Drake thought about it, there was nothing Donovan had said that could be construed as anything even resembling a direct threat. *You've come to the attention of certain people*, he'd said. *The sort who would swat you down like an insect the moment they deem you to be a risk to national security.*

Donovan had told her his words were off the record. In these circumstances, that wouldn't be enough to stop Edna putting them to print. But what did they prove? He would truthfully argue he'd been warning her, not threatening her. That it wasn't the substance of the letter that mattered, merely how it would be perceived if she went public with it.

On its own, the letter didn't justify taking that sort of risk. She needed more. But after her meeting with Donovan, she was starting to wonder if she had the guts to write the story at all.

She should tell someone. But how could she do that without sounding like a lightweight? She considered Mankiewicz; he'd have some useful advice. He also despised female reporters, which was odd for someone whose boss was a woman.

Bazy Miller appeared at that moment, as if on cue. "Edna! What brings you into work on a Saturday? Did you find yourself a scoop last night? Weren't those fireworks marvelous?"

"Hello Mrs Miller. Yes, quite the spectacle." Edna sighed inwardly. Did Bazy know? She didn't have the stomach for this conversation right now.

"Oh dear," said Mrs Miller, reading her expression. "Anything you want to talk about?"

"No. I mean, I'm fine. I'm just...waiting for Ernie's hot tip on race five at Laurel."

Bazy Miller laughed, somewhat condescendingly. She was dressed more casually than usual, but still with the same air of authority. Her wavy brown bob parted in the middle made her look like a librarian. Big tortoise-shell glasses completed the look, so prim and proper. Edna couldn't help feeling her boss worked hard to suppress her natural good looks in the office setting. Bazy certainly didn't approve of Edna's wardrobe choices, which tended to attract attention rather than deflect it. "Tread lightly," Mrs Miller warned. "I find Ernie's hot tips often end up cold motherless last."

"It's for my dad." Which was half true. "But thank you, I'll keep that in mind. What brings you in today?"

Bazy pointed toward Mankiewicz's office. Edna could already sense the features editor staring at both of them. Mrs Miller nodded, and made a beeline for his office without another word. As Mankiewicz closed the door, he flicked Edna a sour glance to make it crystal clear their conversation was not to be overheard.

Bazy Miller was handed the reins of the *Times-Herald* after the death of her aunt, Cissy Patterson. The legendary editor and publisher had run both the *Washington Times* and *Washington Herald* on behalf of owner William Randolph Hearst for almost a decade, before buying both mastheads from Hearst in 1939 and merging them. Patterson then spent the following decade working and drinking herself to death.

Cissy had hired Edna as a photographic assistant back in '47, then appointed her as assistant to society columnist Martha Blair. It was supposed to be a promotion, but it was a job Edna hated with a passion. She'd been too terrified of Cissy's explosive temper to ask for a job on the news desk, which was what she'd really wanted. When Bazy Miller took over in '49, Edna bit the bullet and boldly threw her cards down on the table. Mrs Miller granted Edna her wish, though since then it'd be fair to say Edna had struggled to make her mark. The problem was, all too often Edna found herself at odds with the paper's uncompromisingly conservative agenda. Several of her stories had been spiked because they were seen to be painting the Truman administration in a positive light.

Edna suspected Eldridge was right — if Mrs Miller found out about this letter now, her boss would think picking a fight with the Defense Department and the intelligence community was the best plan of attack. But it would be Edna in the crosshairs. Publish and be damned was fine, but people like Donovan didn't play by the rules. In her experience, when powerful forces locked horns, it was the little people who suffered.

She'd never felt more pathetic and alone in her life. There was no doubt in Edna's mind Donovan would follow through on his threat to sue, but that would be the least of it. General Bill Donovan's reaction almost certainly meant the letter was genuine, but neither the letter on its own, nor her intuition about its authenticity, would be enough to make the story stand up in court. She could do as Eldridge suggested and pursue Admiral Hillenkoetter, but Donovan surely would have cauterized that line of inquiry by now.

What stung the most of all was her suspicion that her reluctance meant Edna lacked the courage to be a real reporter. Because the more she thought about it, the more she felt this story might be better left untold.

# SEVENTEEN

J uly 6, 1952

It was getting late, but Lee Tavon was showing no signs of stopping. Since leaving his room at the Hotel Harrington and hailing a taxi shortly after ten o'clock, he'd been walking empty streets for two hours.

He'd started in Rock Creek Park. Donovan had known he couldn't follow him into the park without being seen. Luckily, he didn't have to. Paolo did the tailing. Donovan had to admit it, in many ways Paolo was the perfect spy. Unless he chose to reveal himself, he was invisible. He could be right beside someone and they'd never know it.

Furthermore, Paolo and Donovan were linked to one another's thoughts as if by a mental radio receiver. When Paolo spoke, Donovan heard his voice like they were sitting next to one other.

From half a mile away, Donovan was now receiving a running commentary on their target's pace and direction. Tavon had followed a walking trail inside the park for almost half an hour before eventually emerging on to Rodman Street, where he continued west for a short way before turning north onto Reno Road and heading for Wakefield. Busy roads were obviously not Tavon's thing — at the first opportunity, he turned west onto Van Ness. There he began threading his way along lonely, tree-lined streets, pausing often to admire the large homes of well-to-do Washingtonians in North Cleveland Park. Most of the windows were dark, but occasionally, seeing a light on, he would stop and stare.

"He's watching a man smoking his pipe," Paolo reported. "He enjoys seeing without being seen."

"Something you have in common," said Donovan, tapping the steering wheel and wondering if it was time to move again. He'd been trying his best to stay ahead of Tavon in the hope that eventually his destination might reveal itself.

But it was starting to look like Tavon was headed nowhere in particular. He maintained the same strolling pace for another half an hour, stopping occasionally to spy on someone for a few moments, before moving on again. None of the homes Tavon watched appeared to be of anything more than passing interest. "What is he doing? Looking for someone?"

"It doesn't feel like a search," said Paolo. "It looks to me like he's merely curious. He stops when he sees an opening."

"What does that mean? He's a peeping Tom?"

"Maybe. I can't be certain. Wait, he's just picked up his pace. He checked his watch and started walking faster. As if he just realized he's running late."

"Which way?"

"He's moving north along 39th Street. He just passed the intersection of Alton Place and he's staying on 39th."

He's changing his pattern, Donovan thought.

"Turning now. West onto Albemarle Street. Crossing Nebraska Avenue and staying on Albemarle."

"He's heading for Wisconsin Avenue," Donovan realized. It was definitely time to move now. He'd been parked outside Woodrow Wilson High School and keeping a safe distance. But if Tavon was on a busy street, Donovan might be able to risk watching him in plain sight.

"You're right," Paolo reported. "He's just turned north onto Wisconsin Avenue."

Donovan took a left onto Wisconsin and began cruising slowly south, knowing he would cross Tavon's path any moment. He pulled his car along the curb opposite a row of shops, noticing the neon sign still glowing in the window of Bishop's Wine and Liquor. Everything else was closed. This had to be Tavon's destination. Donovan turned off his engine and killed the lights.

Tavon appeared on the opposite side of the road less than a minute later and headed straight for the liquor store. As he entered, he waved a friendly hello to the store owner behind the counter, who didn't look up from his newspaper. Bishop's was larger than the average liquor store. It had rows of expensive red wines to serve the discerning tastes of its wealthy local clientele. Tavon disappeared behind a row of bottles just as another man walked into the store. Nearly midnight, and suddenly business was booming.

"I'm inside the store now," said Paolo. Donovan couldn't see him. He had no idea how Paolo actually moved through space — whether he walked or simply floated. "This doesn't look good, Bill. This man is very agitated. I think you need to see this for yourself."

"Oh God," Donovan muttered. "Really?"

"Close your eyes," said Paolo. He was suggesting a mind merge. They'd done it before, but Donovan always found it extremely disconcerting. He could only do it with his eyes closed — experiencing two realities at once gave him terrible head spins. But by sitting perfectly still with his eyes clamped shut, Donovan would momentarily see the world through Paolo's eyes.

"OK," said Donovan, "go."

His world abruptly snapped from darkness to bright light, and he found himself inside Bishop's Wine and Liquor, staring at the man who had walked in behind Tavon. He was up to no good, it was written all over his face. Then he pulled out a gun.

Without saying a word, he walked behind the counter and smacked the store owner across the mouth with the butt of his pistol. "Money!" he yelled. "Now. All of it."

The store owner stood his ground. Blood was dripping from his mouth, but he didn't move a muscle. Donovan thought he looked like a soldier; he wasn't afraid. It was probably not the first time he'd been robbed, either. He appeared to be sizing up his assailant, trying to work out how to give him the least of what he wanted.

"Booze," he said. "Take whatever bottle you want. There's nothin' in the till, I just took it to the bank a half hour ago."

The man with the gun shook his head; he wasn't falling for that. "I been out there, watchin'. You ain't gone nowhere, old man. Don't mess me around, or I'll paint your brains all over the window."

"What's your name, son? Mine's Jimmy. Jimmy Peterson."

"Shut up!"

Perhaps it was one last act of defiance, or maybe a final awakening to the fickle pointlessness of existence. Either way, Jimmy Peterson decided to step up. Tonight, he wasn't going to back down. The owner took one step forward and reached for the robber's gun. But youth and desperation were the only two things this guy had going for him. He was too quick. He shot old Jimmy in the head.

"No!" yelled Donovan. But nobody reacted to his cry, because he wasn't really there. He was still inside a car, a hundred feet away across the street.

The murderer ripped open the cash register drawer, pulled out a handful of bills, and shoved them into his pocket. Gun still smoking in one hand, he grabbed a bottle of Old Grand Dad Kentucky bourbon in the other and moved to leave. Which was when he found himself face-to-face with a new problem.

A witness.

Lee Tavon stepped forward. Did he have a death wish? For a moment, the killer looked ready to point and shoot again. But Tavon was way ahead of him. "It's time to leave now, Jeb."

"How'd you...?"

"I know all about you, Jeb Stanton. Jimmy was one of ours. Put the gun away now. You don't want to make it any worse than it is already."

Jeb's thoughts were writ large on his face; he was terrified. He knew in the pit of his faltering heart he should accept Tavon's advice, if he knew what was good for him. But Jeb had never known what was good for him. He held the gun up to Tavon's face. "One dead, two dead. Ain't no difference to me."

Tavon stared back at him coolly. "You shoot me, you're the dead man. That much I can promise you."

Donovan believed him. So did Jeb Stanton; he lowered his gun, turned, and ran out the front door without looking back. Tavon stared after the killer for an uncomfortably long period of time, though it could only have been seconds. Then he stepped over Jimmy's body to look behind the counter for the store's telephone. "Operator? Get me the police. Yes, hello? I'm at Bishop's Wine and Liquor on Wisconsin Avenue. I'm sorry to say the owner of the store has just been shot dead. It's terrible. There's blood everywhere. You better come quick." Tavon pushed down the receiver then lifted up his finger. "Yes operator, can you put me through to the *Times-Herald* please. Hello? I'd like to speak to Edna Drake."

# EIGHTEEN

July 6, 1952

Donovan opened his eyes and he was back inside his car. He watched as Tavon left the liquor store, crossed the road right in front of him, and disappeared down a nearby side street. "You're still with him, aren't you?" he asked Paolo.

"I'm right beside him. He stopped as soon as he got around the corner. He's waiting."

"He wants to see who's coming," Donovan realized.

Tavon was still there, peering back at the liquor store, when the police arrived a few minutes later. Two uniformed officers found Jimmy Peterson's body. Donovan didn't know what to do. For a moment, he considered getting out of the car to speak to the police. But what would he tell them? He'd seen the whole thing, and that another witness had conveniently identified the shooter? The cops wouldn't buy that for a second. Who would? He'd be arrested on the spot. Donovan sat tight. Less than five minutes later, a plain-clothes detective arrived.

"What's Tavon doing?" he asked Paolo.

"He keeps peering around the corner."

Was this another peeping Tom thing? Did he somehow set up that shooting? Donovan observed the uniformed officers stiffen as the detective walked into the murder scene. They were either afraid of him, or they didn't like him. Maybe both.

Another car pulled up. It was Edna Drake with a photographer. The snapper immediately began firing off his flash. The streetscape strobed like it was being hit by lightning.

One of the uniforms greeted the reporter out front. She must have known him. Somehow, she talked her way inside the liquor store to get a look at the murder scene. The photographer took two more shots before the detective yelled at them to get the hell out. Edna tried to ask him some questions, but the detective gave her the brush off.

Donovan wound down his window to listen in as Edna returned to the pavement.

"Your detective's a real ball-breaker," she told the uniform boys.

They smiled. "Don't I know it," one of the replied.

"What's his name?" she asked.

"Kaplan." The young policeman spat out the name like a swear word.

She started grilling them for information. They assured Edna they didn't know any more than she did.

"Tavon's leaving," said Paolo.

Donovan realized at that moment one of the cops had spotted him. He moved to cross the street, but a truck roared past the liquor store, giving Donovan the chance to start his engine and hit the road before the policeman could get to him. If they tracked him down, he'd truthfully tell them he never saw a thing.

# NINETEEN

July 7, 1952

It was nine in the morning. Start of the working day, for some. Edna had been at it all night, and she was pushing the front-page deadline on the next edition. Though with their printing schedule, there was always another edition if she missed this one. But they'd held the page for her, and Edna had assured the chief sub-editor she would get it done. She had plenty of material after spending hours at the crime scene, but Edna was playing it smart and holding back a lot of good material for a follow-up story. She was keeping this one simple, focusing on the police investigation, even though the cops had given her next to no detail to flesh it out. What they did have were exclusive photos of the crime scene. She was pleased to see the *Washington Post* had no more than a few lines on the murder, relegated to page two of their morning paper.

She was tantalizingly close to handing off her copy when the phone rang. She considered ignoring it, but couldn't bear the thought of missing another good story. "Newsroom. Hello?" She was too stressed to hide her annoyance.

"Miss Drake? Oh dear, it sounds like you're busy."

"Who is this?" she demanded.

"It's Gordon Gray. We met on the Fourth of July."

"Mr Gray?" She softened her tone. "This is a surprise. I was going to call you this week." That didn't sound in any way convincing. In truth, she'd just about written him off as another waste of time.

"Well, I'm glad I beat you to it." She was completely lost for words. General Donovan had almost certainly put him up to the call. "Listen," he said, "I can tell you're busy."

"Yeah, I, uh... Actually, I'm right on deadline."

"I'm back in town tonight. I'd like to buy you a drink."

"Would you?"

"Yes. If you're still interested."

"Uh, sure. I guess."

"It would have to be late, I'm afraid."

"I'm on the graveyard shift. I'm due back in the newsroom from midnight. I can meet you any time before then."

"Good, then let's say ten o'clock at the Jewel Box — do you know it?" Gray asked.

"Who doesn't?"

"Tonight then. I look forward to it." He hung up.

How strange. Gordon Gray, playing good cop to Donovan's bad cop. In public, so no danger there. Besides, she doubted Gray was capable of delivering Donovan's style of simmering menace. Her intrigue was now matching pace with her apprehension.

Story filed and sub-editors placated, Edna Drake placed a call to the one person who might be able to shed some light on Gordon Gray's motives. Lady Norma Lewis sounded delighted to hear from her. "Thank you so much for your wonderful hospitality on Friday night," said Edna, "I enjoyed myself immensely."

"You're too kind." Norma Lewis never tired of having her social events complimented. "I saw some wonderful photographs in your social pages. Did you have a hand in that?"

"I helped them out with a few words." A bald-faced lie.

"Splendid. Now my dear, what can I do for you?"

"It was something you said the other night. When I asked you for introductions, you said 'who else?' It's just dawned on me — did you mean Gordon Gray? Does he have intelligence connections too?"

"Oh, I'd assumed you already knew that," she said.

Edna heard the note of hesitance creeping into her voice, a confirmation all of its own. "I'm not asking you to betray a confidence, but is there anything more you can tell me about him?"

"Wonderful man. Very highly regarded, you know. Very clever. Truman hangs on his every word, as he should, the silly little man."

Lady Lewis was no Democrat.

"Are you saying Mr Gray retains an active role in government?"

"Oh dear, yes. But you didn't hear that from me."

"If I was to assume, for instance, he's on the books for the CIA, would I be barking up the wrong tree?"

Lady Lewis went quiet for a moment. Edna waited her out, knowing it was human nature for Norma Lewis to want to fill an awkward silence. "That's my understanding. But I really don't know any more than that."

"No, of course, I understand," Edna said. She felt that familiar rush of excitement at having an intriguing suspicion confirmed. "I assume you'll be watching the Republican Convention today?"

"How would I do that?"

"They're covering it live on the television. It's the first time ever."

"Are they now? I must have a listen."

Edna smiled. Lady Lewis was of that generation who saw television as radio with pictures. "General MacArthur is delivering the keynote address. I'm sure he'll have some colorful words about the current administration."

Lady Lewis laughed. "I don't doubt it."

# TWENTY

J uly 7, 1952

The glittering baubles that adorned the Jewel Box ceiling were mere colored glass, but the joint was all the richer for it. The bar's allure was all about the shameless tart vibe. Its patrons were happy to slum it, at the same time enjoying a sense of thumbing their nose at the highest authority.

The Jewel Box squatted proudly amid wealth and privilege on the corner of 16th and L streets, stared down by the White House a mere three blocks away. Many an overworked West Winger had drowned their sorrows here. Edna suspected many must be present tonight, lamenting the excoriating denunciation of General Douglas MacArthur's keynote speech to the Republican National Convention. MacArthur had accused the Truman administration of flagrant materialism and excess, then gone on to suggest they were all communists hell-bent on turning the American republic into a totalitarian state. It was a laughable overreach, but there were people taking it seriously.

A piano player in a bright purple suit was singing bawdy limericks to the tune of Al Martino's *Here In My Heart* — a peculiar and ribald riff on modern jazz that hit the right notes all wrong. It was just what the doctor ordered.

Normally, Edna knew exactly what a man had in mind when he suggested they meet at a lowdown watering hole at a time of night when good girls were safely tucked into bed. This place was undoubtedly well below Gordon Gray's standard, but she was guessing that Gray had assumed nobody would look twice at them here. The Jewel Box had earned its stripes as a place where people could meet incognito, no questions asked. Of course, since being named by *Washington Confidential* as one of the city's livelier hangouts, the place had been run off its feet. But it maintained its status as a cool hangout for hep cats, reefer heads, and political dissidents. The sort of joint Senator Joe McCarthy condemned as a haven for commie sympathizers. Those squares in Joe's camp tended to stand out like dog's balls and never made it past the doorman. Yet the Jewel Box never got raided. Word on the street was the police were paid generously to stay away. In here, people of all political colors knew they could let their hair down. It was the D.C. version of Rick's Café Americain.

Three barmen were working the crowd. Two of them were black. Beverley and Wendell, according to their name badges. The third was a white man; he had to be the owner. Edna knew she'd seen him before somewhere. His clientele, of course, were exclusively white. Washingtonians had no problems with having their booze served up by colored folk, but they weren't always so liberal in their choice of drinking companion.

Edna caught the owner's eye. He smiled engagingly, and it hit her — this was the labor hire man she'd observed at Lady Lewis's party. She found him to be one of the oddest, most fascinating people she had ever seen, yet she didn't know why. He was talking to Gordon Gray, who was planted on a stool at the far end of the bar. Mr Gray seemed to fit right in; he waved when he saw her. He was dressed in a light linen jacket, blue shirt and no tie, and looked like someone happy to lose himself in a crowd. As she drew closer, she saw the jacket was well cut and expensive. Gordon Gray was out to impress.

"Edna! Good to see you," said Gray. To her surprise, he held out his hand. She offered him a firm grip in return, then sat down beside him at the bar. "I was just telling our host you had your eye on him the other night."

"Yes, that's right," she said, smiling at the barman. "I was admiring your work ethic."

"Lee Tavon," the man said, holding out his hand. "Very pleased to meet you. I hope you don't mind, I made you a Tom Collins."

Were they trying to make a girl feel special? Edna raised an eyebrow in surprise. "That's one of my favorite drinks."

Tavon smiled and nodded at Gray as if to say 'I told you so'. Tavon had the reassuring patter of a seasoned host, someone who knew how to provide a welcome sense of reassurance.

"He does that," said Gray. "Knows what you want before you do."

"Mark of a good bartender," said Tavon, placing her drink on the bar.

She took a mouthful and nodded her approval. "That is very good."

"Miss Drake — Edna — is a reporter for the *Times-Herald*."

"We don't normally like your type in here," Tavon said. "For you, I'll make an exception."

She found herself staring deep into by Tavon's eyes, then realized as much a moment too late. She turned back to Gray. "How are you?"

"Pleased my day is over. It's been a long one."

"Well, this is a new day for me. I sleep through the afternoon when they have me on nights." She lifted her drink. "Couldn't catch a wink today though. Did you watch MacArthur's speech?"

"It's all anyone can talk about," said Gray. "Personally, I thought he went more than a little over the top."

"He droned on far too long in my opinion," Edna agreed. "People started to lose interest. I've heard it didn't go down too well with many of the delegates."

"They seemed to applaud in the right places," said Tavon.

Edna shrugged. "There's a difference between politeness and acceptance. MacArthur's complaints sound too much like sour grapes."

"Ike's the man," said Tavon. "You mark my words." He poured her a second drink, which she accepted gratefully, even though she could already feel the first one going straight to her head.

"I was going to say something, but I've lost my train of thought completely," Edna admitted.

"Something about your big story today?" Tavon suggested.

She nodded, laughing. "Yes, that's right."

"I must admit, I read it this afternoon," Tavon said. "Terrible tale, but very well told. Any solid leads on the killer?"

"Not yet," said Edna. She really did find Tavon's eyes mesmerizing. And it might be the booze hitting her, but it felt like his lips were out of sync with his voice. Like she'd walked into a badly dubbed French movie. Had he slipped her a mickey?

"I do make them strong," he said, somehow picking up on her bewilderment. "Take it slow."

Edna's mouth fell open.

"He reads minds," said Gray. "He's been doing it to me since I got here. It's his gimmick."

Tavon grinned impishly as he walked away to serve another customer.

"How strange," she said offhandedly. She picked up her second Tom Collins. "Come on, let's find ourselves somewhere quiet."

"That's not so easy in here."

Edna led him to booth in a dark corner at the opposite end of the bar from the piano, turning up her nose at the pianist. "God he is terrible. They need some jazz in here."

"Agreed," said Gray.

"Chet Baker just joined the Gerry Mulligan Quartet. Now there's a band that can draw a crowd."

"Probably scare away this lot though," said Gray. "You're a jazz fan then?"

She nodded. "It's so much better than the rubbish they play on the radio. Doris Day singing about the creep who tails her home. She's so impressed she marries him."

"I quite like Johnny Ray," said Gray.

"Have you heard *I'm Yours*?" she asked. Gray nodded. "You can't miss it, right? Eddie Fisher and Don Cornell both sing it. The two versions are indistinguishable, yet they're both in the Top Thirty."

"Maybe that's why," said Gray.

"It's all maudlin pap," she said, "but the little ladies sure do love it."

Gray shook his head and chuckled to himself. "You are a piece of work."

Edna smiled coquettishly in self-mockery. "Now, Mr Gray, is there something in particular you wanted to talk about tonight?"

"I heard about your chat with Bill Donovan."

She nodded. "I thought as much."

"He was very hot under the collar. I assured him I wasn't your source."

"The General told me my story is a risk to national security. He was menacing, and I don't use that word lightly. Are you gonna be menacing, Gordon?"

Gordon Gray held his hands up in surrender. "No, not me." He was no oil painting. Skinny, nearly bald, way too old for her. But there was something about him. He had kind eyes. Like he didn't have a menacing bone in his body.

But Mr Gray clearly knew how to keep a secret.

"I bet you'd like to know if I'm still chasing the story," Edna offered. He nodded. "None of your business. Though I must say, having the two of you pursue me tends to underline my belief that I'm onto something."

Gray held his hands up again. "I'm not here to fight about it."

"Then why are you here?"

"To be perfectly honest," he said, "I was simply after a bit of company. My family — my wife and sons — are back in Chapel Hill. I find my time in Washington is often solitary."

"And you figure I'm the type of girl to comfort you in your solitude."

Gray smiled, but shook his head. "I'm not trying to proposition you, Miss Drake."

"Oh," said Edna. With a certain degree of surprise, she felt disappointed.

"Don't get me wrong," he said, "you're a funny and vivacious woman. If I wasn't married... But I am. Happily, as it turns out."

"Then you're one of the lucky few."

"I'm not looking to do anything to wreck that."

"Nobody ever is."

"It's just that when we met, you impressed me."

"Really? Because the other night I thought you couldn't get away quickly enough," Edna pointed out.

"See, that's what I'm talking about," Gray explained. "You're a plain speaker. That's a rare commodity in my world. It takes some getting used to. But it can also be refreshing. Actually, I was rather hoping you and I might be friends."

"Now that is definitely a rare commodity in Washington," Edna said, unsure whether to believe him.

"I'm not entirely sure how to explain it," he confessed, "but I felt compelled to ring you. It wasn't because Bill Donovan asked me to. He didn't, by the way."

Edna knew that must be a lie. "Friends need to be honest with one another, Gordon. General Donovan accused you of being my contact, but you haven't asked me anything about my story. I think you know exactly what I have in my possession. You're better connected in this town than you'd have me believe."

He'd been holding her gaze, but now he looked away. "OK, you got me. Bill did ask me to come see you. But the thing is, it gave me the perfect excuse to do what I might otherwise not have been brave enough to do for myself."

Curiously, Edna wanted to believe him.

"I'm in unfamiliar territory," he continued. "I've never done this sort of thing before. If I'm being brutally honest, my motives aren't *entirely* honorable. There's something about you. That sounds like a pick-up line, which is not exactly the way it's intended."

"Not...exactly?" Edna offered. He was playing her, using physical attraction to cover his tracks. She had nothing to lose by playing along.

Gray was abashed. "I'm sorry, I'm probably confusing the hell out of you. Can I get you another drink?" He waved at Tavon, who nodded and immediately placed two glasses on a tray like he'd been waiting for the signal. He walked their cocktails to the table, offered a slight bow, and departed without a word. More than a little Bogart.

"Have you ever been in love, Edna?"

Her eyes widened; it was the last question she'd expected. She took a sip of her drink while she pretended to think about it. "Maybe once."

"You're not sure?" Gray asked.

"It was a long time ago. And it was over before it began."

"The war?"

Edna nodded. "I knew him from home. At school, we hadn't paid each other much attention. But there he was, a paratrooper with the 82nd Airborne. I was so proud of him, and it was wonderful to see a familiar face. I don't know if I'd call it love at first sight, but he was another kid from Rockaway, and suddenly that meant a lot. I sewed up his arm. He was wounded in an artillery blast, just after D-Day. Our hospital unit was still on Omaha Beach. I was in a pretty bad place at that particular time, after those first few days up to my elbows in blood and guts. I'd been given a couple of days off and Danny arrived in the last wave of casualties, but he wasn't nearly as badly hurt as a lot of his buddies. We clung to one another for two days like our lives depended on it. Happiest two days of my life. I heard later he copped it bad for staying at the hospital with me when he could have been back with his company."

"You never saw him again?" Edna paused, unsure of how to put it into words. She finished her drink. "I saw him one more time after that, about three months later. I'd all but forgotten about him by then. Operation Market Garden was underway in Holland and it was going badly. I dunno, I guess maybe I'd already assumed the worst.

"Our hospital had moved to Nijmegen. We were only a couple of miles from the front line. The worst cases came to us in waves. I'd been on my feet for fifteen hours, running triage and getting the boys we could save into emergency surgery. Many didn't make it that far and we were losing one in three on the table. After a while, you don't see them as human beings. They're slabs of meat. You try your best to piece them back together so they can be airlifted to a hospital with better facilities. It sounds awful now, but I didn't *want* to think of them as people. For me, the only way through it was to treat the whole thing like a production line. We were mechanics, making running repairs."

Without wanting to, she'd taken herself back to the moment. Covered in gore from head to toe. The stench of pain and death in the air. The taste of it. "I'm holding a perforated bowel. I hear someone say my name. I'm thinking it's one of the other nurses. But I realize it's the man we're treating. It dawned on me who I'm looking at. In that terrible moment, the wall I'd built around myself came crashing to the ground and it was like waking up in the middle of a nightmare. It can't have been more than a few seconds, but it felt like an eternity.

"My name was the only word to leave his lips. He died before I could bring myself to respond. We both knew he was dying. I had nothing to give. No words of comfort nor recognition. I just stared at him, my mouth hanging open, as he died in front of me. I felt so terrible about that. I should have held his hand, even just said his name. All I could do was look away. I couldn't even cry.

She saw nothing but empathy on Gordon Gray's face and it was almost too much to bear. Too ashamed to maintain eye contact, Edna focused instead on the cars passing them by. "Now, every time I think of Danny, all I can remember is that foul stench from the moment he died. It disgusts me. And I hate myself for it."

# TWENTY ONE

July 8, 1952

It was Donovan's habit to park his car on 18$^{th}$ Street. From there, it was just a short walk to both Dupont Circle and his actual destination. It gave him a chance to look for anyone who might be tailing him.

Today Eloise Page was with him, which prompted a more circuitous route. He'd become complacent with his trade craft; her presence was a reminder to remain on the alert. She was also a useful second set of eyes on the street.

After about half an hour, Eloise signaled that she thought they were clear.

The Verus Foundation was headquartered in a nondescript townhouse beside a disused carriage house in Church Street. It was a quiet laneway where nobody took much notice of comings and goings. A side street people peered down briefly while headed somewhere else, noting its quaint old-world charm before forgetting about it a moment later.

It was also in one of the safest neighborhoods in Washington, owing to the security attached to all the embassies nearby. Bill Donovan and Donald Menzel had picked the building themselves, ensuring it was visible from none of those embassies and thus hiding in plain sight. They paid for it in cash, "generously" donated by former president

Herbert Hoover. Truman told them at the outset that the Verus Foundation had to be financially self-sufficient. He urged Donovan to ask for Hoover's help in making that a reality. As the sixth richest man ever to serve as president, Hoover had plenty to give. Donovan took sly delight in shaming Hoover into a sizeable donation by alluding to a broken promise. On his ascendancy to the White House, Hoover had vowed to honor Donovan's support by appointing him Attorney General. Under pressure from anti-Catholic southerners, he'd reneged on the deal. More than two decades later, Hoover still seemed happy for a chance to clear the ledger.

Purchasing the property had ensured the Verus Foundation would never be troubled by tenancy problems. It was intended that the foundation remain in place long after their deaths; this required a solid asset base. Hoover's dollars had taken them a good way down that road. Operational expenses did, however, require additional streams of income, hence Donovan's determination to maintain strong ties with the Vatican Bank. He had made the most of his favored status with Pope Pius XII, pandering to the Church's fondness for knowledge, secrecy and, above all, financial gain. Here, Father Clarence Paulson had become an invaluable associate.

The Verus Foundation was dedicated to an honorable purpose. With so many layers of secrecy pervading the nation's security services, President Truman had foreshadowed a time when the Government would begin to lose track of its own secrets. Verus was created as a one-stop storage house of all such clandestine knowledge.

It was also in the business of historiography: looking beyond acknowledged accounts to record facts that were sometimes edited out of official history by the dominant paradigm. Of course, Verus remained committed to keep these things classified, until such time in the future when secrecy was no longer required.

From outside, the building was not much to look at. Donovan opened the front door and ushered Eloise inside ahead of him.

"I love what you've done with the place," she said.

Paint was peeling from the walls, and the carpets were threadbare and long overdue for replacement. It was perfect.

"I'm quite proud of our low-rent décor," he said.

"If you wanted an opium den vibe, I'd have to say well done," Eloise complimented.

To date, security had not been a problem. But for anyone who might inadvertently find their way inside, it created the impression that the building owner lacked both money and clout, and might even be toying with insolvency. Nothing to see here.

Of course, the real work went on in the basement. It was stacked with filing cabinets and the plain wooden desks of clerks who might just as well be selling life insurance as collating America's deepest secrets.

But one room in Verus HQ told a very different story. Donald Menzel had ensured his book-lined den at the rear of the terrace was plush and comfortable. It could not be seen from the street, and Menzel always kept his door locked when not in attendance. Virtually no one even knew the Verus Foundation existed. Donovan suspected this might not always remain the case, just another reason they had chosen to hide in the shadows of ambassadors and foreign dignitaries.

Donovan knocked on the door to Menzel's study, then entered without bothering to wait for a response. This was the astrophysicist's private retreat; no one in academic circles was aware of his other life. As far as the broader world was concerned, Donald Menzel was an avuncular and plain-spoken man of logic and science: a vocal debunker of the flying saucer phenomenon. He looked no different here; still immaculately dressed in his dark brown suit and black tie. His hair was neatly combed, and his familiar horn-rimmed spectacles reflected the air of a kindly grandfather. Three walls of the office were lined with books and journals. Behind Menzel's large desk, a floor-to-ceiling window revealed an overgrown garden that flooded the room with natural light. Donovan was quite sure Menzel would live in this room if he could. The only thing missing was one of his beloved telescopes.

"Bill. Right on time. And you must be Miss Page. Pleased to meet you. Clarence not with you?"

"Here soon," said Donovan. "He's been keeping an eye Roscoe Hillenkoetter in New York. I asked Gordon to join us."

Menzel frowned. "You told him where we are?"

"He's on our side, remember?"

"Yes, but... Anyone else you've told?" Menzel asked.

"Secret's safe with me," Eloise assured him.

But Donovan knew Menzel wasn't talking about Miss Page. "I haven't said a word to Ike about any of this."

"But you do speak to him all the time."

"Yes, Donald. That's what friends do. I've promised to work on the campaign if he wins the nomination."

"I heard as much," said Menzel. "Mr Truman is perfectly thrilled about it."

"I've been a Republican all my life. I didn't always see eye to eye with FDR either, but the man knew he could trust me, even if he did have his spies watching from time to time. Truman can't seem to get past regarding me as an enemy in the ranks. But I must admit, I do believe Eisenhower will make a much better president. Maybe even a remarkable one."

Menzel's eyes widened in surprise. "A true believer — after everything you've seen and done."

"Bill's been an enthusiast as long as I've known him," said Eloise. "Never one to do anything by halves."

"You're too kind. But honestly, belief doesn't come into it so much as common sense, which is precisely what this country needs. Pragmatism and a firm hand to ward off the Russians." The doorbell chimed. "That must be Gordon. Look relax Donald, OK? I won't be whispering state secrets in Ike's ear," Donovan promised.

At least, not before Ike was president.

Donovan ushered a bemused Gordon Gray inside and pointed him toward Menzel's office.

"Nice place you have here," Gray said.

"You never saw it," said Donovan. "You were never here."

"Of course."

Donovan did the introductions, while Menzel tried to play host, mostly for Gray's benefit. "Can we get you anything? A coffee?"

"No thanks, I'm fine."

"Good call," said Donovan, "Donald makes terrible coffee."

"Well, I don't have a secretary," Menzel explained apologetically, his eyes darting in the direction of Miss Page.

"Don't look at me," she said, "make your own damn coffee."

Donovan laughed out loud. Menzel was clearly put out, but did his best to remain civil. "Please, all of you, sit down." Donovan pointed toward a couch and two armchairs in the corner of the room. "How did you go last night, Gordon?"

"To cut to the chase," Gordon Gray began, "I don't think Tavon is Edna Drake's contact."

"Is that so?" said Menzel.

"I was there when she walked in. I watched them both very closely. I'm quite sure they met for the first time last night. Unless they were both putting on a very convincing show."

Donovan wasn't buying it. "She's pulling the wool over your eyes."

"I don't think so," Gray argued. "There aren't that many layers to her. She's young. And honest. Wears her heart on her sleeve, says what she thinks. In fact, she said a good deal more than I'd expected. She's still deeply troubled by her time in Europe. Nobody uses those sorts of experiences as a distraction unless they've been trained to do so. We didn't train her. Who would that leave? The Russians? I don't think so."

"She spent time with Martha Gellhorn in Berlin," said Miss Page. "Gellhorn's known to be a communist sympathizer."

Donovan shook his head. "Why would a communist work for the *Times-Herald*?"

"Because it's the perfect cover?" Miss Page suggested.

"No, that doesn't feel right," said Donovan. "But it's a hell of a thing — Tavon rang the paper and asked for her by name. Why would he do that if he didn't know her?"

"If there was any connection between them," said Gray, "I would have spotted it in their body language the moment she walked into the bar."

Donovan couldn't bring himself to believe Gordon Gray had a better read on Drake than he did. "Eloise said she heard Drake ask you about Tavon at Norma Lewis's party."

"She didn't know him then either. She was observing him organizing his negro waiters."

"A man of many colors," said Donovan — pun intended — "aviation investor, caterer, barkeep. I don't know how he gets it all done."

"People used to say the same about you," said Menzel.

"I dunno, Gordon," Donovan continued as if he hadn't heard him. "She must know who you work for. Don't you think there's a chance she just didn't want you to know her connection with Tavon?"

"Anything's possible, I guess," Gray admitted. "Though I doubt it."

"Maybe you're letting your emotions cloud your judgment. You find her attractive, don't you?" Eloise noted.

Gray blushed.

"That's enough," Menzel protested. "Gordon's a married man."

"I bet Edna sees it too," said Donovan. "Which is good. She must have been suspicious about you ringing her out of the blue. Did she question your motives?"

"Yes, she did. I'm sure she thinks I'm trying to play her, but she's going along with it anyway."

Menzel asked, "What about FS-1? How much does she have?"

"She didn't say."

"Why the hell didn't you ask her?" Donovan demanded.

"Softly, softly," Gray replied. "It's not an interrogation."

Donovan demurred, "Then just get her into bed."

"I'm not doing that," Gray said.

Menzel stared at Donovan in amazement. "Nor should you ask him to."

"Ignore him," said Miss Page. "He's just being vulgar because he's trying to shock me."

Donovan was incredulous. "I'm dead serious. This is no time for personal scruples. Do I need to remind you about the stakes of what we're dealing with here?"

"What's the point of any of this if we throw all our moral convictions out the window?" asked Menzel.

"Oh, for God's sake," Donovan barked. "Where did morality figure in us fire-bombing Dresden? Or dropping atomic bombs on Hiroshima and Nagasaki?"

"We did those things knowing they'd save the lives of Allied soldiers," Miss Page explained.

"Precisely," said Donovan. "We killed hundreds of thousands of innocent civilians to save British and American lives, and shorten the war. We did what we had to do."

Gray stood up. "I'm sorry, but we do this my way or not at all."

Donovan knew he'd pushed the man far enough. "Relax, will you? Just tell me you'll be seeing her again."

"I'm taking her out to dinner tomorrow night."

Menzel still had his eyes on Donovan. "Bill, you're still watching Tavon?"

"Like a hawk. I got a chill down my spine watching him in that liquor store, cool as a cucumber. He had a gun in his face and he calmly says, 'Jimmy's one of ours'. That little prick Jeb Stanton almost shat himself. Ran out of there like his life depended on it. Tavon has to be Mob-connected."

Menzel frowned. "I hope to God you're wrong about that. If the Mafia have infiltrated a top-secret government operation, we are in deep trouble. We might need to arrange for Mr Tavon to put a gun to his own temple."

"First, we find out who he's connected to," said Donovan, noting how quickly Menzel had retreated from his moral high ground.

"Fine," said Menzel, "but for God's sake keep a low profile. You can't just go around threatening people. It draws attention."

"If she prints that story," said Donovan, "we'll have more attention than we know what to do with."

"Are you going to give the killer's name to the police?" Gray asked.

"I'm not going anywhere near the police," said Donovan. "We were never there."

"You could do it anonymously," Gray said.

"Which would suggest there's some sort of conspiracy. I'm not going to do that. The police will have to catch Stanton on their own."

Gray clearly thought otherwise, but on that point Menzel and Miss Page agreed with Donovan.

"Bill, are we any closer to identifying who leaked that letter?" Menzel asked.

"It's Hillenkoetter," Donovan replied. "Has to be."

"You better be certain of that before you confront him," said Gray.

"That letter was only distributed to a handful of people," said Donovan. "No one else read it. Hell, no one else should even know it exists. Vandenberg and Smith both confirmed they have their copies under lock and key. We can assume the same goes for the President.

I actually think Harry destroys MJ-12 and FS-1 memos after reading them. He doesn't want them lying around."

"Maybe this one got away from him," said Miss Page.

"Wouldn't be the first time something leaked from the Oval," Gray pointed out. "The President's staff is anything but watertight, and many of them will be out of a job soon."

Donovan couldn't bring himself to believe anybody close to the President would leak something this sensitive. "Nobody in the White House other than Truman himself is cleared to Majestic level. He created Majestic more than four years ago, and there have been no leaks in all that time. Verus is this President's legacy. He wants our secrets protected."

"A security probe at the White House would also be problematic," said Gray. "Once we start asking questions over there, word will get out. We won't be able to keep a lid on it."

"No," Menzel agreed.

"We won't go down that road until I've eliminated all other possibilities," Donovan assured them.

Menzel nodded. "Start with the Admiral."

"Wouldn't Roscoe be a fool to leak a letter with his own name on it?" Gray inquired.

"Not if he figures he's got nothing to lose," said Donovan.

"He's spoken up before," said Menzel. "Thinks we should go public about the alien presence."

Donovan tried to imagine that Presidential message to the nation: *We are in contact with visitors from another planet. We don't understand their technology or why they're here. But we believe they mean us no harm. Your government remains in charge.*

Miss Page scoffed, "I'd give it a week before the nation began tearing itself apart."

# TWENTY TWO

July 8, 1952

It had been a quiet night. Edna didn't mind that so much; she was still basking in the glory of her front-page exclusive on the liquor store murder. It invited an easy follow-up story on the murdered man.

In the words of his near neighbors, Jimmy Peterson was salt of the earth, one of nature's gentlemen and a fearless veteran of the war in the Pacific. His violent death was variously a terrible shock and no surprise at all to those who knew him. He'd been robbed three times in the past six months. The story had virtually written itself. She'd knocked it off quickly from her notes of the previous night, given she'd already spoken to the people who'd appeared on the street in the aftermath of the murder. This left Edna free to spend the rest of the pre-dawn hours pondering her next move on that other story, which was starting to seem way too big to ignore.

Problem was, she still had next to nothing to go on. She had no idea whether the letter was genuine, and not the vaguest idea who had sent it to her. Donovan's reaction told her it was the real deal, but that on its own wasn't enough to go to print. If she chased an official response now, it would be the usual doubletalk and denial. She needed something more. Something they couldn't simply reject out of hand.

The appearance of Gordon Gray was an intriguing curiosity. Edna didn't think she had anything to fear from him, though she didn't trust him for a moment. But right now, he was the only reliable source talking to her, and she figured she had nothing to lose by spending time with him. It had been refreshing to find herself in the company of a man whose motivations weren't immediately obvious. The friendship line was cute, maybe even partly true, but he had to know she wasn't buying it. Still, if he wanted to take her out to an expensive restaurant for dinner, what was a girl to do?

As the light of a new day dawned, she ended her shift with an uncomfortable necessity. The Tune Inn was one of her favorite early morning dives. She had ordered bacon and eggs; Joe Eldridge opted for a breakfast beer. That might have been understandable if, like her, he'd just come off the night shift. But political reporters worked business hours, and his day was just about to start.

They sat by a street-front window because it was Edna's longstanding habit; she liked the glow of the neon sign. Yet she was starting to think she'd have been wiser to sit somewhere less conspicuous. She had begun by telling him about her night at the Jewel Box. Eldridge sucked back hard on his beer and stared back at her like she ought to be ashamed of herself.

"I didn't sleep with the man, if that's what you're worried about. Not that it's any of your business if I did."

Eldridge tried to laugh, but just succeeded in blowing suds over the table. He was a mess. He looked like he'd gone to bed drunk, then picked up where he'd left off.

"Look," Edna ordered, "shut up and listen for a moment, I'm trying to tell you something here. My little get-together with Gordon Gray was no accident. General Donovan has already tried to warn me off the story. He'd pretty much succeeded until Gordon showed up."

"Gordon," said Eldridge, like he was trying to make fun of the name. He put the beer down and reached over to touch her arm. "Eddy, we're partners now, you and me."

She calmly removed his hand from her wrist. "Come on Joe, I'm asking you what I should do next."

"Leave it with me," he said. "As I said, I know someone who knows Admiral Hillenkoetter."

Edna shook her head, frustrated. "Did you hear what I said? Donovan will have warned him about talking to me." He finished off his beer, then stared at her without speaking. "What?" she asked.

"I was just thinking how beautiful you are first thing in the morning."

"For God's sake, keep your voice down."

He laughed. "When did you become such a prude?"

She knew it was the beer talking, but she was getting angry. "Listen, about that… It's not going to happen again."

That wiped the smile off his face. "You don't mean that. I mean, it's nothing I don't deserve but… You're going to make me say it, aren't you?"

"No Joe, I'm really not."

He reached over and touched her gently on the cheek. "I'm falling for you, Edna."

Edna Drake gasped aloud and pulled away from him. "Jesus Christ. Go home, tell your wife. I bet she could do with the attention."

"No. You don't… I mean…"

The arrival of her bacon and eggs stopped Eldridge in his tracks, but she had lost her appetite. "I'm tired, Joe. I need to get some sleep and you need to go to work." She leant forward and whispered, "So do me a favor and fuck off, will you?"

He rose to his feet indignantly. "Yes, well, I'm not giving up that easily."

"I'm telling you here and now, there's nothing to fight for. I don't love you. I think you're a good reporter, but to be honest you're a fairly lackluster human being, and you drink too much to be a decent lover."

"You wouldn't get all worked up like that if you didn't like me. I'll quit drinking."

"Oh, for Christ's sake..."

"I'm going, I'm going." He threw a few coins down on the tabletop, muttering "breakfast's on me," then headed for the door.

She didn't dare turn around, sensing that every eye in the place was staring at her. Edna sat there cutting up her eggs in red-faced mortification.

It never for a moment occurred to her that the man across the street holding a camera might be anything to worry about.

# TWENTY THREE

July 9, 1952

"It's only a flying visit," said Donovan.

"That's funny," said Tony LeVier, struggling to find a comfortable position for his leg cast as he sat down on an unforgiving metal chair. "You're a real comedian."

They were seated at the rear of the makeshift hangar, constructed by Lockheed at White Sands to ensure the saucer stayed out of sight to any aircraft that strayed over the test site. LeVier was on crutches for his ankle, which had been fractured in the aftermath of the saucer crash.

The hangar might have been constructed hastily after the accident, but no expense had been spared. It had a concrete floor and a mechanical roof that allowed the saucer to exit vertically as well as through the main doors.

If it ever flew again.

The saucer itself was tethered to the ground in the center of the space, a move deemed necessary because the craft never touched the ground: it hovered about three feet in the air.

While LeVier himself failed to see the funny side of it, there had been some degree of amusement within the FS-1 Project that he hadn't been injured in the saucer crash itself. There were some who argued they were dancing with death, attempting to fly an object they knew so little about. Yet the project was buoyed by the knowledge it had been successfully flown before, by Bill Donovan.

They had even learnt a lot from LeVier's crash, even while knowing next to nothing about how it worked. The ship's propulsion system generated a strong gravitational field around its exterior, as well as a powerful inertial dampening effect inside the cockpit. This had ensured that when it slammed into the New Mexico desert, neither pilot nor craft was damaged. The force of the impact had created a large crater, a result of the ship's gravity field hitting the earth. It had sent a massive plume of sand and dust into the air, and the sand walls of the crater caved in almost immediately, leaving the saucer half buried.

A hasty excavation ensued; a crane had to be brought in to remove the craft from its resting place. But none of this could be communicated to LeVier while he was still trapped inside the saucer, because radio communication had been severed in the crash. He had been met with a wall of sand when he tried to exit the ship and realized it would be folly to try to dig his way out. So he had waited for a rescue team to do it for him. Maybe it was stress, maybe some degree of oxygen deprivation, nobody knows for sure. Regardless, LeVier had failed to realize the ship was hanging ten feet in the air when he made his exit. He'd hit the sand below hard and off balance, fracturing his leg.

He was embarrassed and pissed off about making the mistake. But the ignominy of it had cemented LeVier into a perpetual bad mood since he'd learned Truman had grounded the project indefinitely.

Not that this had stopped work entirely. There was still plenty of research to be done.

"From everything I know about that ship, it shouldn't have allowed you to fall like that," said Donovan.

"Allowed me? I wanted out," said LeVier. "To be honest, it felt like the ship threw me out."

Donovan rubbed his chin. Could the ship actually be that responsive to the whims of its pilot?

Nothing about the ship in their possession accorded with the wreckage of other crashed saucers in American possession. Of course, before now they had precious little to work with. Wreckage from Roswell; and from later retrievals at Kingman, Arizona; and the Great Sand Dunes, Colorado; had left them with mere fragments — nothing in the way of a functional propulsion system. It was as if the critical elements of those crafts deliberately self-destructed on impact.

"Can't you persuade that friend of yours to pay us a visit?" LeVier asked. He meant Paolo. "It'd sure speed things along if he helped us understand what we're dealing with here."

"I've tried," said Donovan. "He refuses. Says he won't break our promise to the Russians."

"No, of course not," said LeVier bitterly. "Stalin being a man of such high moral principle, an example to us all."

"Are the boffins any closer to understanding the gravity generator?" Donovan had tried to stay abreast of scientific analysis on the saucer, but in truth most of the analysis papers written thus far were beyond his grasp.

LeVier sniffed dismissively. "How much do you know about nuclear physics?"

"I'm a lawyer, what do you think?"

LeVier said, "The periodic table of elements goes all the way up to ninety-two, which is uranium, the radioactive substance we dig out of the ground."

"I know what uranium is."

LeVier smiled. "It's the heaviest element we've found existing in large quantities in nature. But there's also a group of what they call transuranium elements. There used to be only two of these, neptunium and plutonium, elements ninety-three and ninety-four. But in the past couple of years, they've been able to generate all the way up to element ninety-eight in the laboratory. So they tell me. Now here's the thing: beyond plutonium — element ninety-four — none of them exist at all in nature. They're all highly radioactive and unstable. They're only produced in laboratories as rapidly decaying by-products from smashing particles together. And when I say rapidly decaying, I mean fractions of a second. Still with me?"

"So far," said Donovan.

"The boffins here at White Sands say the substance that powers the saucer's gravity generator is a stable form of element a hundred-fifteen. It's so stable, it's not radioactive at all. You can hold it in your hand."

"How is that possible?" Donovan questioned.

"How indeed. We can't begin to know how to create such an element even as the momentary product of an atomic reaction, far less generate it in a stable form. The boffins reckon it must be the product of a technology that's thousands of years more advanced than ours."

"Who have you been talking to about this?" Donovan asked him.

"Nobody. Why?"

"You sure about that? No sly suggestions to your buddies late at night? No bedtime chat with your wife?"

"Of course not," said LeVier. "To be honest, it's insulting you even feel the need to ask."

Donovan held up his hands. "I mean no offence." He decided to bait the hook one more time. "But come on, just between you and me, doesn't all this secrecy worry you?"

"How else are we gonna get this done?" LeVier argued. "You said it yourself, if this project goes public, all bets are off. The world could go to hell, real quick. What would people do if they thought their governments were no longer in charge? We could have the armed forces going rogue. Maybe not here, but what about other countries? It terrifies me to think about it."

"You and me both," said Donovan, who nevertheless felt oddly relieved.

# TWENTY
# FOUR

J uly 9, 1952

It was just after dusk, and the street lights were already glowing along 5th Avenue as Donovan made his way into the lobby of Roscoe Hillenkoetter's apartment building. The man's residence overlooked Central Park on the Upper East Side. It was wonderful to be back home in New York, but Donovan couldn't stay long.

The doorman asked to see his identification after Donovan announced he had an appointment with the Admiral, who had just taken command of the Third Naval District. For a man of Hillenkoetter's experience, it was not a troubling role in peacetime. It left plenty of room for extracurricular activity.

Satisfied with Donovan's ID, the doorman informed him the Hillenkoetters could be found in apartment C on the 18th floor. He didn't bother to call Hillenkoetter to ensure the appointment was genuine.

Donovan smiled as Jane Hillenkoetter opened the front door, then leant in to give her a kiss. They'd always gotten on well. "You're looking good. New York must suit you."

"Nice to see you, Bill. Roscoe said you'd be paying a visit. Come on in." She was polite, if a little standoffish. Perhaps Mrs. Hillenkoetter counted Donovan among those in Washington who had turned their backs on her husband after his fall from grace as Director of Central Intelligence. It wasn't true, but there would be no convincing her of that if she'd already made her mind up. She directed Donovan to the study without a word of inquiry as to the nature of the visit; she knew better than that.

Hillenkoetter was still in uniform. He finished a phone call and rose from behind his desk to offer a warm greeting. "That was Pearl on the phone. I left Korea nearly a year ago, but they value my insights after time on the frontline."

Hillenkoetter had been in charge of the Pacific fleet cruiser-destroyer force in Korea.

"Offering your pearls to Pearl, eh?"

Hillenkoetter chuckled. "Something like that. Grab yourself a whiskey."

"I'm fine."

"I guess I know what this is about."

"You do?" Donovan questioned.

"You're keen to get that sucker back up in the air, am I right?"

"Well, that is true," Donovan admitted, "but it's not why I'm here."

"Stamford assures me Tony LeVier is keen to go up again. Balls of steel, that man. There's just that small matter of the President giving us the nod."

They both knew this was no small matter. "Haven't you heard? The project's on hold indefinitely, Roscoe."

Hillenkoetter moved toward the side cabinet and pulled the stopper on his whiskey decanter. "Why?"

"We have a security problem."

The news caught Hillenkoetter off-guard. "How so? And why is this the first I'm hearing of it?"

"There's been a leak. A letter. Written by you, as it turns out."

"Me?"

"It found its way into the hands of a reporter."

"Jesus," said Hillenkoetter. "How did that happen?"

"This, my friend, is the question on everybody's lips," said Donovan.

"Our correspondence is held in the strictest confidence," Hillenkoetter insisted. "I haven't told a soul."

"The letter concerned is dated May fifth of this year. It's your request for permission to conduct the test flight."

"Yes, I remember," said Hillenkoetter, "I have that on file here."

"How widely was it circulated?"

"Only to the people named on the letter itself."

"That's what I thought."

"Surely you didn't come here thinking it was me..."

"To be perfectly honest, I'm not sure what to think," Donovan admitted. "But I'd very much like to cross you off my list."

"Then I am a suspect."

"No, I didn't say that. I said I'm here to cross you off the list. If you could just show me your copy of the letter, I'll get out of your hair."

The Admiral looked around the office. There was a filing cabinet in one corner, but several boxes stacked beside it. Though Hillenkoetter was unaware of it, Paolo was standing right beside him. He'd followed Donovan into the apartment. Donovan watched as he moved silently around the office, searching for anything untoward.

*It's not here.* Paolo's words in his head were as clearly as if they'd been spoken aloud.

Donovan said nothing. He hadn't asked Paolo to be here. Lately, though, he'd been turning up uninvited. It had become more than a little unnerving.

"We only moved in a week ago," said Hillenkoetter. "I'm afraid my files are still a little bit disorganized."

"Take your time, Roscoe." Donovan realized he wanted his friend to find the damn letter, if only to prove Paolo wrong.

He suspected this was in vain.

"I moved the classified material here myself," the Admiral said, troubled by the idea that Donovan could suspect his private documents had been tampered with. He unlocked his filing cabinet and pulled open a drawer to search an alphabetical list of files. He pulled out the one he'd been looking for and began flicking through papers. "I'm sure it should be here…"

Still looking.

"You sure you have the right folder?"

"Yes, yes," Hillenkoetter said tersely. He got to the end of the file and started again from the top. "May fifth you said?"

"That's right."

Finally, color drained from his face, Hillenkoetter looked up. "It's not here."

"Meaning what?"

"Meaning it's been removed."

"Somebody accessed to your files while they were in transit?"

Hillenkoetter shook his head. "Impossible. These files haven't left my custody. I lugged those boxes myself."

"You had movers helping you?"

"Of course. But that would have been a very limited opportunity, a minute or two here and there. And for someone to do that, they'd have to know exactly what they were looking for and where to find it."

Donovan thought that seemed far-fetched. The moving company would have been Navy-approved. Defense contracts were a license to print money for moving firms: it was in their interest to keep their employees on tight reins.

"The only other possibility that springs to mind is our cocktail party. Jane threw a housewarming the night after we arrived. It was just a few close friends and one or two old Navy buddies, but we booked catering."

"Who was that with?"

"A fellow Garrick Stamford recommended."

This was it. "Did you notice anything strange while they were here?"

"Not at all. In fact, everything ran very smoothly."

"I assume you have a back door?" Donovan asked him. Most lavish New York apartments had a separate entrance for staff.

Hillenkoetter nodded. "It opens right off the kitchen."

"What was the name of the catering firm?"

Hillenkoetter moved over to his desk. "I have their card here somewhere. Yes, here it is. Harmony Events." He handed the card to Donovan.

Lee Tavon's operation had a branch in New York.

# TWENTY FIVE

J uly 12, 1952

Gordon Gray smiled into his vodka martini as he watched Edna walk slowly to the table and sit down. She nodded to him without saying a word, and it was probably the coolest thing he'd ever seen. Pure Lauren Bacall. A drinks waiter appeared like he'd been waiting to take her order. She went for her usual.

"I was going to order that for you, but I didn't want to presume," he said.

"I never say no to a Tom Collins. I bet they make a good one here. Maybe even better than the Jewel Box."

Martin's Tavern was a Georgetown landmark. It served classic American food in the ambiance of a French bistro and the class of a five-star hotel, with a clientele to match. They were seated outside. The night air was clear, the temperature perfect. It was pure romance. Once more, Gordon Gray was out to impress.

Edna liked him, even if she didn't trust him. He had a quiet confidence that stopped well short of swagger. He had money (never a bad thing in her opinion) and he knew how to dress with understated dignity and class. But what impressed her the most was his authenticity. If Gordon Gray was faking that, he was so good at it she almost didn't care. Despite everything else going on here, Edna Drake enjoyed his company and felt free to simply be herself.

"How was your day?" he asked.

"Lord, don't hit me with that one. I'll start thinking we're married."

Gray blushed a little. She didn't need to look too hard to see the man was smitten. But she also knew him to be an honorable man. He had to be torn by his attraction to her, and sitting here against his own better judgment.

Her drink arrived, and it seemed like the perfect moment to change the subject. "Well then, Dwight Eisenhower for president, eh? He might be hard to beat."

"You're right," Gray admitted. "Mr Truman certainly rated his chances back in '48 — he tried to get him to run for the Democratic nomination."

Edna's eyes widened. "Truman has always denied that."

"It happened," said Gray, "believe me. It's why Harry's so torn about Ike going to bat for the other team." Edna made a mental note to follow that one up in the morning.

"Eisenhower's smart," she said. "The Democrats have held the presidency for twenty years and, if you'll excuse me for being so blunt, Mr Truman has tarnished the brand with his handling of the war in Korea."

Gray raised an eyebrow, but didn't argue the point. "The next few months will certainly be interesting."

She took a sip of her Tom Collins, determined to take it more slowly tonight, then pulled a cigarette from a pack in her purse. Gray produced a lighter from his pocket and leant across the table with the flame. She nodded gratefully, then sat back in her chair, readying herself for what was about to come. "I heard something interesting the other day."

"What was that?"

"A little bird told me you work for the CIA."

Gray didn't bat an eyelid. "But you knew that already."

She shook her head and smiled wryly. "No, I didn't."

"Lady Lewis told you," he said. "She rang me to apologize for giving the game away."

"In her defense, she didn't give you up. Not really. She just said nothing when I made the suggestion."

Gray shrugged. "It's no big secret. I'm a consultant, not a field operative."

"And all this? It's just two people enjoying one another's company?"

Gordon Gray took his time with his martini before telling her, "I don't know about you, but I'm enjoying your company immensely." He meant it.

Edna laughed. "What if I told you my newspaper would like to pay for dinner?"

"I'd say your newspaper can save its money for a more worthy pursuit. This is not work, Edna. It's pleasure. At least, it is for me."

"Curiously, I'd have to agree," she said. "But it's not just pleasure, is it? I mean, come on Gordon, can we talk about this? There's more going on here than two people sharing a romantic dinner by candlelight."

"Romantic...?" He began to blush again.

"I know you want to ask me about my story. So, go ahead and ask."

Gordon picked up the menu. "Maybe we should think about ordering. It's getting busy."

"I'm having the sirloin," she said. "I hear it's to die for."

He didn't react. "I think I'll go for the lamb chops. Would you like an appetizer?"

"The steak will do nicely," she said. "Medium rare."

He waved the waiter over, delivered their food order and asked for two more drinks. Job done, Gray looked her right in the eye and said, "General Donovan did mention something I want to ask you about.

Regarding our friend at the Jewel Box, Lee Tavon. Are you aware it was Mr Tavon who tipped you off about the liquor store murder?"

Edna was stunned. "What?" It wasn't the question she'd expected.

"Apparently not," said Gray.

"He never said anything about it the other night," Edna promised.

"No, I thought that was odd," said Gray. "General Donovan is of the opinion you two must have known each other already."

"Wait, how does General Donovan know it was Tavon who tipped me off?"

"I'm afraid I can't answer that question," said Gray. "But I told him that, in my opinion, you met Tavon for the first time at the Jewel Box. I'm right about that, Edna, aren't I?"

What sort of strange game was this? "Yeah — I had no idea who'd rang me that night. And I'm not sure I'd take General Donovan's word on it being Tavon."

"Bill is right about that, I assure you."

"What's your point?"

"My point," he said, "is that you can't trust Lee Tavon. He has his own agenda. He's hiding something."

"Be that as it may," she said, "it was a good tip. There were no other reporters at that liquor store when we arrived."

"Doesn't that tell you something? How does a man like Tavon have firsthand knowledge about a murder?"

It was a very good question. She was starting to lose her appetite for this conversation. "Excuse me, will you? I won't be a moment." Edna made her way into the busy tavern and followed her nose to the lady's room, aiming to collect her thoughts.

Someone strong grabbed her arm when she was two steps from the door. Edna felt a stab of fear in her lungs as she turned around to find a burly black barman looming over her. "Easy pal," she said coolly. "My arm's not a cocktail shaker."

He didn't appear dangerous, but he wasn't letting go of her arm. "Please, Miss Drake," he said, "don't be scared. Mr Tavon wants to speak with you. He waitin' outside. Will you come?"

She sighed. "Now?" If he knew where she was, why didn't he approach her himself?

"Please miss, he can't be stayin' here long. He say folks be watching."

"OK then, lead the way."

The barman took her through the kitchen and out a back door. It opened to a poorly lit alley, full of empty beer bottles stacked in boxes, and a set of garbage bins that smelled like they were harboring last week's catch of the day. When Tavon emerged from behind the bottles, the barman retreated indoors.

The night was getting odder by the minute.

Edna hit him with it straight up. "It was you who called me about the liquor store murder."

Tavon nodded solemnly. "That's right."

"Why didn't you say anything the other night at the Jewel Box?"

"I wanted to," he said, "but you were with Gordon Gray."

"You do realize I'm here with him tonight?"

"I'm sorry to drag you out here like this, but he and his people are watching me. When I heard you were here, I availed myself of the opportunity. You can't trust him."

"Funny," Edna said. "He says the same thing about you."

"I gave you that tip to prove you *can* trust me. I wanted to demonstrate to you that I know things. My information is solid."

"Did you murder an old man to make that point?"

Tavon looked disappointed. "No. I had no hand in the demise of the liquor merchant."

An odd turn of phrase. Quaint, not quite right.

"But I do know who killed him," he said.

"How do you end up being the first person to know about a murder without being involved?"

"I'm well-connected."

Edna figured he meant the underworld. She scanned the alley; if she was about to be ambushed, now would be the moment. But it was just Lee Tavon and the dead fish.

"I want you to tell the police," he said.

"Why can't you do that yourself?" Edna asked.

"They won't believe me."

"Who *are* you, Mr Tavon?"

"A businessman. A concerned citizen." His eyes narrowed, like he was trying to make up his mind about something. "I was there, OK? I saw it happen. But if I tell the police, they'll find a way to blame me for it or charge me with being an accomplice, which I'm not."

"That sounds a bit screwy to me. Like you have something to hide."

Tavon grinned half-heartedly, a worried expression creasing his brow. "Doesn't everybody?"

"It's a serious matter, not coming forward to assist in the investigation of a murder."

"You place a high value on the truth, don't you?"

"It's my job," Edna said.

"Yet there are many in your profession untroubled by the facts if they get in the way of a good story."

Edna shrugged. "What's your point?"

"I assume you have a good reason for not publishing the Majestic letter?"

Tavon floored her with that one. "*You* sent that?"

He nodded. "Which is why I want you to trust me. That letter is on the level."

"I've worked that much out already. I've been threatened with lawsuits and personal ruin. Bill Donovan says that letter is a threat to national security."

"Because he's one of the men tasked with keeping the secret."

"I need more," she said. "You need to talk to me. Tell me everything you know."

Lee Tavon took a step back, shaking his head. "If I do that, I'm a dead man."

"Off the record. No names. I can attribute it to Capitol sources."

He considered it. "Leave it with me. Now, you better go. Gordon Gray must be starting to think you've run out on him. Tell the police their murderer is Jeb Stanton. And be aware, Gordon Gray and William Donovan are working together."

"Tell me something I don't know."

"They're photographing you and recording everything you say. You have to get this done quickly. Publish your story. Find a way, or they'll shut you down for good."

"Then you have to talk to me."

Tavon's eyes widened like an animal sensing danger. "Enjoy your steak. I hear they're good." He disappeared into the night with the stealth of an alley cat.

As Edna made her way back through the tavern, the barman gave her a brief conspiratorial nod.

She hit Gordon Gray with the warmest smile she could muster so as not to look like the cat who'd got the canary. Edna stared deep into his eyes. Still seeing a man of integrity, she wondered how Gordon Gray negotiated the minefields of compromise and obfuscation that lay between the many worlds he inhabited.

She also knew how to corner him. "All right Gordon, let's stop beating about the bush and lay some cards down on the table. I assume at this point you know it was Lee Tavon who sent me the letter. Are you and General Donovan going to persist with this nonsense about it being fake? Because we both know it's a lie." She saw it in his eyes immediately. Gray had no defense against the plain, honest truth. She let the question hang. He took his time to frame a response and so she waited, determined to let him speak first.

Finally, Gordon Gray said, "I have no comment to make on its authenticity. It's in the best interests of both myself and the Government that I decline to say anything further."

"Interesting choice of words," Edna remarked, scribbling them down on a napkin.

"You can't quote me on that."

"I don't have to," she said.

If it was a fake, he'd have no hesitation in telling her so at this point. This was his way of confirming the letter was authentic. Of course, whether or not that would be good enough for the *Times-Herald* lawyers remained to be seen.

# TWENTY SIX

J uly 12, 1952

"Tavon's here," Clarence Paulson declared quietly via two-way radio. He was leaning against a store front, alongside an alley off N Street, fifty yards from Martin's Tavern.

Donovan cursed. "Are you sure?"

"He walked right past me. It's him, no doubt in my mind."

Donovan was just across the road, hidden on the first floor of a men's clothing store and looking down on the tavern. It wasn't entirely unexpected that Tavon had shown up, but why was he being so obvious about it? "He must want us to see him."

*Paolo — are you still at the Jewel Box?*

*Yes. Tavon isn't here. He vanished from the bar about ten minutes ago.*

Donovan didn't bother to point out this would have been useful information ten minutes earlier. Besides which, it didn't add up: that wasn't enough time for Tavon to get this far across town.

"What's the deal?" asked Paulson, who didn't share the dubious pleasure of having Paolo's voice inside his head.

"Clarence, are you following Tavon?"

"He's long gone. He had a car waiting."

Shit. They'd never find him now. "He came here to see Edna," said Donovan, "meaning either Gray is wrong about her, or he's been lying to me to protect her."

Donovan was going to have to split the operation in half. While he chased Tavon, Miss Page would have to keep a close eye on Gordon Gray.

Without Gray knowing about it.

# TWENTY SEVEN

July 14, 1952

"Welcome to tire town," said Donovan.

The clock on the Firestone factory chimed midday as they made their way toward downtown Akron in a brand-new Ford Crestline rental. The vinyl seats still had that new car smell, though there were plenty more noxious odors in the air that competed for their attention.

"Is this what people call Middle America?" Paulson asked, clearly less than enamored by what he was seeing.

"I guess so," said Donovan, "though I haven't spent a lot of time in Ohio."

According to information furnished by Wally Smith, courtesy of the CIA, Lee Tavon had moved to Akron with his family shortly after the war. They'd settled into a small suburban cottage, bought with the proceeds from selling the Tavon family farm. It was a move that had precipitated a career change from primary producer to businessman for Tavon. Contrary to Donovan's suspicions, there were no clear links between Tavon and bootlegging during the prohibition era. On paper, it looked as if the proceeds of the farm sale were what he had used to bankroll a highly successful move into high finance and diversified investment. Lee Tavon had interests in a range of areas, from aviation and banking, to bars and catering.

They hadn't caught a whiff of Tavon's movements since the night Paulson had watched him drive away from Martin's Tavern. Donovan strongly suspected — perhaps hoped was more accurate — they would find him hiding out in the family home.

They parked a few doors down from Tavon's remarkably unimpressive two-story home in the inner suburb of Middlebury. Here, if appearances were to be believed, Lee Tavon lived with his wife Maeve and the youngest two of their four children. Their two eldest boys were away at university. It was a very middle-class house in a middle-class suburb of Middle America. A completely unremarkable home for a family who paid their taxes and were otherwise unknown to authorities.

"Over to you," Donovan told his partner in crime. Paulson had considered presenting himself as a man of God, which was true enough up to a point. He had remained a priest, albeit one who had lost his religion. But Donovan reasoned it was all too easy to slam the door in the face of someone spruiking Jesus door-to-door. They needed a compelling reason to engage the lady of the house in conversation, knowing it was highly unlikely Tavon himself would answer the door.

Clarence Paulson knocked twice before Maeve Tavon opened the door to greet him. For a moment, he thought she was the hired help. She was far younger than he'd expected.

"Can I help you?" she asked.

Paulson flashed his phony ID. "John Wilkins, madam. I'm with the State Department. Are you Mrs Lee Tavon?"

"That's right."

Paulson had figured he could hold a credible American accent for a few minutes, before he was likely to say something odd that raised her suspicions. Donovan told him not to bother; he'd said it was always better to sound natural. "I'm wondering if your husband is at home?"

Mrs Tavon's pretty smile gave way to a look of concern. "He's in Washington. Is there something wrong, Mr Wilkins?"

"That's a shame. I'd been hoping to catch him. But since he's not here, would you mind if I asked you a few questions?"

Maeve Tavon took half a step forward and peered out at the street, perhaps wondering whether their exchange was being observed by her neighbors. "Ah, no, I guess not. Please, come in." She ushered him through the door and into an adjacent sitting room. "Take a seat, Mr Wilkins."

Paulson sat, trying to get a handle on the woman's emotional state. She didn't seem particularly agitated by the notion her husband was being pursued by the Government. That, at the very least, was odd. Maeve Tavon also looked at least twenty years younger than a woman who was supposed to be in her late fifties. She had a nice white apron over a blue floral frock, not a hair out of place. He could smell brownies baking in the kitchen. It would be hard to imagine a more ideal version of the modern American housewife.

"Is this about taxes," she asked, "because I'm certain we have that all taken care of."

"No, no, nothing like that," he assured her. "It's just that, well, we're seeking your husband's input on an aviation project. As you might be aware, he's a major shareholder in Lockheed."

"Lee doesn't talk to me about these things," said Mrs Tavon. "He says a lot of what Lockheed does for the government is secret, so I know not to ask him about it."

"No," said Paulson. "Of course. Very good. But I'm also wondering why it is you and the family have remained here in Ohio, when your husband spends so much of his time in Washington and New York."

"This is where we want our kids to grow up," she said. "Lee moves around a lot. He'd be away from home no matter where we were."

"How often do you see him?" Paulson asked.

"Most weekends. Sometimes he stays on for a day or two into the following week and works from home."

"He has a home office?"

"Yes, that's right. Mr Wilkins, is there something in particular I can help you with?"

"Well, I'm just a bit confused. As you say, he's here most weekends and he'd told us we might find him here today, yet there's no sign of him. Did he leave early this morning?"

"Actually," she said, "we didn't see him this weekend. He said something had come up in Washington and he needed to stay. I'm sorry if there's been some confusion."

"Not at all," said Paulson. "I guess we'll have to track him down in D.C. Thank you for your time, I'm sorry to have troubled you."

She stared at him for maybe a second too long. "Not at all." It was just long enough to make the moment awkward. Nothing Paulson could put his finger on, but Maeve Tavon was certainly hiding something.

It finally hit him when he got back to the car. "She didn't ask me about my British accent. Doesn't that strike you as odd?" Paulson asked Donovan.

"Maybe she's just polite," Donovan shrugged.

"A perfect stranger shows up at your door claiming to work for the government, but he's not American. Who wouldn't ask a question about that? It's always the first thing Americans remark on when I meet them."

Curiously, Donovan didn't seem to care. He already had the engine idling and hit the gas the moment Paulson sat down beside him. "While you were talking to Maeve, Paolo was taking a look around. Tavon's not in there."

Paulson was less than happy to hear this. "Then what the hell was I just doing? Why did you drag me to this stinking backwater, if Paolo can do your dirty work for you?"

Donovan patted the priest on the arm. "It wasn't for nothing. Now we have more of a handle on his wife. Whatever he's up to, she's in on it for sure."

"Meaning what?" Paulson asked.

"Meaning the Tavon family are not the stalwart American family they claim to be. This middle-class suburbia routine is a cover."

"You think Tavon's a spy?"

For a long time, Donovan said nothing, but his silence spoke volumes. There was only one nation on Earth with the audacity to attempt an infiltration of this magnitude on US soil. The only other nation that knew the saucer existed. "If he is, his ties with Lockheed are a serious problem."

"And now he knows we're onto him," said Paulson. "You have to take this to the President. Or the FBI."

Donovan shook his head. "Truman's a dead man walking. In a few months, he'll be gone from the Oval Office. It's time we cut the apron strings." If Donovan dumped this at Truman's feet now, he'd become the little man's scapegoat. Harry's final act as President would be to make damn sure Donovan's days among Washington's intelligence community were brought to an abrupt and inglorious conclusion. "As for the FBI...they don't have the security clearance."

Paulson wasn't going to let it go. "Please tell me you don't mean to tell General Eisenhower instead."

Donovan thought about that for a moment, but quickly dismissed it. "Ike's not there yet. We can't expect him to think like a president until he's in the Oval Office. Until the election's won, he's first and foremost a politician — and there isn't a politician alive who could resist the temptation of going public with this. It'd blow the Democrats out of the water. But it could also start World War Three So, we tell no one."

"You're talking about concealing a suspected traitor."

"Clarence, we have no real evidence an act of treason has been committed here. All we have is suspicion and guesswork."

"You've had men killed for less, you told me so yourself."

Donovan sighed as he ran fingers through his thinning hair. "It might yet come to that."

# TWENTY
# EIGHT

July 14, 1952

Monday morning, and no news was decidedly not good news. Edna stared at Joe Eldridge's empty chair at the desk in front of hers, wondering if his absence might have anything to do with her.

For the fifth time that morning, she tried calling the Jewel Box. Still no answer. Edna almost wished Eldridge *was* here, so she had someone to talk to about this. Her confrontation with Tavon on Saturday night had, if anything, left her in even more of a dilemma. She wasn't at all sure she trusted Lee Tavon enough to put her entire career on the line, for a story based solely on his word. On the other hand, Gordon Gray had notably failed to deny it when given the chance; at least now she knew her source. Yet her reporter's curiosity told Edna she still needed to drill down further into the story.

"Drake." The familiar note of disdain in the voice of Theo Mankiewicz filled her with dread. She looked up to find the features editor standing right in front of her desk. "Boss wants to see you in her office."

"Why?" Edna asked.

"Damned if I know," said Mankiewicz, grinning like a hyena. "But she doesn't look happy. Best not keep her waiting." He clearly relished the prospect of Edna being raked over the coals.

Bazy Miller remained behind her desk as Edna entered her office. "Shut the door," she said tersely. Edna did so, her guts clenching. The publisher's face grew darker. "I'm going to ask you a question, Edna. I need you to think very carefully before you answer. I want you to be completely honest with me. Can you do that?"

Edna nodded, already feeling like she was about to lose her job. She and Bazy might not see eye to eye on many things, but they had never actually clashed openly.

Bazy looked like she was about to blow her stack. "I think you know what this is about, don't you?"

"Honestly Mrs Miller, I have no idea."

First lie.

Which served to make Bazy Miller even angrier. "Sit down, for God's sake." Edna did as directed. "I've just received a letter from a prestigious Washington law firm informing me one of my junior reporters — that's you — is having an affair with my senior political reporter, Joe Eldridge. A married man. The letter came complete with photographic evidence."

Edna's stomach hit the floor. Bazy threw the prints down on her desk. Edna picked them up. The first one was her and Eldridge, arm-in-arm outside the apartment building where they'd spent the night. A series of shots showed them together again at The Tune Inn, one image showing him touching her affectionately on the face. Another with his hand on hers. Two people sharing a moment of intimacy.

"Are you sleeping with Joe Eldridge?"

In an odd way, Edna was relieved. She had immediately imagined the worst — shots from a secret camera hidden somewhere in the bedroom. These pictures were hardly salacious. They were even open to interpretation. She considered denying it but, staring into her boss's furious glare, Edna didn't have it in her.

"It was one night."

Mrs Miller nodded but remained silent, waiting for the rest of the story.

"It was the Fourth of July," said Edna. "We went to Lady Lewis's Independence Day party. You know that, you were there. We'd both had too much to drink. It was a mistake." She pointed at the most recent images. "This is me calling it off, telling Joe it wouldn't happen again."

Mrs Miller sat back in her chair and sighed. "Do you know who also received a copy of these photos? My uncle, the Colonel. I've just been on the phone to him." Edna went white. Bazy meant Colonel Robert McCormick, the owner of the paper; Edna guessed the discussion hadn't gone well. "He told me to sack you on the spot."

The words hit Edna like a punch in the ribs. "I see."

"I really don't know what to do. He's probably right, I should fire you. But the thing is, it'd make me a terrible hypocrite."

So, the rumors were true.

"You mean...?" Edna couldn't bring herself to say it.

"Good God, don't turn prudish now. You know very well I've been sleeping with Garvin Tankersley. The newsroom gossip can't have passed you by."

"I did hear something to that effect," Edna admitted. Tankersley was the paper's news editor. "Martha Blair told me. But I wondered if she was just being a bitch."

Bazy Miller laughed. Her cheeks were wet, and they weren't tears of joy. "The Colonel also received photographs of me and Tank."

"Oh. Fuck. Bazy... Mrs Miller, I..."

"I'm not ashamed of it," her boss said. "In fact, I plan to divorce Max and marry Tank. But that particular news item has come as quite a shock to the Colonel, let me tell you."

"I see."

"He thinks Tank is beneath my social status. He also says he disapproves of divorce, which is pretty rich considering his first wife had to divorce to marry him."

"You're a woman," said Edna. "We're the bearers of shame."

"That might be overplaying it a little," said Bazy. "I wouldn't be in this chair at all if not for the Colonel."

"Put it this way," said Edna, "I'm assuming he didn't order you to sack Joe Eldridge."

Bazy sat back in her chair and sighed. "No, that's true, he didn't. On the other hand, I'm sure I haven't heard the last of the matter. Do you have any idea what's behind all this? Clearly, someone has it in for the both of us."

"The photos," said Edna, "were they perchance issued by the law firm Chance, Whittle and Spence?"

Bazy's eyes brightened ever so slightly, then narrowed. "They were. What the hell have you been up to?"

Edna told Bazy about the letter, her meetings with General Donovan, Gordon Gray, and Lee Tavon. How Tavon had outed himself as her source for both the letter and the liquor store murder. "But he has gone to ground," she explained. "Nobody's seen or heard from him since Saturday night."

Bazy Miller took her time weighing up the tale, without offering Edna the vaguest hint of a response. "Why didn't you bring this to me earlier?"

"I should have," Edna admitted. "Joe talked me out of it. He said you'd want to publish before we had the full story. Though I didn't get a chance to tell him about General Donovan's threat. To be honest, in the face of that I think the story is still a bit light on."

"Well, let me tell you Bill Donovan is no supporter of this newspaper. In the last year of the war, J. Edgar Hoover sent us a copy of

Donovan's proposal for the creation of a civilian spy agency. I believe our story described the idea as an American Gestapo."

Edna raised an eyebrow. This would have been good to know before she'd stumbled into her meeting with Donovan. "I had no idea."

"You would have been in Germany at the time, so I can hardly hold that against you. But our story prompted Roosevelt to shove the whole idea under the rug, and he died before it could be resurrected. It was another two years before Truman was finally convinced the idea had merit, but he's never liked Bill Donovan much and kept him at arm's length from the CIA."

"There's more to this than one man's bitterness," said Edna.

"Indeed. I think we can safely assume the letter to be genuine."

Edna nodded. "Gordon Gray pretty much confirmed as much."

"Tell me you're keeping it somewhere secure."

Edna blanched. "It's in the bottom drawer of my desk."

"Lord save us, are you mad?"

"The drawer's locked."

"Those desks aren't secure; the drawer locks are useless. Jesus, Edna — bring it in here, I'll put it in my safe."

By the time she'd retrieved the letter and returned to Bazy's office, Edna knew she needed to cut some kind of deal. "If I give this to you, do I have your word I won't get the boot? I need to know, boss."

Bazy nodded grimly. Both of them knew it was a promise Bazy Miller might not be in a position to honor for long.

"They may keep coming for us," said Edna. "Things could get worse before they get better. They obviously don't want this story published."

Bazy Miller thought about it, sitting back in her chair and staring at the ceiling. "We need to be strategic. The Colonel's photos came with a letter of demand saying that if I don't sack you within twenty-four hours, Joe Eldridge's wife gets her own copies of the photos. We need to do something about that. I suspect it's the main reason the Colonel wants me to sack you."

"That's Joe's problem, not mine," said Edna, though she could hardly believe she was hearing herself say the words.

"No honey, this is most assuredly your problem. You don't want your private life splashed through the *Evening Star* gossip pages. You'd be a laughing stock in that newsroom. It'd be a knockout punch for your career." Bazy let the words hang in the air for a moment, before she continued. "But I think there might be a way around it, if you're willing to play ball."

"What do you have in mind?"

"OK, here it is: As of this moment, you are sacked. Unofficially." Edna's mouth fell open. Words failed her. Bazy held up her hands defensively. "I said unofficially. Just for appearances. I'll tell everyone here you've resigned, but I'll keep you on the payroll. You'll have to take a bit of a break, then probably work from home until we sort this out."

Edna placed the letter down on her boss's desk. Bazy picked the letter up and read it, whistled in surprise and approval at the contents, then placed it inside her wall safe and locked the door.

"I think they're watching me," Edna cautioned. "Maybe even listening to my telephone calls."

"Let them listen," said Bazy. "As far as they're concerned, you're now an out of work reporter. You can't publish. Just watch what you say over an open line. We'll have to establish some sort of protocol for communicating."

Edna asked, "Any thoughts on where to start?"

"For starters, go see that murder cop downtown. He'll want to look into the name Tavon gave you. It's Kaplan, isn't it? Detective Kaplan?" Edna nodded. "He's a good man. Incorruptible, so I've heard. But you scratch his back on this, he might just scratch yours back. Ask him to take a look at Tavon. I'll make a few discreet inquiries of my own in the meantime. I'll get word to you in a day or two on a place you and I can meet up. This is our little secret, OK? No telling Joe Eldridge or anybody else out there. If it's going to work, nobody can know."

"Agreed," said Edna.

"All right then. You're fired! Go pack up your desk and get the hell out of here.

And for God's sake, try to look upset about it."

# TWENTY NINE

July 14, 1952

Edna felt well and truly out of place as she approached the imposing glass entrance to Metropolitan Police headquarters downtown. She had no doubt the stone edifice was a fine example of art deco architecture, but it made her feel like she was part of the criminal fringe merely for venturing inside.

At the inquiries desk, a brass name plate proudly declared Liam O'Dwyer to be the desk sergeant of the day. He looked her up and down solemnly. "Can I help you?"

An Irishman. "I'm here to see Detective Vincent Kaplan."

O'Dwyer grimaced. Apparently not a Kaplan man. "What would a pretty thing like you be wanting with the likes of him?"

Edna bit down hard on her instinctive desire to chew the moron's ear off. "He's expecting me, so if you'd be so kind, Sergeant." She stared O'Dwyer down, and made sure he was the first to look away.

"Take a seat. I'm sure he won't be long."

Edna had taken Kaplan's file from the *Times-Herald* library shortly before she'd fled the newsroom, trying her best to look bereft.

Theo Mankiewicz had taken it upon himself to escort her to the door. "Go home to New York, kid. Find yourself a man, settle down. But maybe avoid the married ones this time." His words might have been well-intentioned, but Mankiewicz was always so condescending when he spoke to her it was hard to say for sure. Edna had nodded and said nothing in response, more worried he'd spot the pilfered file under her arm.

Kaplan's exploits were well-documented in the *Tribune* and the *New York Times*. It had been just over a year since he'd traded New York for Washington. He brought with him a reputation as a fearless corruption fighter from two years in the service of New York prosecutor Julius Helfand, chasing down cops on the Mob payroll. Kaplan had personally delivered an ultimatum to his own police commissioner, William O'Brien, telling his boss to quit the force, or face the full force of the law. O'Brien had resigned his commission the following day. Little wonder the likes of Sergeant O'Dwyer screwed up their noses at the mere mention of Kaplan's name. Cops and robbers had one thing in common: they hated a rat in the ranks. Problem was, too many of them also shared a fondness for dirty money and easy women.

Corruption had become so endemic during Prohibition that even now, twenty years later, it remained a serious problem dogging every major metropolitan police service in the country. It was being addressed with varying degrees of urgency, often resulting in warring factions that split whole departments right down the middle.

But Kaplan's corruption fighting days appeared to be over, at least for the time being. It looked as though he'd landed in homicide as soon as he'd arrived in Washington. On the night of the Peterson murder, they'd only exchanged a few words. He'd come across as a humorless stiff with a rod up his ass. But now it made sense. When your colleagues treat you like a leper, you need a thick skin. Something Edna Drake thought she could relate to.

He'd told her that night it looked like a robbery gone wrong and that there were no witnesses. She was here to tell him he'd been mistaken on the latter point.

Kaplan recognized her immediately when he appeared in the foyer. He pointed at the front entrance. "Let's take a walk," he said. "I could use some fresh air."

He had a cigarette in his mouth, which he lit the moment they were outside.

Fresh air.

"I've always preferred smoking outdoors. In the squad room, sometimes I can't see six feet in front of me for the smoke. Nobody ever opens a window. I swear, one day they'll ban this stupid habit as a fire risk." Detective Kaplan pointed her toward the pavement, and they started to walk. Kaplan said nothing for a minute or so, seemingly keen to make sure they couldn't be overheard. "Sorry to hear you lost your job." He sounded like he meant it.

"Long story," she said. "But I'll be OK."

"Woman of your resources? I have no doubt. You said you had something?"

"Possibly more than one something. I've been reliably informed your man for the Jimmy Peterson murder is a street hood by the name of Jeb Stanton."

"Who told you that?"

Edna pondered that for a moment. "Normally this is when I tell you I can't name my source. But I'm willing to break that golden rule in the hope of some quid pro quo."

He raised an eyebrow. "You freelancing? I told you I won't comment on the case."

"I'm not after a story. That is, I'm not after this story. I'm interested in knowing more about this source of mine. I need to know if he's reliable."

"He witnessed the shooting?" Kaplan asked.

"That's right. He was there in the store when it happened. Told me about it in gruesome detail to prove his point."

"The sort of detail a murderer would remember," said Kaplan.

"My thoughts exactly, although in this case I think he's telling the truth about Stanton. What I'm wondering is how my man knew Stanton's name at all. I've never witnessed a shooting, but I'm guessing most murderers don't wear name badges. Yet somehow my man knew the shooter's name. He survived the encounter without a scratch, and then calmly called our paper and asked to speak to me — despite the fact that at that particular moment, we'd never even met."

"What's his name?" asked Kaplan.

"He's a businessman. Lee Tavon. In the liquor trade himself, as it turns out."

"I know the guy," said Kaplan. "Runs the Jewel Box."

"That's him." She didn't ask how Kaplan knew him, but hoped like hell it wasn't because Kaplan had rolled over since leaving New York.

"And what, you think he hired Stanton to do the shooting, then called you to brag about it?" Kaplan asked.

"I dunno. Something like that, maybe."

Kaplan stubbed out his smoke on the pavement, then immediately pulled out another from the packet in his coat pocket. He offered her one; Edna shook her head. He lit up and started walking again. "Why didn't you tell me about Tavon at the scene? Stanton's probably in the wind by now. I should book you for obstructing justice." "Tavon only revealed himself to me two nights ago. When he rang the paper, he never gave his name — he just gave me the tip."

Detective Kaplan looked her up and down. It might have been lewd, if he wasn't so suspicious. "I wondered how the hell you got there so quickly." He turned to watch the passing cars lost in thought. "I've heard whispers about Tavon, nothing solid."

"What sort of whispers?"

Kaplan gave her that world-weary look. "Let me check into Jeb Stanton and maybe I'll get back to you," he said.

"I'm starting to think you might actually be one of the good guys, detective."

"I like to know who I can trust."

"That can be a lonely business," she said. "A man like Tavon knows a lot of people. Pays a lot of people, if you get my meaning. Tread carefully."

Kaplan smiled. This wasn't news to him. "Duly noted. What's he to you, anyway?"

"He's given me another story. A big one. He's trying to convince me it's on the level. Wants me to trust him. Look, I know he's not squeaky clean, but I want this story. I'd just like to know what strings are attached."

"You might not like the answer."

"Tavon knows things. Dangerous things. That's useful for someone like me. Plenty of people in this town don't talk to dame reporters."

"All right," said Kaplan. "Give me a few days. I'll call you. And thanks."

Edna nodded. "Tavon's gone to ground since I saw him the other night. He said people were following him."

"What people?" Kaplan asked.

"I don't know who exactly," she said, hoping he'd buy the lie. "But dangerous people, from the sound of it."

Kaplan looked wary; he was good at reading people. "Wouldn't have anything to do with this other story of yours, by any chance?"

"Maybe," she said. "Probably. Government people. The ones who don't like their secrets coming out into the light."

Kaplan stopped in his tracks. "Is this what got you fired?"

Part of her wanted to tell him everything. She sensed she could trust him, that maybe it would be a good thing to have someone else in on the deal. But Edna hardly knew Kaplan, and it would be asking a lot. "It's complicated," she said finally.

"What good is this story if you don't have a job?" She couldn't help it then, she smiled. In a way, that told him all he needed to know. "I see," Kaplan said. "Say no more."

"So, I'm not under arrest?"

"Not today."

"Pity."

"Go home. Keep your head down. I'll call you in a couple of days."

"No," she said. "My telephone's probably bugged. I'll call you."

Kaplan looked at her sharply, wondering if she might have a screw loose after all.

# THIRTY

J uly 16, 1952

The Lockheed Aircraft Corporation was based in Burbank, California. In just over a quarter of a century, it had spread its wings far and wide across America, becoming a big wheel in the business world and wielding huge power in Washington. This was thanks in no small part to a long and successful partnership with the Department of Defense. Lockheed had its own airport at Burbank, purchased in 1940 after antitrust laws forced the break-up of the United Aircraft and Transport Corporation. Lockheed had snapped up the airport for the princely sum of $1.5 million. Since then, government contracts had seen it expand into an aviation company that eclipsed UATC in power and influence within the aviation sector. But Lockheed didn't own an airline, so nobody was talking about breaking it up.

In the past five years, Garrick Stamford's investment in Lockheed had made him an incredibly wealthy man. He'd also built a network of business and political connections, nearly as impressive as his wealth. Donovan had known him since the war; Stamford had been one of Donovan's OSS operatives in Italy.

For some time now, Stamford had been privy to many of the Verus Foundation's most closely held secrets. Lately though, Donovan had begun to wonder if Stamford had been deliberately keeping them in the dark on the finer points of Lockheed's classified research program.

Stamford's office building at Burbank was alongside the main terminal. A smiling and extremely attractive young secretary greeted Donovan warmly as soon as he walked in the door.

"Good to see you again, General Donovan" she said.

"Thank you, my dear." Donovan couldn't remember her name, but wondered whether Stamford liked to keep her working back late.

Her smile was so engaging it sent a short sharp thrill down the back of his neck. "Go straight in," she said.

The office was huge, bathed in sunlight from floor-to-ceiling windows on three sides with a panoramic view over the airport tarmac. Stamford stood up from his desk to offer his hand. "General, get in here. How are you? Did you have trouble finding the place?"

"No, no," said Donovan. "You're well sign-posted."

Stamford laughed. It was an old spy joke. The French resistance would often switch road signs around to confuse the enemy.

Stamford pointed him in the direction of two lounge chairs by the window, opening a cigar box on the coffee table between them in offering. Donovan took one so as not to appear ungracious. He was prepared, for the moment, to extend his old friend the benefit of the doubt.

But Bill Donovan had questions.

"That was quite the night in Atlantic City," said Stamford. "I had a sore head the next day, I can tell you."

"A remarkable man, that Lee Tavon," said Donovan. "Remarkable. Also, as it turns out, hard to find. Don't suppose you've heard from him lately?"

"No," said Stamford warily. "Not for a couple of weeks, actually. I tried to call him the other day. I've been wondering about investing in IBM. Have you heard of it?"

"Can't say I have," said Donovan.

"They build machines that process data. They're called computers."

"Is there money in that?" Donovan asked skeptically.

"Some people think so. Lee's so good with R&D; he's never led me astray. Actually, I'd say he's a bit of a magician."

"Tavon gives you financial advice, is that right?"

Stamford tapped his nose. "Tips. Always well-timed. Always on the money. He's made me a fortune. I don't know how he does it. Sometimes I think I don't want to know. If this IBM thing pans out, I'll let you know."

Donovan shook his head. "Thanks, but no thanks. Garrick, you do know it's not magic, right? It's called sleight of hand. Sometimes, it's also called stock market fraud."

Stamford smiled. "No, it's nothing like that. He just knows things. The sort of things other people couldn't possibly know."

"What does he get out of this little arrangement of yours? He must get something. The saucer project, for instance — I gather you talk to him about that?"

"We talk about it," Stamford admitted. "Lee's a shareholder. He knows what I tell him is for his ears only."

"Does he?"

"Sure he does. We run a tight ship. There are no loose lips at Skunkworks. What are you suggesting, Bill? This is starting to feel like the third degree."

"Oh, I'm just keen to know more about the elusive Mr Tavon. Ever met his wife?" "Maeve? Yeah, sure. She's a doll. He's a lucky man."

"It's never occurred to you this knowledge he dispenses with such generosity might come from an illegal source? Like the Mob, for instance?"

Stamford half grinned, nodding his head in comprehension as he turned to stare at the runway. "Nucky Johnson's not in the Mob. Not anymore."

"But if he knows Nucky, he knows other people," said Donovan. "Paul D'Amato is connected, isn't he? Who else has Tavon introduced you to?"

"The man is friendly with a few ex-bootleggers and the odd illegal casino owner. They make for colorful companions. That doesn't make him a master criminal. What's the matter, Bill? What's he supposed to have done?"

"Apart from betray his country by breaking the Espionage Act? Nothing at all, Garrick. Nothing at all. What I'm trying to work out is whether he'll take you down with him."

Stamford shifted uncomfortably in his seat and was about to raise an objection, only to change tack at the last moment. "I've done nothing wrong. I have complete discretion on who's in the loop on our little project. I'll have a word to him, OK? Next time I see him?"

Donovan placed the Harmony Events business card on the coffee table. "Seen this before?"

Stamford picked it up. His eyes shifted from the card to Donovan, then back again. He knew damn well what that card meant, and where it had come from. Stamford was an easy man to read. "Is this the card I gave Roscoe?"

"Tavon caters at a New York cocktail party for Admiral Hillenkoetter, right around the same time a top-secret document goes missing from the Admiral's private papers. Quite a coincidence, wouldn't you say?"

The window behind Stamford darkened. Donovan knew without looking up it was Paolo entering the room. Donovan didn't need him here, didn't want the distraction. But Paolo pleased himself these days.

"Hillenkoetter's just moved," said Stamford, who had gone pale. "The paperwork could have been lost in transit, right?"

"No chance. I know for a fact Tavon took it."

"Jesus Christ," Stamford muttered.

Paolo tutted, knowing Donovan hated people taking the Lord's name in vain.

*Play hardball,* Paolo told him. *You cannot trust a word that leaves his mouth.*

Stamford's air-conditioned office was as cool as a December dawn, but the man was starting to sweat.

Donovan said, "I've kept this off the President's desk for now. But I need your full cooperation on this. I'm sure I don't have to tell you what's at stake."

*Good, good.*

Stamford sat forward. "Of course, Bill. Whatever you need."

"I need to know the full extent of your dealings with Tavon. Copies of every financial transaction. The full paper trail. Then, and only then, might we have a shot at keeping you out of jail."

Stamford nodded in acquiescence. Prison was a bluff. There was no way in the world Truman, or anyone in MJ-12, would want to kick up that much dust. But Stamford was scared now, backed into a corner.

Paolo was nodding his approval.

# THIRTY ONE

July 16, 1952

The knock on the door scared her. Nobody ever visited Edna Drake at home, and there was no peephole to see who it was. Then again, if someone wanted to hurt her, wouldn't they just kick it in?

She opened the door to find the whiz kid grinning at her. "Hey there, Edna. How you doing?"

"Johnny. How'd you find me?"

He tapped his nose conspiratorially, then peered over Edna's shoulder into the apartment. "Gonna invite me in?"

She sighed and waved him through the door, taking a quick look down the stairwell to make sure he was alone before closing it behind him.

"Mrs Miller tells me you're undercover. Pretty cool."

She wasn't at all thrilled Johnny was in on the deal. "What are you doing here?"

"I'm your messenger boy." He sat himself down on her couch. "So... Got any booze?"

Johnny Galbraith's father had secured his job as a cub reporter. Around that same time, the senior Galbraith had made a point of diverting his textile company's advertising spend to the *Times-Herald*. From what Edna had seen of Johnny's writing, he was no Hemingway, yet he'd convinced some at the paper that he was God's gift to journalism. He had the sort of brash confidence that could kick down doors, though in her opinion he lacked the street smarts to back it up. Johnny Galbraith never had to fight for anything in his life.

"You shouldn't drink on the job, kid. It's a bad habit to get into." But Edna could tell her words were falling on deaf ears; Johnny didn't give a damn about her views on day drinking. "What's the message?"

"Boss wants to see you. She's booked a suite in the Hamilton Hotel under the name of Mrs Geoffrey Black. It's a made-up name."

"No shit."

Johnny offered her a lift, but Edna figured it was safer to make her own way there, in case they were watching her apartment.

Bazy Miller's hotel suite was plush, the walls a strident emerald green, drapes in basic black. It wasn't to Edna's taste at all. The furniture was art deco throwback; the sort that looked beautiful and was dreadfully uncomfortable to sit on. Which was probably apt. Places like this always delivered the same message: "Don't get comfortable, you won't be here long."

"I've left my husband," Bazy Miller declared. "I'm here for the duration."

"Oh," said Edna, rather shocked.

"I guess I have you to thank for that."

"Oh dear."

"Don't worry, you've done Tank and me a favor. Take a seat."

They discussed the letter and Edna's progress in authenticating it, as well as the fact that she'd been spectacularly unsuccessful in raising anybody at the Pentagon. Edna explained how Helen Barber had pointed her toward Project Blue Book, but that Major Fournet wasn't taking her calls.

"How about you let me have a chat to Helen Barber?" Bazy offered.

"No, I don't think so."

Bazy looked put out. "Why not?"

"She's a nervous woman. Doesn't even really want to talk to me. If I send you after her, she'll think I've thrown her to the wolves and we'll burn her completely. Sorry, nothing personal, Bazy."

"No, don't apologize for wanting to protect your source."

"Anyway, she's helped me all she can. We need someone with clout who'll talk to us. Cold-calling people at the Pentagon is a waste of time. Sooner or later, the word will be out on us. I was wondering about calling Bob Ginna at *Life* magazine." He'd co-authored their investigative story on saucers.

"You can't tell him about the letter," Bazy instructed.

"No, of course not. But I think it's worth a shot. Ginna spent a year chasing that story. He spoke to a lot of people."

Bazy pointed to the telephone. "What are you waiting for?"

"What, now?"

"You got something better to do?"

Ginna took the call. Edna baited the hook without getting specific. Said she had something big, and needed to talk to someone in Blue Book about it.

Ginna didn't even have to think about it. "The man you want is General Chuck Cabell. He's the Director of joint staff for the Joint Chiefs of Staff."

"Wow, a tautological job title," said Edna. "I guess that means he's important?"

"Until the end of last year, he was head of Air Force intelligence. Cabell personally set up Project Blue Book."

"You didn't mention him in your story."

"No, because he's smarter than that. Cabell is deep background," Bob Ginna explained.

"Here's the thing Bob, I've been having no luck getting to people at the Pentagon."

"That's because General Samford is head of Air Force intelligence now."

"Is that bad?" Edna asked.

"Samford has cracked down hard on all contact with the media. You've got to avoid all channels that lead to Samford, which means you can forget about the Pentagon switchboard. You need to call the Blue Book office direct at Wright-Patterson Air Base in Ohio. I'll give you the number. Say you were speaking to me, and that I suggested General Cabell would want to speak to you."

"But you don't even know what it's about," said Edna.

"Are you going to tell me?"

"No."

"Didn't think so."

# THIRTY TWO

J uly 18, 1952

For two days, Edna had worked hard at doing nothing. She slept late. She caught up on dirty laundry, read trashy magazines, and kept *Young Man With A Horn* — the latest Miles Davis masterpiece — on high rotation. Lay low and look defeated, Bazy Miller had told her. So, Edna Drake had dutifully given it her best shot at playing a woman cast adrift by the world.

There were times it all felt way too real. She was starting to wonder if she'd made a big mistake in urging Bazy to call Cabell. At the time, she'd thought it made perfect sense; a serving General was more likely to take the call of a newspaper editor. But the more Edna thought about it, the more she worried it had been a mistake to hand this important step in the investigation to a woman who had, to all intents and purposes, given her the sack.

As far as everyone else at the *Times-Herald* was concerned, Edna Drake been fired for misconduct. Nobody from the office had called to check on her, not a one. It had only taken two days for Edna to realize how lonely her life had become. There was no one at the paper she could call a close friend. They were colleagues, not confidantes. While the *Times-Herald* boasted a number of female reporters and correspondents, Edna had never found much in common with any of them. They all still thought and behaved like interlopers in a man's world. The younger ones were obsessed with finding a husband, the older ones with keeping theirs and climbing the Washington social ladder. Apparently, news of her brief affair with Eldridge had not gone down well.

She did, however, savor a certain enjoyment from the idea of working undercover. It made Edna feel special, a cut above the Joe Schmoes out there going about their daily grind. She was going to make the rich and powerful quake in their hundred-dollar boots. Men like General William Donovan.

She was dying to stick it to that smug old bastard. He was nothing more than a bully. Like those boys back home in Queens, who used to strut around Rockaways' Playland like they owned the place.

The amusement park had been her whole world before the war. She'd lived two streets away. Her father Paddy had worked most of his life as a roller coaster mechanic. From the age of eight, Edna had spent her Saturdays in the ticket booth of the Atom Smasher, learning the hard way about boys who aimed to get a free ride by playing rough with a little girl. She'd learned to stand her ground. When that didn't work, she could hit them with fairground invective, colorful enough to make a nun blush. Half the time, she didn't even know what the words meant. Usually, it was enough to make them pay. Nobody had ever matched Edna for trash talk before or since.

But there was that one time...

Ronnie Jamieson wasn't used to people talking to him like that, and he certainly wasn't going to put up with it from a grubby little girl like Edna. He'd dragged her out of the booth and slapped her hard across that big mouth of hers, like it was his God-appointed right to put her in her place. She still remembered tasting the blood, feeling the swelling in her lips and that moment of panic when she realized she was in over her head. Ronnie was a nasty, spoiled rich kid three years her senior. Being insulted by the hired help demanded reparation. He'd ordered Edna to let him and his friends on the rollercoaster for free. Not that money was a problem; Ronnie had plenty of that. He was making a point of showing Edna she lived in a world run by people like him.

There had been three of them. She didn't want to be hit a second time. She'd waved them straight to the front of the queue, ignoring the half-hearted objections from other patrons, and sitting them down in the front carriage for their free ride.

On weekends, the boys at the controls of the Atom Smasher were her age. None of them had been about to defend her honor if it meant taking a beating from Ronnie and his friends. Everyone knew how the Jamieson kid loved to throw his weight around. Nobody liked him, but no one had ever stood up to him.

Edna's father, Owen 'Paddy' Drake, was a minor deity among the working folks at Rockaways' Playland. He could fix anything. The Atom Smasher itself was built to his design.

Word that little Edna was being slapped around had spread from ride to ride through the fairground staff. After their first turn, she was waiting for them at the bottom. Smiling through bloodied teeth and fat lips. The boys had laughed at her, like she was the joke. Until they'd noticed the small mob of angry carnies gathering at Edna's ticket booth.

Whenever they'd tried to get out of their carriage, a posse of sun-scarred, toothless roustabouts pushed them back down. Bony, work-scarred fingers tapped them on the forehead and leather-necked grinners yelled crazily at them to "sit down boys, safety first." Nobody ever laid a glove on them; the threat was enough.

Ronnie had said his father would get them all fired. Nobody cared. Then he'd offered them money. They'd laughed. He had no answer to the quiet menace of men whose lives were worth so little they had nothing to lose.

To this day, Ronnie and his friends still held the record for the longest continuous run on the Atom Smasher. Two hours and fifteen minutes. For much of the second hour, Ronnie's friends were covered in puke and begging for water and mercy, yelling at him to apologize. He did, finally.

Which was when Edna had let them out.

She hadn't thought of Ronnie Jamieson in years. Not until Bill Donovan had brought it all flooding back with his overdeveloped sense of entitlement.

Except now Edna Drake felt like the one trapped in the coaster, unable to get off.

Two nights ago, she'd noticed a man out there watching her. She'd glanced out the window, purely by chance, and saw him standing there on the other side of the road, looking up toward her apartment. He wasn't from the neighborhood, and he was too far away to be a peeping tom. She'd seen him again yesterday morning, pretending not to watch as she came down to breakfast at Mamma Rey's.

This morning, she skipped breakfast and took a walk down M Street to the corner of 4th, trying her best to look like someone with time on her hands headed nowhere in particular. As far as she could tell, the only thing stalking her was the pungent stench of the fish markets.

Bazy Miller pulled up in a gun metal Packard, a brown trilby pulled down over dark glasses. Edna jumped into the front seat beside her, and Bazy screwed up her nose at the stink. "Nice neighborhood."

"Works for me," said Edna. "I don't get paid a whole lot." The rich bitch probably never saw the inside of a fish markets her whole life.

"I assume you made sure nobody followed you?"

Edna frowned. "Not that I could tell, but I'm no expert." She felt her boss was enjoying the cloak and dagger a bit too much. "Where are we going?"

"University Yard."

"OK," said Edna, "let's not take any chances. Head up past the Library of Congress and park somewhere near Union Station."

"That's nowhere near University Yard."

"Exactly," said Edna. "If anybody is following me, we'll keep them guessing.

Bazy threw a copy of the morning paper on Edna's lap. "Check out page three." Edna opened the paper to a banner headline: SAUCERS KEEP COMING. She glanced back at Bazy, who was smiling like a proud mother. "We're going hard on this, Edna."

"With or without me, it would seem." Joe Eldridge had written the story. "I'm starting to feel like I'm being left behind on my own project."

"Not at all," Bazy assured her. "This is all down to you. You've sparked my interest. Something very strange is going on here. We're running another story tomorrow. Joe spoke to a Civil Defense Director in Dayton, Ohio. One of General Cabell's suggestions. He gave us one heck of a quote. Get this, he said, 'There is something flying around our skies and I wish we knew what it was.' How do you like that?"

Edna nodded compliantly. She didn't like it one little bit, but said nothing. They turned left onto Pennsylvania Avenue and drove most of the way toward Capitol Hill, before turning right on $2^{nd}$ Street, taking them north past the Library of Congress and the Supreme Court. Bazy parked a block from Union Station and Edna led her in through the front doors. Once inside, Edna glanced over her shoulder. Nobody was following them that she could see. She made a beeline for a side entrance door nearest the station's cab rank, and hopped into the back seat of the car at the front of the line. "George Washington University Law Center," Edna told the driver, "to the H Street side of University Yard."

It might have been overkill, but she figured it paid to be careful. The taxi took them southwest, back across town. University Yard was a park lined by trees with paths cut like an asterisk through a wide lawn; each led to one of the law school buildings that surrounded the square on three sides. Edna observed students milling about, mostly right outside the buildings. Bazy paid off the cab driver and they started walking, past the George Washington statue and onto a diagonal path toward a park bench.

Two men were waiting for them, both dressed nearly identically in navy blue trousers and white open-necked shirts. Like Mormons on vacation. Edna assumed the older one was General Cabell. The other man was at least two decades his junior and rather funny looking. His big ears stuck out like radar dishes, drawing unwanted attention to his receding hairline and making his face look huge.

Bazy introduced herself to Cabell. Edna did likewise. He shook their hands warmly. "I hope you don't mind," he said, "I thought it'd be useful to have Major Fournet join us. Dewey is Blue Book liaison at the Pentagon."

The women shook Fournet's hand, then sat down on either side of the two men.

"I tried to call you," Edna told Fournet.

"Yes, I know. I'm sorry, but I'm under orders to avoid reporters," the funny looking man apologized.

"Not from me, you understand," said General Cabell.

Edna realized Bazy wasn't saying anything; her boss was waiting for her to take the lead. "All right then Major," Edna began, "how about you start by telling us a little about your work with Blue Book?"

"I work closely with Captain Ed Ruppelt, who's the officer in charge."

"You're ranking officer, but he's in charge — how does that work?" Edna asked.

"It's complicated," Cabell acknowledged.

Fournet continued. "We've developed a systematic approach to analyze and assess unexplained aerial sightings across the United States. It's a comprehensive screening process that takes into account every possible source of information that could help us explain them."

Edna pulled out a notebook and started furiously scribbling notes as Fournet continued.

"We gather all current information on weather balloons, aircraft, and astronomical bodies. We coordinate with the Air Force Air Weather Service, Flight Service, Research and Development Command, and Air Defense Command. We also communicate daily with the Office of Naval Research, the atmospherics branch of the Bureau of Aeronautics, the Civil Aeronautics Administration, the Bureau of Standards, and several astronomical observatories."

"Wow," said Edna. "Sounds like a lot of work."

"I asked them to be thorough," said Cabell, "and they're getting very good at it."

"By doing this," Fournet explained, "we account for the vast majority of sightings. These are cases that have rational explanations — balloons, aircraft, planets, meteors or weather events, that type of thing. The cases that have no rational explanation are added to the unexplained list. Then, after *Life* published their story in April, we started to record a spike in sightings."

"You're saying reports rose *because* of the story?" asked Bazy.

"Exactly," said Fournet. "But the funny thing is, we've also noticed no matter how many cases are reported, fifteen to twenty percent of them always defy rational and scientific explanation."

Edna questioned, "These ones are the real deal? They're flying saucers?"

"That's one possibility," said Cabell. "They're unexplained. We don't know for certain what they are."

"The point is, they *can't* be explained," Fournet clarified. "They are reliable sightings, often observed simultaneously by a variety of sources — for instance, we have many cases of visual sightings from observers on the ground and in the air, that were simultaneously observed on radar. In many instances, these objects are observed doing incredible things. They perform impossible aerial maneuvers, they fly at incredible speed, they change direction on a dime and climb to impossible altitudes in a matter of seconds."

"General Cabell," asked Edna, "what's your take on all this?"

"I can't talk on the record. Nothing I tell you today is attributable to me."

"I'd hoped you could speak freely to us," said Bazy. "We're trying to cut through all the Pentagon bullshit, if you'll excuse the French. If you don't want us to quote you directly, we won't name you as our source. But I want to know what we're dealing with here."

"*Life* magazine was on the money," Cabell stated. "The only explanation for what we're seeing is visitation by spacecraft not of this Earth, with capabilities far in advance of any human-built aircraft. But that's not an admission I'm willing to make on the record. There's been hell to pay since that story in April. Our Chief of Staff, General Vandenberg, has made it abundantly clear any official answer to this problem that mentions flying saucers is the wrong answer."

Bazy laughed and shook her head; this was a game she knew all too well.

Edna just felt a rising sense of anger. "How can he just stick his head in the sand?"

"He can't," said Fournet. Cabell gave him a gentle warning tap him on the arm.

"Vandenberg is nobody's fool," said Cabell. "He's concerned about causing panic. A lot of the senior ranking officers are worried the saucer frenzy plays into the hands of the Russians."

"How so?" Edna asked.

"The theory goes," said Cabell, "that the Russians could build their own replica saucers and fly them into US airspace to cause a big panic, making it easier to invade."

"That assumes they want to invade us," said Edna.

Cabell nodded in agreement. "Which they probably don't. Unbridled expansionism is what lost Hitler the war. Nobody knows that more than the Russians. They lost seventeen million people in helping us defeat the Third Reich."

"I'm not so sure," said Bazy. "Stalin and Hitler are two sides of the same coin."

Edna was sure her boss was about to start parroting Joe McCarthy, and jumped in ahead of her. "Blue Book must be locking horns with them by keeping this debate on the public agenda."

"Our information often isn't welcomed," Fournet admitted.

"Who sees your reports?" Bazy asked.

"They go up the chain to General Samford," said Cabell. "But all public posturing aside, there is a group of people sufficiently concerned with what's really happening, and what it all means. They want to know the facts — and they know it's not the Russians we need to worry about. A few weeks ago, Samford arranged for Captain Ruppelt to deliver a briefing to Air Force and Navy intelligence men in Washington. Ruppelt told them we still had no proof the UFOs were anything real. He admitted that by making certain assumptions, it was possible to find rational explanations for all the sightings. Then a colonel from Samford's office pointed out it would be just as plausible to make slightly different assumptions, and conclude the UFOs were interplanetary objects. And Ruppelt had to agree. Believe me, it put a chill through the room. It was the first time I'd heard someone put voice to the growing concern inside the Pentagon: that Blue Book might be trying too hard to find answers where there were none."

"Ed Ruppelt is trying to apply scientific rigor," said Fournet. "The bottom line is, we can't say with scientific certainty these things are saucers from outer space."

Cabell continued, "But for many people, logic and gut instinct suggest otherwise. Look, I have no idea if we're being visited by aliens from outer space, I really don't. But even if the chance is one in a thousand — hell, even one in ten thousand — the Department of

Defense would want to know. We just fought a war. We're not led by men prone to sticking their heads in the sand."

Edna turned to Bazy and caught her eye; now was the time to come clean. Bazy merely shrugged. "General Cabell," Edna asked, "how well acquainted are you with General Bill Donovan?"

Cabell didn't react to the name in any obvious way. "I've met him once or twice. I know he's still pretty well plugged into the CIA."

Bazy asked, "Could he be working freelance for them?"

"I'm not sure. Why, what have you heard?"

"Nothing in particular," said Bazy, "but he's been very heavy-handed with Edna in response to a story we're pursuing."

"What is this story of yours, anyway?" asked Cabell.

"I have a letter," said Edna. "Written by Admiral Roscoe Hillenkoetter, stamped Top Secret Majestic, asking for presidential permission to conduct a test flight of a craft designated FS-1."

"As in, 'Flying Saucer One'?" Fournet suggested.

"That was my line of thinking, yes," said Edna. "The Admiral's letter says this craft was 'acquired' in April 1951, that it's made of some unknown material and is powered by a science our engineers don't understand."

"We believe the letter to be genuine," said Bazy.

"It probably is," Cabell admitted.

It was quite an admission. Even though she'd already decided as much for herself, it made Edna's pulse race. "Do you know about this project?"

"Not officially," said Cabell. "But in my job, you hear things you're not supposed to hear, when the bourbon is flowing and men with star clusters are trying to impress one another."

"Please go on, General. This is news to me too," said Fournet.

Cabell smiled apologetically. "What I'm about to tell you must never be traced back to me."

"Understood," said Bazy, riveted now.

"That test flight went ahead, but it failed," said Cabell. "It's some kind of alien craft we retrieved intact. But we don't know how to fly the damn thing, and our test pilot crashed."

"Holy shit," said Edna. "I knew it."

Fournet was shocked to hear this. "You've never mentioned any of that before."

"The reason for that, Major, is it has no bearing on the work of Blue Book. Because whatever strange objects are up there in the sky, we're not the ones flying them." Cabell shifted his gaze back to Edna and Bazy. "You mentioned Majestic. I've heard the name. I'm not in the loop, but I'm guessing General Vandenberg would know about it."

"We believe so," said Bazy.

"His name is on the letter," said Edna. "It was addressed to the President. But there's no way Vandenberg will talk to us."

"I might be able to help there," Cabell told her. "I've been talking with General Vandenberg's secretary, Wendy Angwin. She wants to move. He's a hard task master. Expects her in the office twelve hours a day, six days a week."

"Someone should tell old Hoyt we won the war already," said Edna.

"Wendy wants out," Cabell continued, "and that might be your way in. If Vandenberg is conducting top secret business off the books, he'd need to do it face-to-face outside the Pentagon. He won't record meetings like that in his diary, but there's always one person who knows where he's going."

"His secretary," said Edna, impressed.

"Leave it with me," said Cabell.

# THIRTY
# THREE

July 18, 1952

Edna rode the bus back home and hit Friday lunch hour on M Street. She resisted the urge to head for Mamma Rey's, and took a left turn into 4th Street at the corner drug store and did her best to mingle with the crowd; though she was the only white face in a sea of ebony. While that had never bothered her in the least, it did make her easy to find. Then again, anyone tailing her would probably be just as easy to spot.

The Jackson Grill was so busy there was a queue of would-be diners waiting outside. She ignored the rumblings and headed to the front of the line, where a stressed waitress was playing door bitch. Edna gave her the magic words. "I'm meeting a friend at the bar." The waitress waved her through. Drinkers don't need tables.

Three steps inside and the atmosphere was so electric she had to force herself to walk past the barman. There were two phone booths at the back near the bathrooms. They were both free. She shut herself inside one and knew the noisy patrons would make it impossible for anyone to listen in, while the glass doors made it easy to spot a tail. She dialed the number.

"Homicide, Kaplan."

"Hello detective, it's Edna Drake. I thought I'd check back in, see how you're doing."

"We got Stanton. He was in hiding, but it didn't take a lot to shake him loose. I think he was relieved it was us who found him."

"Who else is looking?" she asked.

"He wouldn't say. Just that they wouldn't be so friendly. I asked him about Lee Tavon. I don't think he's heard the name. But whatever Tavon said that night has Stanton rattled."

"Any idea what that was?"

"I get the impression Stanton thinks Tavon is Mob-connected. I've seen that same look of terror too many times. I sent a couple of my guys to ask around, people I trust. All we got were the usual denials. I went down to the Jewel Box, spoke to a barman. Beverley King. He wasn't too happy to hear his boss is wanted in connection with a murder."

"I don't blame him." She'd seen how cops treated black people in her neighborhood.

Kaplan didn't take offence. "You might like to know Mr King had nothing but words of praise for his employer. Said Tavon's bar staff were the best paid colored folk in town."

"I've heard that before," she said.

"Which got me to thinking. A few months back, we interviewed a colored waiter name of Jerry Thomas, on staff at the Salle Du Bois." Arguably Washington's most exclusive restaurant. "We were chasing down another murder. Old Jerry wasn't our man for that, but we did find out he had a side hustle in marijuana cigarettes."

Back in November, President Truman had signed the Boggs Act into law, making marijuana possession a mandatory two to ten in prison with a fine of up to $20,000, even for a first offence. Edna was partial to a toke; she thought the Boggs Act was jackboot governance. "There's been no dope bust at the Salle," she said. "I'd have heard about that. Which means you let him go. Why would you do that?"

"Jerry's employers hired a fancy lawyer to keep him out of jail, and I wasn't inclined to trouble myself over a bit of reefer. I just kept him on the hook in the hope of catching a bigger fish."

Maybe Kaplan agreed with her about the Boggs Act.

"Anyway, he said, "I paid the Salle Du Bois kitchen a visit last night. Jerry was most forthcoming on the topic of Lee Tavon."

"You telling me Tavon is your marijuana marlin?"

"Got it in one," said Kaplan. "But we still can't find him. He's in the wind."

"Don't I know it."

"There's no sign of him anywhere. I think he's getting help from someone, though Christ knows who."

"His business associates?"

"The sort who shoot first and don't ask questions later," said Kaplan. "I'd keep clear if I were you, Miss Drake."

"I don't have that luxury," she said. "This story's big, detective."

"Then go speak to Beverley King," said Kaplan. "He won't talk to me, but he might be more inclined to help you out. I got the feeling he knows more than he told me. Listen, if you do find Tavon, tell him I'll let the dope wrap ride if he testifies against Jeb Stanton."

"Meaning you don't think Tavon had anything to do with the murder?"

"I can't say that for sure," Kaplan admitted. "But an innocent man would be highly motivated to make a deal. Then again, innocent men don't need to hide from the police."

Edna knew all too well why Tavon was hiding, but she wasn't ready to tell Kaplan. "I'll let you know if I have any luck," she said, then hung up. Edna picked up the phone again to dial the Jewel Box, but changed her mind. If Donovan and his people were after him, the bar's phone would almost certainly be tapped. They'd be watching too, meaning it would be risky to go there in person. She'd be telegraphing the fact she was still chasing the story.

Edna Drake had a better idea. She retrieved a notepad from her handbag and found the number she was after.

Lady Lewis never answered her own telephone, but she did take the call. "Lovely to hear from you again, my dear."

"I know this might be asking a lot," said Edna, "but I need your help."

"If it's in my power dear, it would be my pleasure."

"I'm afraid it involves telling a bit of a lie. A harmless one," Edna added quickly. "More sleight of hand, really."

"How terribly naughty," said Lady Lewis. "Do tell."

Edna smiled. "I'd like you to hire someone for the afternoon. You're having a tea party and you must insist this man is the only person for the job. He works for your caterer Lee Tavon — his name is Beverley King. When you call, I'd like you to use these precise words — you say, '*Mr Tavon insisted Beverley King is the only man you should trust with your cups and saucers.*' You must insist Mr King is the only man for the job."

"Is it a secret code?" asked Lady Lewis.

"Why yes," Edna replied, "it is."

"Marvelous."

The kitchen in Lady Lewis's mansion was bigger than Edna's entire apartment. There was enough copper cookware hanging above them to run a phone line to California, with enough left over to rustle up a meal fit for kings and queens. The woman of the house liked to entertain, though her cook was not at all pleased at being chased out of his own kitchen. Yet in a Georgetown mansion the kitchen was, alas, the best place for a black man to be seen without raising eyebrows.

Not only did Edna want their conversation to be private, but the fewer people who knew she was meeting Beverley King, the better. It was a gamble to show up at Lady Lewis's mansion at the same time as a black servant with known connections to a man wanted by authorities. Edna was banking on most white men thinking all 'niggers' looked alike. She hoped anyone tailing her would fail to peg King as Lee Tavon's barman, if seeing him out of context.

At first, Edna feared Lady Lewis might insist on listening in, but the woman was discretion personified. She left them alone without a word said about it.

King appeared to be taking it all in his stride. "Tea party for one, is it?" he asked.

Edna smiled. "Something like that. Does Mr Tavon know you're here?"

"Who askin?" Beverley King wanted to know.

"Edna Drake." She held out her hand.

He stared at it a moment, then shook it gently, like it might explode on impact. "I ain't seen Lee since last weekend," he said.

"Pity," she said. "I thought the cups and saucers routine might have clued him in." She'd hoped Tavon might show in person, but knew it was a long shot.

"He did mention your name last time we spoke. Said you might come callin'."

"Can you get a message to him?"

"Depends," said King. "That detective put you up to this?"

"Not exactly," said Edna. "Although he did ask me to pass on a message to Mr Tavon if our paths crossed. He's willing to look the other way on the reefer business, if Mr Tavon helps him nail that liquor store shooter."

"That cop. Kaplan? He thinks Lee had something to do with it," said King. "It ain't true. Mr Tavon is one of the most peace-lovin' people I ever met."

"He also has a lot of secrets," said Edna. "Which makes him hard to trust."

King shrugged. "I'd trust that man with my life. What's your cut in all this?"

"I need to see him," she said. "In the flesh. I'm a reporter. He's given me some very valuable information, but it's only half the story. I need the other half."

"I don't know nothin' 'bout that," said King.

"Believe me, you're better off," she said. "The people chasing Lee? They're chasing me too. Look, he wants to talk to me, I know he does. I'm hoping you can make that happen, Mr King."

He laughed. "Mistuh King? Shit girl, don't lay it on too thick. Point me to a telephone and I'll make the call."

# THIRTY FOUR

J uly 19, 1952

East Potomac Park jutted out into the Potomac River like a massive claw, spreading south from the Thomas Jefferson Memorial. Most of it was taken up by the golf course, but at this time of night the links were a ghost town, a dark and lonely place for a woman on her own.

"How far along here did you want to go?" the taxicab driver asked nervously as he headed south down Ohio Drive.

"I'm going all the way," Edna said. "Right to the point."

It must be the loneliest place in Washington, which was obviously the point of meeting here. Nobody could tail her without being seen. The tip of the park, known as Hains Point, was a picnic area by day. In the evenings, it was a place where young couples occasionally came to watch the submarine races. But tonight, it appeared to be devoid of human life. She paid the driver, promising a big tip if he came back for her in a half hour. He hit the road like a startled jackrabbit and Edna Drake knew she wouldn't see him again. From here, the road looped back around the other side of the peninsula, but there was a long expanse of grass leading to where the headland met the river. She stepped onto the grass, thankful she'd worn sensible shoes and a jacket. There was a wind blowing north up the river, and it was starting to feel chilly. To her right, a light flashed on the horizon: a plane taking off from Washington National Airport directly across the river, less than a mile away.

A shadowy figure emerged from the trees lining the riverfront. Though the light was dim, she knew it was Tavon. "Thanks for coming."

"I'm fairly certain sure my taxi driver thinks I'm a hooker," Edna said, then regretted it. She hoped he didn't take it as a come-on.

"I love it out here," Tavon said, oblivious.

"Are you a golfer?"

Lee Tavon shook his head. "I come here at night to collect my thoughts. Beverley is always reminding me about the club's whites-only policy. Back in '41, a group of negro men got special permission from the Secretary of the Interior to play there. People lined the fairways to throw rocks at them."

"I'd believe it."

"I've heard there are moves afoot to desegregate all golf courses in Washington."

"You can bet your white dimpled balls that won't end well."

"Well, progress comes in small steps, I suppose."

"Forgive me," said Edna, "but you don't seem terribly agitated for a man on the run from the law."

"They'll catch up with me soon enough, I expect. But Edna, I assure you I have nothing to hide."

Said every guilty man she'd ever met.

"You should call Detective Kaplan downtown. He wants you to testify against Jeb Stanton."

"I try to avoid the police whenever possible. Particularly the honest ones. I find they can be so quick to judge," Tavon explained.

"That letter you sent me, what else can you tell me about it? About the FS-1 program?"

"It's run by Lockheed," he said. "At a remote airbase outside Las Cruces in New Mexico. You really stirred up a hornet's nest by going to General Donovan. He's part of it, you know. He's the man who found the flying saucer."

Her eyes widened; no wonder Donovan was so pissed at her. "What's your connection?"

"Mostly financial. I have a lot of money in Lockheed stock. But I also know a lot more than they think I know." He seemed pleased with himself.

"Such as?"

"Such as the reason I brought you all the way out here tonight." He started to walk back toward the trees. "It's such a clear night. That's good." He reached the fence on the river bank and pointed over toward the airport. "You're going to love this."

"Why?"

"You're about to see something that will change your life."

But she couldn't see anything.

"On Monday night, there were eight of them," he said. "They were just south of D.C. A Pan Am pilot saw them. They were back again on Wednesday, heading north that time. Seen by reliable witnesses. Moving closer to the Capitol."

"What are you talking about?" Edna thought she knew, but she wanted him to say it.

Lee Tavon pointed across the river again. "See for yourself."

At first, she thought they were planes. Two, maybe three of them, moving slowly in the sky above the airport tower. Their lights changed color slowly from white to red. But as they circled, a plane took off and its lights were easy to distinguish — they were blinking constantly.

The other lights were much brighter and seemed to be dancing around one another. Edna had never seen planes do that, not even during the war.

She heard Tavon laughing beside her, an odd kind of a noise expressing his unabashed delight at the aerial spectacle. "Are they...?"

"That's right," he said, nodding and laughing again, like it was all some grand Halloween prank. More lights joined the dance. Edna counted seven of them, weaving in and out of one another. Then, as if to demonstrate their movements were precise rather than random, they all froze in the sky simultaneously.

"Flying saucers," she said.

"In the nation's capital," said Tavon.

"How did you know?"

"Like I said, they've been here all week."

"But how did you know they'd be back?"

He didn't answer. The lights began to move slowly in a formation toward the city. Toward Capitol Hill. Getting faster, but still moving as one.

"I've got to tell the paper," she said.

"Yes, you must. Go to the air traffic control tower at the airport. They will have seen them too. They'll have something to say about it."

Edna felt like she was dreaming. She needed to leave, but couldn't move her feet. She was held mesmerized as the lights moved closer to the Capitol.

"I have my car here," said Tavon, "I'll drive you myself. Perhaps one of your colleagues could meet you there."

The lights were further away now. They began to dissolve into the ambient light of the city. She turned around. Everything around her began to spin. "Phone," she said. "I need a phone." She stumbled, and in a moment she would pass out.

Tavon grabbed her by the arm. "Easy now. Deep breaths. Big night ahead. You'll want to be awake for it."

# THIRTY FIVE

July 19, 1952

There were no signs of life at the golf club. By the time they reached the Jefferson Memorial, Edna Drake, knew the nearest phone would be the one in her apartment. That would mean throwing caution to the wind, but there was no time to waste worrying about whether or not her phone had been tapped. She told Tavon to pull up around the corner from the entrance to her building.

"You can go if you like," she told him. "I can get a taxicab to the airport."

"Don't be silly. I'm driving you," he said. "I'll wait here for you. Go make your call. Don't worry, I can take care of myself."

Edna considered asking him to walk with her to her apartment, but that would only attract unwanted attention. "OK. Great," she said, hopping out of the car.

A man answered the phone when Edna was put through to Bazy's hotel room.

"Oh I'm sorry, I was looking for Bazy Miller."

"You got her," said the man. Then Edna twigged — it was Tank. Awkward. He handed the boss on the phone without another word.

Bazy Miller heard the excitement in Edna's voice and didn't waste time asking for detailed explanations. She said she'd have photographer Carl Ogden and the whiz kid meet Edna at the airport.

Tavon was still waiting for her outside.

"See anyone?" she asked, hopping into the front seat beside him.

He hit the gas and swung the car into reverse. "Not a soul."

"There," she said, pointing toward the Capitol. "They're moving south." She stared at him, wondering what Lee Tavon knew about it that he wasn't telling her. "Is this some secret spy plane program, playing war games with Congress?"

Tavon shook his head. "No. This is something else."

"What do you know?"

He glanced over at her, but said nothing more as he put his foot down. The roads were almost empty, but he was driving way too fast for Edna's liking. Tavon tore along Independence Avenue at sixty miles per hour and fishtailed through the turn onto Arlington Bridge.

"You want to slow down there, Fangio?"

The highway to the airport took them right past the Pentagon. Edna wondered if anyone in there was awake to the light show.

"I bet they have no idea what's happening," said Tavon, as if reading her mind. "Our military bureaucracy isn't known for its rapid response. Admiral Yamamoto once called us a sleeping giant. Right now, the giant is face down in the pillows and snoring."

Tavon thankfully slowed to a more sedate pace for the last mile to the airport terminal. "I won't stay, obviously," he said. "I'll try to find a way to speak to you in a day or two."

Edna knew she should have firmed up another meeting with him, but for the moment the FS-1 leak was shunted to the backburner. She thanked him for the lift, happy he wouldn't be the one driving her home.

The airport was all but deserted. Planes still flew at this hour, but flights were few and far between after midnight. She could see no staff in the terminal to speak to. Edna took a few minutes to scope the building layout inside and out. She discovered a separate entrance to the control tower on the exterior concourse. By the time Ogden and Johnny Galbraith showed up, Edna had a rough plan of attack.

"Good to see you again, Edna," said Ogden. "But didn't Bazy fire you?"

She grinned. "Long story."

"We really chasing flying saucers?" Ogden asked her.

"We are," she said. "I've seen them. But let's start at the control tower, see if we can talk our way in." She was already walking in that direction. The tower entrance was unlocked. She opened the door and ushered Ogden inside. "Johnny, hang here and keep an eye out for trouble, and for God's sake yell out if you see anything strange in the sky. And I don't mean a DC-3."

He nodded and stayed put.

A set of stairs wound up four flights in a windowless stairwell, opening right up into the air traffic control center. Right away, it was obvious they were in the middle of something big. Six men were staring intently at radar screens, gesturing excitedly. For a long time, nobody even noticed them standing there.

"Capital Airlines has seen something," yelled one of the air traffic controllers.

"Bring it up on the speaker," ordered the man in charge. They heard the voice of a pilot through a loudspeaker. "It's there in the sky just near us, off to the right," the pilot said. "And there it goes!"

Edna checked her watch. It was a quarter past twelve.

"Who the hell are you?" The chief traffic controller had just seen them.

Edna smiled and stuck out her hand. "Edna Drake, *Times-Herald*. We heard there are some strange objects over the airport?"

"You can't be in here," the man said.

"Sorry, what's your name? For the record," said Edna.

"Harry Barnes. I'm in charge here. I need you out."

She was writing, pretending not to notice Barnes trying to shuffle them back down the stairs. "Is that Barnes with an 'e'? And what's your actual title, Mr Barnes?"

"With an 'e', that's right. I'm the senior traffic controller."

"Can you tell us what you've been seeing on radar, Mr Barnes? We heard your exchange with the Capital Air pilot just then. Sounds like he saw something pretty unusual."

Barnes appeared to be in two minds. He was in a state of high agitation, but clearly wanted to talk. "We don't know what the hell they are. But two of them flew right over the White House and the Capitol building. They move slow then fast. Real fast."

"How fast, if you don't mind me asking?"

"I clocked one of them at seven thousand miles an hour," a man behind Barnes yelled.

"Not a plane then," said Edna.

"No damn plane I've ever seen," Barnes admitted. "We've checked our equipment. It's working fine. The guys over at Andrews and Boling are seeing them too."

The two Air Force bases that were both close by.

"What about a temperature inversion, boss?" another traffic controller suggested.

The man next to him shook his head. Barnes agreed. "It's not an inversion. They look totally different on the scopes. Plus, we've got eyewitnesses."

"I saw them earlier, out the window," the guy in the headset yelled.

"Shut the hell up, Zacko," Barnes yelled.

"Right here," said Zacko, too excited to be deterred by his boss's anger, "when we first saw them on the radar." He was grinning like he'd just confirmed the existence of Santa Claus.

Edna had no idea what they meant by an inversion, but she wrote it down and made a note to check it later. The room flashed white like a lightning strike as Ogden took a photograph.

"Jesus Christ," said Barnes. "No pictures in here. I need you to leave now, we're real busy here."

Edna nodded. "Of course. We'll go." She had more than enough for Monday morning's front-page lead.

She was laughing uncontrollably by the time they reached the bottom of the stairs. "Holy hell Carl, can you believe this? I don't know how easy it's going to be to photograph these damn things, but I need you to do your best."

"I might try getting further away from the terminal, away from the floodlights. I'll have the airport itself for perspective then too."

"Sounds like a plan," she said.

Johnny Galbraith was waiting for them on the road outside. "See anything?" He shook his head. "How about you scour the terminal building to see if you can track down any more witnesses? Air crew, cleaners. Anyone you can find. This is going to be your story, kid. I'll help you all I can, but this one won't have my name on it. You just hit the big time."

Galbraith grinned, grabbed her by the cheeks, and gave her a big smacker on the lips. "Miss Drake, I think I love you." Cheeky little fucker.

He ran off in the direction of the terminal before she had time to close her mouth from the shock.

Edna looked up into the sky and thought she saw a light disappear at impossible speed right as her eyes hit upon it. Like it knew she was watching, and suddenly got shy.

# THIRTY SIX

July 21, 1952

"You need to interview me," Edna said.

"No, you need to write an observation piece as a breakout," said Galbraith.

"I'm not putting my name on this, remember?"

The kid smiled wearily. "I remember all right, but you haven't told me why they're after you."

"You're better off that way," she said. "But this story needs an eyewitness account, and you have one sitting right in front of you."

"How exactly does that work when we're not using your name?"

"I'll pick a pseudonym. You and I will be the only people who'll know."

"Christ Edna, I don't mind stretching the truth to sell a few papers, but that would be a flat-out lie. We're the ones who are supposed to catch the liars, not join them."

Edna sighed. "I commend your ethics, but these are special circumstances. And we're not lying — every quote I give you will be an honest response. You just change my name to protect me."

He shook his head. "I don't like it. If Bazy finds out, she'll sack me. She can't sack you twice."

"The story needs me," said Edna. "An eyewitness is the closest thing you have to a photograph." Ogden had failed them on that front; they had no shots of the UFOs. "Look Johnny, the only way Bazy will find out is if one of us tells her. It's not conventional, but it's not unethical. You're just protecting your source. Reporters do that all the time. I'll use my middle name and my mother's maiden name, that way it's not completely made-up. How about that?"

Finally, Galbraith nodded reluctantly. He began asking her questions, and Edna rattled off what she'd seen at the park. The images flooded back into her mind almost like she was seeing them again for the first time. "Describe my excitement, my agitation."

"And what exactly were you doing in East Potomac Park around midnight?"

"I was taking a walk with a friend."

"Had you been drinking?"

"What? Why the hell would you ask me that?"

"It's a fair question Miss... what's your name again?"

"Madeleine Shaw," said Edna.

"Had you been drinking when you saw the lights in the sky, Miss Shaw?"

"No," she said. "I was completely sober. That's the God's honest truth."

"So, you're just batshit crazy."

"OK, you've clearly got enough now."

Most of Sunday morning was spent chasing official comment. She didn't dare make the calls herself. Johnny put in the calls to the Pentagon and the White House. It might have been a mistake using the phone in her apartment, but she'd already done so the previous night to call Bazy; the damage was done. If they were listening, they knew exactly what was going on. One way or another, she'd know soon enough.

Johnny was only a cadet reporter and nobody knew him from Adam. The government spokesmen on duty gave him nothing. He had no better luck at the Pentagon. She wasn't particularly surprised, and a part of her harbored a certain guilty pleasure at his failure. Besides, they didn't need government comments to make the story work. The authorities would be forced to talk when their story hit the front page.

They wrote it up at her dining table. Edna didn't know where else to go, given the newsroom was still officially off limits. They'd been up all night and all morning by the time they sat down at the typewriter, and she knew they needed to work fast before weariness took its toll. She held it together on coffee and adrenalin, but knew from experience that by about two in the afternoon her pithy prose would turn to gibberish because she'd be asleep on her feet.

Job done, she told Johnny it was up to him to get the piece to the sub-editors on the production desk. Which was when the little shit tried for a little icing on the cake. "There's still plenty of time for that. How's about you and me take it into your room to celebrate?"

She laughed out loud at his audacity. "I date men, not boys."

"Old men," Johnny said. "Come on, you want to show me the love too, don't you?"

Edna Drake was remarkably close to losing her cool. "Swear to God, Johnny, I'm about to punch you in the mouth. Get the hell out of here and if you come back, I'm calling the cops."

Johnny Galbraith just smiled. He didn't seem in the least bit contrite, but was at least smart enough to know it was time to leave.

\*\*\*

Edna staggered out of bed early on Monday morning and threw on some clothes to find a copy of the newspaper. Tyrell the paper boy was yelling at the top of his lungs on the street corner; he saw her coming and had a copy of the *Times-Herald* ready for her.

"Big news," he said, grinning. "Everybody in my house saw the lights. Flying saucers over Washington, sure was amazing," he beamed. She briefly wondered why a seven-year-old boy would be awake so late at night, but her attention was caught by the front-page headline; it was cheesy, but it would hook their readers in.

# AERIAL WHATZITS BUZZ WHITE HOUSE

*By Jonathan Galbraith and staff*

A SQUADRON of oddly glowing objects were observed flying over both the Capitol building and the White House on Saturday night and Sunday morning, the latest in a string of strange and un-explained aerial sightings around Washington D.C. and nearby areas.

The objects were spotted on radar at Washington National Airport, where air traffic controllers recorded them flying at an impossible 7,000mph.

"We don't know what the hell they are," senior traffic controller Harry Barnes told the *Times-Herald*.

The objects were also observed on radar by the Air Force at both Andrews and Boling bases, and it's understood traffic controllers at Andrews also witnessed what was described as a "huge fiery orange sphere" hovering directly over the base range station.

Washington resident Madeleine Shaw was out taking a late-night walk with a friend and observed the lights over the airport.

She said it was the strangest thing she had ever seen.

"I saw seven of them, they were flying in circles around one another and around Washington Airport.

"At first, I thought they were planes, but their lights were too bright, and they pulsed through different colors — red, orange, and green.

"Then they began flying toward Capitol Hill, and I knew that whatever they were they were being intelligently controlled."

***

For once, Edna was glad her name wasn't on the story. She knew what sort of a kick Johnny would be getting out of having his name on the front-page lead, and wished she was there to see it. She also knew she'd have to find something to keep him in check. Johnny Galbraith was way too cocky for his own good; he would probably see her rejection as a minor battle in a war he could still win.

He was wrong about that, but Edna wasn't particularly worried about it. Johnny Galbraith was nothing she couldn't handle. In fact, for the first time since Tavon had sent her that damn letter, she was starting to feel like she might finally have things in hand. The saucer drama would be a welcome distraction for Bill Donovan and his cronies. After today, she couldn't possibly remain Donovan's main preoccupation. All over Washington, the big men in charge would be picking up the paper and getting themselves very hot under the collar as they tried to figure out a way to keep it all under control.

It would be too little, too late. The cat was out of the bag.

Edna picked up the phone and rang Bazy. "It's me," she said. "I want back in. Reinstate me. This thing's taking on a life of its own. I can't do this from home, and I'm sure as hell not going to let Joe Eldridge and Johnny Galbraith take all the credit for my hard work."

Bazy said nothing, but Edna could hear the wheels turning in her boss's head. "The Colonel won't be happy," Bazy spoke at last. "Then again, he's probably forgotten your name already. And he's insisting he'll sack me if I refuse to give up Tank...so maybe he can just go to hell. Get yourself down to the Roger Smith Hotel. We've just heard Captain Ruppelt from Project Blue Book is flying into D.C. today from Dayton. He always stays in the same place. If you get there quick enough, you might catch him checking in. Everyone else in the Pentagon has clammed up."

# THIRTY
# SEVEN

July 21, 1952

It had been a long twenty-four hours, and Donovan was feeling more than a little ropey. He had always prided himself on his ability to manage on very little sleep, but lately it felt like the years of driving himself past the point of fatigue were finally starting to catch up with him. These days, Bill Donovan needed a solid seven hours to function normally. He didn't feel anywhere close to his best today, with a little over half that amount.

He'd been in London when he'd heard about the Washington saucer flap. He knew he'd have to head home immediately, and had commandeered a US military C-54 out of Berlin. But even with Hoyt Vandenberg's help, it took a frustratingly long time to find a plane.

It was a far cry from the war, when he'd always had an aircraft and pilot at his disposal.

The Military Air Transport Service finally agreed to divert an airplane to London and fly him to New York. He'd arrived after midnight and fallen into bed at his Manhattan townhouse around 2am, hoping to sleep late before his lunchtime flight to Washington. But Ike's campaign chief Sherman Adams had called at 6am, urging him to get to D.C. as quickly as possible. Donovan had landed just before midday and headed straight to Dwight Eisenhower's hotel.

He had two days before he needed to be back for the Privy Council in London, where Donovan was acting as senior counsel on a legal challenge to a convoluted Hong Kong Supreme Court decision; it had effectively gifted a fleet of American-owned planes to China's communist regime. Donovan was determined to have the ruling reversed, but now found himself needing to be in two places at once on opposite sides of the Atlantic.

Ike's retinue had commandeered a suite on the top floor of the Wardman Park Hotel in the leafy and affluent Woodley Park, just far enough from the downtown diplomatic belt to satisfy the candidate's desire to remain under the radar before the campaign properly kicked off. The place was a hive of activity.

Eisenhower's urbane grey-suited campaign director Sherman Adams marched into the room, looking very much the man in command as he held out his hand for Donovan to shake.

"How's it coming together?" Donovan asked.

"Not bad for a candidate who knows next to nothing about politics," said Adams. "Did you know he's never even registered to vote? That's got to be a first — a presidential contender who's never marked a ballot paper."

Donovan smiled. "A man of the people."

"This way," said Adams, directing Donovan past a dining room full of young women cheerfully folding "I like Ike" flyers. "Thanks for getting here so quickly, Bill. He keeps asking questions about this I can't answer. I'm starting to feel like a fool."

"I'll do my best," said Donovan, "though I'm not sure I'm the man with answers today." He was beginning to wish he'd found an excuse to be unavailable for this meeting.

The candidate's office was the size of a small bedroom, with just enough space for a medium-sized oak desk and a floral two-seater lounge on the wall beside it. A large window behind the desk offered a view of the homes of Washington's gentry.

Ike was still in his golf gear. He loved nothing more than getting the day started by teeing off at the crack of dawn. Donovan had wondered to himself on more than one occasion how the man would manage to shoehorn presidential business around his golfing commitments. Today didn't seem like the day to make that observation. Eisenhower looked perplexed as he greeted his old war buddy with a manly hug.

"It's getting crazy out there, isn't it?" Ike said, pointing back through the door.

"Action stations." Donovan was both surprised and impressed, given the campaign had barely begun.

Ike asked, "Are you ready to join this circus when we hit the road?"

"Raring to go, sir. Raring to go."

That put a smile on Eisenhower's face and he nodded at Sherman Adams.

"I'll leave you to it," said Adams. "My phone list is getting longer by the minute." He pulled the door closed behind him, and the campaign machine's chaotic roar dimmed.

Ike said, "I guess you've seen the papers."

Donovan nodded.

"Word is they're pretty riled up at the Pentagon. Not that General Samford is taking my calls right now. We were hoping you could shed some light on it, Bill."

"Samford has Air Force intelligence looking into it. They have that special unit of theirs."

"Blue Book," said Eisenhower.

"That's the one. Nobody's saying anything much beyond that, from what I can tell. I think the incident caught them on the hop. They don't know what to make of it."

Ike smiled. "Come on, you and I both know that's not true. This has been going on for weeks. Don't tell me you've forgotten I was

Army Chief of Staff in '47 when that flying saucer crashed in New Mexico."

Donovan kept his cool. "The Air Force said that was a weather balloon."

Eisenhower sighed. He wanted straight answers, not the usual runaround. Donovan sympathized, but his position with Truman and MJ-12 was tenuous. He wasn't about to throw top secret information into the mincer of an election campaign.

"General Ramey himself told me that weather balloon story was baloney," Eisenhower challenged. "It was just to get the press off their backs. I remember being surprised by it at the time, because I knew there was so much more to it. But when I saw Ramey months later, he dismissed the whole affair. Didn't want to talk about it."

Donovan said, "Talk to Blue Book. Often these sightings really are just weather balloons. I've heard temperature inversions can upset radar around Washington too."

"Is that who you're talking to?"

"I was in London until the early hours of this morning. But that's who I'd be calling. They're at Wright-Patterson in Dayton, but I believe they have a man at the Pentagon."

"Sherm tried the Pentagon already. No luck. And you're playing dodge ball, Bill."

"My contacts in defense intelligence aren't what they used to be," Donovan said. A bald-faced lie to the man who could be the next president. "Why not pick up the phone yourself and go higher up the chain? I'm guessing you still know how to throw your weight around."

"Give me your candid opinion — is this something I need to be concerned about?"

"I...don't know what to tell you, sir," Donovan replied, trying to work out how best to respond without breaking the law, or fanning the flames of Truman's wrath. "It's most likely nothing. But there are people inside the Pentagon who have their concerns about these matters."

"These matters?"

"That's right." More than people like General Samford would want to admit to a political candidate, Donovan thought.

"OK, Bill. Thank you." Eisenhower could see he'd been choosing his words carefully, and let him off the hook.

Donovan felt like he'd just fallen at the first hurdle. He decided to come at it from a different direction. "What about Wally Smith at the CIA? He must owe you a favor or two. Why not give him a call?"

Ike nodded. "Yes. Good idea." Donovan sat down on the lounge and watched as Ike took great delight in asking the hotel operator to put him through to the Central Intelligence Agency. He put his hand over the receiver. "Bill, if you pick up that phone next to you, you'll be able to listen in."

Walter Smith had been Ike's Chief of Staff during the war. Donovan put the phone to his ear just as Smith took the call.

"Wally, it's Ike. How are you?"

"Very well, sir. Congratulations on winning the nomination. I think you'll make a fine president."

"Thank you, Beetle. I've been meaning to call to thank you for your generous note of congratulation."

"Well, I'm very pleased for you, sir. You have my vote," Smith replied. His tone betrayed the fact that he was well aware Ike was calling for a different reason entirely.

"We're just getting the wheels in motion over here," said Ike, "but I look forward to catching up with you in the near future."

"Is there something I can do for you, General?"

"Look, I'm just wondering what you can tell me about this aerial incident over the Capitol."

"Oh. Yes. Well, I afraid there's really nothing I *can* tell you. I mean, I haven't heard anything just yet. We're still investigating."

"There's something to it, is that what you're saying?"

"No, that's not... I'm sure there is nothing to worry about."

"Are you certain of that, Beetle?"

"I'm certain, sir. Rest assured, if there was an imminent threat to national security, you would hear about it. Now I'm afraid I have to go, I'm already late for a meeting. Let's get together soon. Goodbye."

The phone line went dead before Ike had a chance to respond; he hung up the receiver. "I know bullshit when I hear it," said Eisenhower.

Donovan had one more suggestion, knowing it could come back to bite him. But he needed to prove his usefulness. "There's always Plan B. What about President Truman?"

"Do you think that's really necessary?"

"If you do call him, please don't tell him it was my idea."

Eisenhower raised an eyebrow at the remark. "I assume he knows you'll be campaigning with me?"

Donovan nodded. "And he's not happy about it. But he knows he can't stop me."

Eisenhower's expression shifted. He understood Donovan's reluctance. "Don't worry, we never had this conversation."

Donovan stood up and started for the door. "I'm sorry I can't fill in the blanks, sir."

"Don't go anywhere," said Eisenhower. "You can listen in. Who knows, maybe we'll soon have more to talk about."

Donovan knew he'd just been outwitted. "All right. Let me find a cup of coffee while you place that call." He made his way to the kitchen. It wasn't big, considering the size of the dining room. It was assumed guests in suites preferred to order in. A filter coffee machine was the only sustenance on offer; thankfully someone had just refilled it. He poured himself a cup, threw in a sachet of sugar and stirred.

"There's milk in the fridge," someone said, a young intern behind him.

"I prefer black," he said. "Old Army habit." She nodded with no more than a dim level of interest; the war was ancient history to her.

By the time Donovan got back, Ike had the phone to his ear. He pointed to the other handset. "They're just putting me through — Mr President, how are you, sir?"

The essence of breezy civility.

Harry Truman didn't bother with pleasantries. "What can I do for you, Ike?"

"Well sir, a polite inquiry. I've been seeing a lot of noise in the press about these aerial sightings. I'm wondering whether we have anything to be concerned about."

There was a pause on the line, then a sigh. "Did Bill Donovan put you up to this?"

Eisenhower looked at Donovan in alarm. Donovan shook his head and mouthed "no".

"No," said Ike, "he didn't. Wally Smith didn't have much to say about it, but I detected a note of caution in his voice, so I thought I'd go straight to the top."

"You're chasing pink elephants." Truman was trying to be dismissive, but there was anger in his tone. "I don't believe you for a moment, by the way. Donovan's there with you now, I'd lay odds on it. He's a loose cannon and he'll do you no favors. You'll need a stronger caliber of advisor if you plan to sit in this chair."

"I'm sorry you feel that way, Harry. I hope you know it was nothing personal, me going with the Republicans. I'm sorry it upset you, but it's politics. You know how that goes."

"That I do," said Truman, sighing. "Listen Ike, a word of advice: you'll win neither friends nor respect by giving credence to these ridiculous stories. You want to stop taking this flying saucer rubbish so seriously. Don't go saying anything in public you might later regret."

"I certainly don't believe everything I read, Mr President," Ike replied, working hard to keep his own tone more measured. "But

I don't think it's fair to say the matter is rubbish when it's serious enough to scramble Air Force reconnaissance. I'm simply asking whether you've received any reports from the Pentagon."

"None at all," said the President. "Nor, frankly, do I expect to see any. Now if you'll excuse me, I still have a country to run — at least for a few more months." With that, the President hung up.

Ike slammed the phone down. "God damn pain in the ass." He immediately regretted saying it, and threw Donovan a penitent glance. "What really bugs me is we used to get on well."

Donovan nodded sympathetically.

"I mean, those things buzzed the White House, for Pete's sake. He has to be getting a full report on the matter. The Commander in Chief would want an explanation." Eisenhower was thinking aloud, piecing it together. "He'd want to know whether there's a credible threat."

"Yes sir," said Donovan, "I think you might be right. And that, I'm afraid, is all I have to say on the matter. I'm a loose cannon, remember?"

"Go on," said Ike, "get out of here. Don't let him get to you too."

"Too late," said Donovan.

# THIRTY EIGHT

July 21, 1952

Donovan arrived back to his mansion in Georgetown to discover that his wife, who had come home that morning while he was gone, had since departed for New York. He'd missed her entirely. It was his fault; he'd forgotten to tell her he was returning from London. The gap between them had been widening lately. Ruth's growing resentment of her husband's disregard for their relationship was coupled with Bill's constant roaming about the country in one official capacity or another. She'd hoped this would end with the war — it hadn't.

In truth, Bill Donovan had grown to like his nomadic existence. He always felt happiest when he was on the move.

Of course, he had roamed in other ways, on occasions too numerous to easily forgive. They never really talked about it, but wives always knew these things about their husbands. His years of unending selfishness in this regard meant that now, at a time in his life when he most needed a companion, Ruth was nowhere to be seen.

Donovan stared morosely into the garden through the window in his study. He wasn't sure how long he'd been sitting there, but he felt Paolo's arrival almost immediately. It startled him; it was a peculiar sight in daylight, this apparition that was solid rather than transparent, yet neither blocked the light nor cast a shadow. Even so, the room darkened when Paolo appeared, as if his presence absorbed the light.

"I really wish there was a way to sever this connection of ours," Donovan said.

Paolo's head tilted to one side. "You would prefer I only come when you call."

"I would, yes."

"Yet it never occurred to you to ask my opinion on the matter."

Donovan looked away; he was tired and in no mood for a debate.

"This is the most fun I've had in centuries, William. With you, I'm living a whole new life. I can be part of conversations and join you in your endeavors, instead of merely wandering the world forgotten and unseen. This is your gift to me. Need I remind you, it's also your only way of knowing what the Russians are up to? You can't afford to stop now."

"You're inside my head, Paolo. I need you to give me space. At first, I assumed you had no choice in the matter. But I think you do."

Donovan rose from his chair and made his way to the kitchen to make himself a cup of tea. The maid was nowhere to be seen.

Paolo was waiting by the stove. Always a step ahead. "Two minds are better than one, William."

Donovan slumped against the kitchen bench. "It's paralyzing me. I'm nearly seventy years old, and for the first time in my life I find myself wracked by indecision. I can feel you there, questioning my motives. You've brought me nothing but doubt. It's driving me around the bend."

"Set me free," Paolo suggested. "These Papists treat me like their captive demon."

"You'd still be trapped in that sarcophagus if it wasn't for me," said Donovan.

"You released me only to trap me all over again. They feed me, they read me Bible stories like I'm a child. I tell them I'm six thousand years old, that their Old Testament is a fairy tale because I was there when these events occurred. They don't listen. They play me music and say the composer was inspired by God. I tell them there is not one god but many. They say I'm under the devil's influence. Late at night, the Swiss Guard bring me wine and the Russians send their women to keep me happy and ask their questions. I see the fear in their eyes. And none of it comes close to feeling the sun on my face and the earth between my toes. You know this, yet still you do nothing. I don't care about their secrets. Tell them to let me go."

But they both knew it was just words. It would never happen while Joseph Stalin remained alive. And in truth, Paolo could never be free to walk the Earth. That ship had flown.

Donovan was shaken from his thoughts by the housekeeper. "Sir, there's a Miss Eloise Page here to see you."

Miss Page had her hair pinned back in a bob, and it occurred to Donovan she was deliberately downplaying her better features. "How'd you know where to find me?" Donovan asked.

She raised an eyebrow, as if to ask him if he'd forgotten who he was talking to.

"You're keeping tabs on me."

"Of course I am," Eloise said. "Good Lord Bill, you of all people shouldn't be surprised by that."

"Not surprised so much as insulted."

"Walter Smith is just covering his bases. You'd do the same in his position."

"Is that what you came here to say?"

"What did you tell Eisenhower?" she asked.

"Wow, news does travel fast."

"That's what happens when you piss off the President."

"I told him nothing."

She nodded. "I said as much to Walter."

"What's this about, Eloise?"

"I'm concerned that you asked for my help, but you haven't been keeping me in the loop."

"You already know more than you should," Donovan admitted.

"Do we need to worry about Lee Tavon?""No."

Miss Page stared at him without saying a word. He wondered if she suspected he was lying, or if she knew it for certain.

# THIRTY NINE

July 21, 1952

Carl Ogden broke away from the photographer pack in the Roger Smith Hotel lobby as soon as he saw Edna walk in. "Hey."

"Hey yourself," she said. "Anything yet?" He shook his head. "Don't suppose you know what he looks like?" she asked.

Ogden shrugged. "A man in a blue uniform?"

Within a half an hour, the press throng had noticeably swelled. There was Paul Sampson from the *Washington Post,* along with reporters from all the major wire services — AP, UP, and INS — each of them with a photographer in tow.

This story was officially a big deal.

Edna nodded a polite greeting at Sampson, who nodded back. "This must be real if the *Washington Post* is covering it."

"Probably just a stray flock of birds," said Sampson. "Still, it's all anyone's talking about."

"I saw it myself," she said. "It was no flock of geese up there."

"The readers of the *Post* would love to hear about your observations."

Edna smiled. "No comment."

"I didn't see your name on that *Times-Herald* story," Sampson argued, sounding a little suspicious.

Edna shook her head and smiled again, but said nothing.

Ed Ruppelt arrived in the lobby shortly before midday. The press gang immediately leapt into action mode, surrounding him like moths to a flame. He was younger than she'd expected, handsome in a white bread, clean living kind of way.

"Captain Ruppelt," Sampson called out, "what does the Air Force make of these sightings over Washington?"

Ruppelt was a rabbit trapped in the headlights. "I, er, have nothing to say at this time."

"Captain Ruppelt, Edna Drake from the *Times-Herald* — objects were detected on radar at three separate locations and witnessed flying over the White House. Don't you think the Air Force should have something to say about that?"

Ruppelt waved desperately at the clerk behind the counter, who handed him a key, no questions asked. He disappeared into the elevator under a hail of flash bulbs without saying another word.

"Well, wasn't that worth the wait?" said Ogden sarcastically.

"He's got to come down eventually," said Edna. "He didn't fly here from Dayton to spend the day in his room."

It was almost an hour before Ruppelt appeared again to run the gauntlet to a taxicab. "Come on now," he pleaded. "I need to get past."

"Not until you give us something, Captain," yelled back one of the wire reporters.

"This is a big deal," said Edna. "People want to know what's going on.""We need an official statement," Sampson demanded. "What is the Air Force doing about this?"

Ruppelt looked up at them defiantly. "No comment. There's your official statement." He pushed his way through the reporters as they screamed their frustration at him.

"Where are you going, Captain?"

"Are you going to the Pentagon?"

"What do you know?"

But Ruppelt had said all he was going to say.

Edna was still fuming as she made her way back into the newsroom. It was only as the first look of astonishment hit her that she remembered most people were still under the impression she'd been fired. Theo Mankiewicz almost ran from his office to stop her, holding his hand out like a traffic cop. "You need to leave right now, Miss Drake. The editor made it clear your services are no longer required. Do I need to call security?"

"Go suck an egg, Mankiewicz. Security are the ones who just let me in." She wasn't in the mood for playing nice, and he was out of line. A chorus of laughter rang out nearby, and the man turned red with embarrassment and outrage. Somebody even had the temerity to clap.

It was so awful, Edna actually began to feel sorry for the poor sap. "Look Theo, go speak to Bazy. You'll find I'm right where I ought to be." Mankiewicz marched off in the direction of the boss's office to demand an explanation.

Grateful her desk had not been occupied by anyone else, Edna threw her stuff down and fell into her chair.

Eldridge had his back turned; he was busy typing. "Glad you could make it," he said quietly without missing a keystroke. Obviously, Bazy had clued him in. His chair swiveled violently as he turned to face her, cheeks more than a little red. Drunk again. "Let's try and keep it professional, shall we?"

She stifled a derisive chortle. "Fine with me, Joe." She waved him off, figuring she had bigger things to worry about. His eyes fell to her cleavage and he turned back around, making Edna feel sexy and cheap with a single glance.

She was back. Problem was, thanks to Air Force stonewalling, she had no story to write. She'd considered going up the chain to General Cabell, but guessed he'd just be holding the line. From the look of bewilderment in the eyes of Captain Ruppelt, Edna guessed Blue Book and the Air Force were playing catch-up. It was possible she knew more about what happened than they did. She wondered wryly how Ruppelt would react if she offered herself up for his team to interview.

There was only one other person she could think of who might give her something new for tomorrow's paper. She called the Pentagon, and asked to speak to Major Dewey Fournet, telling the operator it was his sister, Edna. Remarkably, she was put through straight away.

"Listen, I'm rather busy right now. Call back in an hour. No, make it two."

"You're trying to get rid of me."

"No. Two hours. I promise we'll talk then." He hung up without saying her name; there had to be someone in the office with him. Edna checked her watch: four o'clock in two hours. She could wait until then.

Time to check in with the boss. Bazy's secretary Dot offered Edna a conspiratorial smile, waving her straight in. Bazy looked relieved it was her.

"Let me guess, Mr Mankiewicz is giving you hell?" Edna asked.

Bazy pulled a long-suffering sneer. "Theo's a wonderful wordsmith, but he's so holier than thou — and a terrible gossip. I couldn't trust him to keep his mouth shut about you. Sure you wanna be back here so soon?"

Edna nodded, pleased her editor was asking rather than telling. "Events have moved on. For the moment, that letter is the least of their worries."

"Unless this FS-1 Project is somehow responsible."

Edna shook her head. "Not according to Tavon. 'This is something else' — those were his exact words. And now the whole world is watching."

"But in saying that, Tavon is also telling us he knows more."

"Yes, I think he does," Edna agreed. "But he's not easily drawn on it. And he's gone into hiding. We might have just enough now to run with a story, but it'll be thin."

Bazy thought about it. "Let's hold off a bit longer. Just until we've seen how this latest saucer flap plays out."

Dewey Fournet was still in his office when Edna rang him back. "I don't have long," he said. "Ed Ruppelt's in the corridor pacing up and down because the Air Force won't requisition him a car for an investigation. Some genius in the motor pool suggested he take the bus."

"OK, so what have you got for me, Major?"

"About Saturday night? Nothing. No comment is the only response you'll get on that today, I'm afraid." Edna sighed, disappointed. "I do have some other news, though. General Cabell found out Hoyt Vandenberg has one of his off-the-books meetings tomorrow morning."

"Where?"

"His secretary wouldn't say. We think she knows, but won't give it up. It's a hotel downtown at 11am, that's all we know. Are you game to tail him? That's all I can give you — I'm going to be chained to a desk wrangling Air Force intelligence for the next few days."

"Tail him? From where?"

"His car will arrive at the north entrance to pick him up. It's a black Chevy Deluxe. I'd say he'll leave here a little after ten. Got to go." He hung up.

Hang around outside the nation's most secure military facility and follow a general's staff car — what could possibly go wrong?

# FORTY

July 22, 1952

Edna felt ridiculous, worried she was in over her head. She'd never tailed anyone in her life.

After more than an hour of reconnaissance the previous night, she had comprehensively failed to find a spot to park anywhere close to the Pentagon for more than a few minutes without coming to the attention of the military police; they constantly watched the perimeter. In the end, her only option was to pull over on a dirt verge where the Pentagon access road fed onto Washington Boulevard. Edna was pretty sure this was an illegal stop, but she'd probably go unnoticed for a quarter of an hour or so.

She and Bazy had considered using two cars and two-way radios — with one car acting as a roaming spotter — but the risk of being made was too great. In the end, Edna decided to keep it simple. She would follow Vandenberg alone and unassisted, and hope nobody noticed.

Edna hadn't done much driving since the war, but once behind the wheel of Bazy's Packard, it had come back to her fairly quickly. Nothing to do but wait now. She kept the engine running, terrified of stalling the car just as she needed to get moving. Thankfully, Vandenberg didn't keep her waiting long. She saw the car coming from a quarter of a mile away. On a whim, she decided to take a chance and pulled out first, hoping this would appear less suspicious.

Once they were both safely on Washington Boulevard and she confirmed it was the General's Chevy in her rearview mirror, she changed lanes and slowed down to pull in behind. She managed it just in time. Less than a minute later, the traffic slowed to a crawl as they hit Arlington bridge. A policeman was in the middle of the road ahead, directing traffic. There'd been an accident.

She was bumper-to-bumper with Vandenberg's staff car. They crawled along for almost ten minutes. By the time they reached Lincoln Memorial Circle, she was trying to think ahead to where the General might be going. When Vandenberg's Chevy veered away on the 23$^{rd}$ Street turnoff, it caught her completely by surprise. She desperately yanked the steering wheel around to give chase, but hit the gas pedal way too hard. The Packard lurched forward violently. She cursed her own stupidity, certain her poor driving had come to the attention of Vandenberg's driver. Edna hoped he wrote her off as a crazy woman. She stayed with the Chevy, trying to work out what she would do if they got wise to the tail and tried to lose her.

Further and further north, they drove to Washington Circle. The Chevy turned. She let one or two cars get between them, then panicked. Edna was now behind two black cars, and struggling to tell them apart. One veered north back onto 23$^{rd}$ Street. Gut instinct told her it wasn't the right car. She stuck with the other one as it moved onto New Hampshire Avenue, then right onto L Street. They crossed Connecticut Avenue and took the next left into 17$^{th}$ Street. Vandenberg must be headed for the Mayflower Hotel.

Edna pulled up opposite the hotel's rear entrance, watching as the Chevy swung into the driveway. Hoyt Vandenberg, looking decidedly more casual having jettisoned his uniform jacket and tie, strolled inside the Mayflower without so much as a backward glance. A moment after his car pulled away, others began to arrive.

CIA Director Walter Smith was the next inside, followed by several men she didn't recognize. She was surprised when astrophysicist

Donald Menzel appeared; was he here as a skeptic, or as a scientific advisor?

Bill Donovan was watching the arrivals too, from a bedroom window in the hotel suite where the Majestic members were gathering. He'd seen the Packard pull up, but he spotted Edna through his binoculars when she wound down her window to toss out her chewing gum.

An electric chill of panic shot down his spine. He'd been sure he'd dealt with Edna Drake. How the hell had she found her way here?

He figured he had his answer when Edna climbed out of her car and crossed the road to speak to Gordon Gray. Gray appeared eager to shake her off, to which Edna responded like a jilted lover.

An alarm bell rang inside Donovan's head.

Gray walked away quickly, but words had passed between them. There was clearly more to that relationship than he'd been led to believe.

When Edna spotted Gordon Gray, she tossed aside all thoughts of discretion. She was surprised, excited, and in truth a little disappointed, to find him here. She left the cover of the car to catch him.

Gray wasn't pleased to see her. She grabbed his arm, but he shook her off, muttering something that sounded like "sorry," then scuttling away past the doorman and into the hotel's rear lobby. Edna realized then her reaction had come across as a little hysterical.

She was about to follow Gordon Gray inside the hotel, when a black Cadillac pulled up in the driveway beside her. It lacked the requisite American flags and had no motorcycle escort, but there was no mistaking President Harry Truman when he emerged from the back seat. He was flanked by two Secret Service agents. They glanced at Edna briefly as they kept the President moving toward the Mayflower. Truman usually preferred his more flamboyant Lincoln convertible for trips around D.C. Opting for an unmarked hardtop Cadillac was the presidential equivalent of going incognito.

"Mr President?" Edna called. Truman turned, smiling warmly. "Edna Drake, *Times-Herald*..." She saw his expression harden. "Are you here to discuss the saucer sightings over Washington? Do they pose a security threat, sir?"

He feigned a laugh and didn't slow down. "I have nothing to say, I'm sorry." She saw the negro doorman say something to Truman, who gave the doorman a friendly pat on the shoulder in return. They knew one another. The Secret Service closed ranks at the entrance, preventing her from following as the President disappeared inside.

"Oh, come on guys. Do I look like a threat?" They stared past her like she didn't exist and simply stood their ground. She didn't mind so much; she had a story now. They kept the hotel entrance barred for another minute or so before retreating to the elevator, leaving Edna alone with the doorman.

"Hello," she said, smiling.

"Hello Miss," said Stanley.

"I'm with the *Times-Herald*. Edna Drake." She held out her hand for him to shake.

It caught him by surprise, but he shook it just the same. "Stanley Coleman, ma'am. Pleased to meet you."

"Couldn't help noticing you're on friendly terms with Mr Truman."

"He was living here a while, after the '48 election," said Coleman. "He still remembers me whenever he pays us a visit."

"Is that very often? I guess he likes it here."

Stanley gave her a wry smile. "That he does."

"Stanley, is there any particular reason why a lady wouldn't be allowed inside today?"

"I'm sorry, Miss Drake. My orders are, nobody gets inside today without prior approval."

"Whose prior approval are we talking about?"

"That would be from the President hisself. More than my job's worth to let you in here, I'm afraid."

"Anything else you can tell me Stanley?" She stepped closer and slipped a five dollar note into his hand. "Off the record, of course. I wouldn't want to get you into trouble."

He looked behind him to make sure the Secret Service weren't still lurking in the foyer, then took the money and pocketed it. When Stanley turned back around, he didn't look her in the eye and started talking like she wasn't there. "I don't know all their names. It's not always all of them together at once, but they all here today. I counted twelve men. Other than the President. That's all of them. Nobody ever told me what they do up there. But whatever it is, they don't want nobody at the White House seein' them do it."

# FORTY ONE

July 22, 1952

Donovan nearly threw a chair at the window when he saw Edna Drake confronting the President. After three days of watching Drake's apartment had turned up nothing, he'd felt certain she'd been neutralized as a threat and had called off the surveillance. This was a mistake.

It felt like Donovan's bad calls had started eclipsing the good ones lately. There were bridges on fire all around him. He'd allowed himself to be distracted by the Privy Council hearing in London. Truman would blame him for Drake's presence outside, and the worst part was, Donovan blamed himself for it too. As the head of security for both Majestic and the Verus Foundation, that buck stopped with him, not the President.

It was Gordon Gray's doing, of course, but there'd be nothing to gain in trying to shift the blame. Donovan had never done that in his life, and wasn't about to start now. Besides, Gray was Truman's golden boy: the man who got things done when nobody else could.

Donovan wished he'd been here to tell these old men it would be a mistake to hold a second consecutive Majestic meeting at the Mayflower. They'd grown lax on security because Conrad Hilton always treated them like kings when they came here; they'd sweet-talked the hotelier by telling him they met to discreetly address the communist threat in Washington. To Connie Hilton, that particular c-word was like a red rag to a bull. He'd immediately offered up the lap of Mayflower luxury whenever they needed it, at no charge. He'd also instructed his hotel manager to ensure their meetings were well catered. There were drinks and canapes on arrival, and a full a la carte lunch delivered to the suite for anyone who had time to stay.

Today there would be no grand luncheon; this gathering was more akin to a council of war. The situation itself would be galling enough to Truman, who had wearied of the Washington media treadmill in recent months. Add to that the likelihood of an internal security leak, and the man would be spitting blood. And Donovan still hadn't told the President about the leaked letter; he'd hoped to have that matter sorted before such a thing was necessary.

"What do I do?" Bill Donovan said to himself, realizing too late that it would be Paolo who responded.

*You take care of her.*

Lately, it had begun to feel like Paolo's opinions were merging with his own. It was becoming harder to tell one from another. That realization had begun to fester into a nagging fear that Bill Donovan was no longer his own man.

*You have to get that letter back, by force if necessary.*

Donovan heard the chorus of concerned voices as Truman stormed angrily into the apartment.

"Where is he?" Truman yelled. "Donovan, show yourself."

Donovan made his way into the lounge to take his tongue-lashing. Truman rounded on him like a yapping terrier. "How in hell does a newspaper reporter know the time and location of a classified intelligence meeting?"

Donovan glanced momentarily over Truman's shoulder in the direction of Gordon Gray, who was looking more than a little rattled. "It would appear, Mr President, we have a leak."

"Meaning someone in this room?" said the President.

"That is one possibility, yes," said Donovan.

"Please, General Donovan," Truman spat back at him sarcastically, "do enlighten us with your thoughts on the other possibilities."

"A third-party security breach, for one," said Donovan. "Perhaps somebody here mentioned innocently to a colleague or a loved one something about a luncheon at the Mayflower with the President. Harmless enough on its own, but news like that can travel quickly."

"Or," suggested Wally Smith, "it could be an unlucky coincidence. She was in the right place at the wrong time."

"No," said Truman. "She was standing there like she was waiting for someone. Waiting for me. For the love of God, she asked me about flying saucers."

Donald Menzel was staring urgently at Donovan now, eyes wide, pleading with him to keep his mouth shut. Before the meeting, they had discussed the option of coming clean about the leaked letter. Menzel had been in favor of owning up, but had obviously changed his mind. Donovan was inclined to agree. The security breach that brought Drake to their door needed to take precedence. In a way, it was almost a relief. Donovan knew what he had to do.

"I'll speak to everyone in this room, one by one," Donovan assured the President. "But for now, can I suggest you proceed as intended? It's important you remember you brought these men together because you trust them implicitly. There are critical matters to be discussed."

Truman seemed somewhat placated by this. "All right then. Go. Leave us to it."

"Actually," said Gray, "I'd like General Donovan to stay. I believe his input might be useful." Gray was looking at Donovan with an air of gratitude.

Truman sighed. "All right. But Bill, if I discover anything said here today has found its way back to Eisenhower, I'm going to have you thrown from a fast-moving train."

Donovan had been steeling himself for mention of Ike. "Duly noted, Mr President. I can assure you I've said nothing whatsoever to General Eisenhower or his campaign staff relating to your administration — classified or otherwise."

Truman stared at him for a moment, then decided to believe him. "OK, ok. Sit down and let's get on with it." The tension hadn't completely dissipated, but a sense of relief passed through the group.

Vannevar Bush took the opportunity to pass around tumblers of bourbon, starting with the President who downed his with one gulp. Booze was usually the best way to break the ice between Roscoe Hillenkoetter and Wally Smith — spook chiefs past and present — who were forced to put egos aside and face one another here. It had been that way since Hillenkoetter's unceremonious removal as CIA top dog, and Smith's appointment as his replacement. Matters might arguably go more smoothly without Roscoe, but the top-secret nature of this grouping meant membership could never be rescinded. Each man was a lifetime member, whether he liked it or not.

Bush had bigger fish to fry today. Once everyone had a drink in hand, he directed them to the dining room. With Truman and Donovan both in the room, there were fourteen men in total. Allowance had already been made for the President, but they had to grab an extra chair to squeeze Donovan in. He opted to sit beside Bush, facing Truman from the opposite end of the table.

Donald Menzel kicked it off. "Firstly, for anyone under the misapprehension that the weekend's events over Washington were our doing, let me assure you this is not the case. We still can't fly our saucer with any degree of reliability, and we only have the one. There were seven, possibly eight, craft spotted on radar on Saturday night and Sunday morning."

"Whatever was going on in the skies above Washington," added Bush, "it wasn't us."

"This has been building to a crescendo for weeks," said Vandenberg. "The Air Force has been swamped with sightings up and down the East coast since last month."

"It's like they're sending us a message," said Smith.

"If they *are*," said Bush, "we need to know what it is. And we need to know quickly. The task was urgent BEFORE they started buzzing Washington. Saturday night's performance sounded a red alert."

"Damn right," said Truman. "Find out what they want."

General Robert Montague rose to his feet. He was a ballistics expert, and headed the highly classified Armed Forces Special Weapons Center at Sandia, New Mexico, developing nuclear weapons. He was a quiet man, but when Montague had something to say, it was worth hearing. "Gentlemen, Jerome and I believe they HAVE sent a message... And we think we've determined what it is."

Jerome Hunsaker was the group's aeronautics expert. What he didn't know about manned flight hadn't been invented yet. He was sat beside Montague, and together they unfurled a map covered in red vector lines.

"By analyzing the radar vectors from Saturday night, we noticed there were two distinct behaviors at play," Hunsaker said.

"The bogeys did two things," said Montague. "First they flew at low speed, around a hundred to a hundred thirty knots, before changing direction and disappearing at a blistering pace."

"When they did speed up," said Hunsaker, "they always vectored toward the same point on the map."

"In so doing," said Montague, "we think they've given us two distinct messages. We've pinpointed the spot where all those lines intersect. And then we've cross-referenced it by looking at the distance travelled by the saucers when they were observed on radar at low speed. That worked out to a hundred twenty-five miles. When we follow those high-speed vectors for hundred twenty-five miles, we arrive at that same precise location – where all the vectors intersect."

"We think it's some sort of invitation," said Hunsaker.

There was hushed silence in the room. Finally, Truman said, "You think they want to *meet* us?"

Hunsaker and Montague looked at the President and nodded slowly in unison. "It's about five miles due south of Petersburg, Virginia," said Hunsaker.

"But we don't know when," said Montague.

"A meeting," said Gray. "At this precise moment in history. That can't be a coincidence."

"Explain," said Smith.

"I'm sure I don't need to remind you," said Gray, "President Truman's days in office are coming to an end."

"You certainly don't need to remind me," said Truman. "Part of me can't wait." A ripple of nervous amusement passed around the room.

Gray nodded in deference to the President, but kept talking. "We don't yet know for certain where Majestic will stand beyond the end of this year with a new Commander in Chief. Meanwhile, we might be holding the fate of the world in our hands here and now."

"We need to close ranks," said Vandenberg. "Nobody says a word of this to anyone outside this room. Not even in hushed whispers."

Truman stared at Donovan. One by one, the other men turned and did the same.

"My lips are sealed," Donovan assured them, his tone urging them to make sure they did likewise.

Smith was agitated. "We need to know what we're dealing with, and whether national security is at risk."

Hillenkoetter, for once, was in full agreement with him. "We need to get down there. Do some reconnaissance."

"I will remind you," said Menzel, "there are no indicators the visitors intend us any physical harm."

"Then they won't mind us checking things out," said Vandenberg.

"National security's not the issue," said Menzel.

Smith sighed heavily. "For Christ's sake, just say it, Donald."

"The problem is one of public confidence," Menzel replied. "If word gets out, we lose control of this. We have two case studies for what happens next. I believe they're both good approximations of what we could expect. First, the *War of the Worlds* panic in 1937. Panic gripped the country in the space of a few hours. People believed Martians were invading. The fear of invasion is still right there in people's minds. Panic is a powerful force. Hard to stop once it builds up a head of steam.

"Then we have the movie *The Day The Earth Stood Still*. A realistic take on how military leaders down the food chain could be expected to react in the face with interplanetary visitors arriving in our midst. Most of them believe what we've been telling them, that flying saucers aren't real. But then, what if suddenly they are real and everyone knows it?" Menzel looked around the room at the men's faces, one by one. "There'd be a lot of fear. Loud voices calling it the end times, branding the visitors demonic forces from hell. A lot of people could quickly lose faith in the power of the government to protect them."

"He's right," Bush agreed. "And it can be taken out of our hands the moment they just decide to land on the White House lawn. They were only a few hundred feet away from doing just that on Saturday night."

"Lord save me," cried Truman. All too often with these men, he was out of his depth. His input was limited to colorful humor and exasperation.

"What's stopped them from doing it before now?" asked Gray.

"We have," said Menzel. "They watch us very closely. They understand our moods, our temperament, probably better than we understand ourselves."

Hillenkoetter had been trying to get a word in. "But if their position on public disclosure is shifting, they must see a change in us."

"Precisely," Menzel agreed.

"What's the biggest change confronting us right now?" asked Bush, his tone suggesting he already knew the answer.

"The presidency," said Truman.

"Exactly," said Bush. "A new president, perhaps one not so highly motivated to keep these things a secret."

Gray nodded.

Smith was aghast. "Surely you're not suggesting our alien visitors are trying to influence the outcome of the election?"

Menzel couldn't help letting loose a wry laugh. "That sure would be one for the history books."

"No," said Bush, "I'm saying they may already know who the winner will be."

"God dammit," said Truman. "Even the space men like Ike."

Donovan got up from his seat to peer over Hunsaker's shoulder at the vector map. "You said it was a little way south of Petersburg?"

"That's right," said Hunsaker, pointing. "About five miles south."

"I was afraid of that," said Donovan.

"What's the problem?" Truman asked, without bothering to mask his irritation.

"The farm right there is owned by Lee Tavon."

"Jesus Christ," Menzel muttered.

"On paper," said Donovan, "it's actually the property of Garrick Stamford from Lockheed."

"Your friend," said Truman accusingly.

"Yes, sir. Stamford bought it on Tavon's behalf," Donovan explained. "Apparently, Tavon didn't want to have his name on the title deed.""This just gets better," said Truman.

Vandenberg was exasperated. "Why haven't we heard about this before now, Bill?"

"I only found out myself a few days ago. Until five minutes ago, I had no reason to suspect it was anything more than a shady land deal."

"What exactly are we to make of this?" asked Bush.

"That's not clear yet," said Donovan.

Vandenberg placed his hands on the table. "Bill, I think you and I are taking a little drive in the country this afternoon."

It was the last thing Donovan wanted to do. He'd hoped to be on the next flight to London, but he knew Truman was staring at him.

"First things first," the President said. "I'm not leaving here while that reporter is out there. Neither are you, Hoyt."

"All right," said Donovan.

# FORTY TWO

July 22, 1952

Donovan hit the street at full stride and zeroed in on Edna Drake, who was leaning against the hood of her car. She watched him approach, but didn't move a muscle. Why was she still here? He saw her grin and itched to slap it off her face.

*Not a good idea. She knows how to handle herself. She'll hurt you, old man.*

He slowed himself down a fraction and reached for his revolver, savoring the fear it evoked.

"What the hell?" she demanded, angry and alarmed.

"You're taking me for a drive, Miss Drake. We have an appointment with your boss. She's expecting us."

"OK fine," said Drake, trying to sound cooperative. "So why don't you put the gun away? One of us might get hurt."

The broad had a smart mouth. "Just do me one favor — shut up and drive."

Drake started the engine as she climbed into the passenger seat beside her, gun held low and pointed at her stomach. The Packard started moving slowly.

"You're a man of God, aren't you General? You do know kidnapping is a sin, right?"

Donovan couldn't help smirking. "As in, thou shalt not abduct thy enemy at gunpoint? I can assure you I'm doing God's work here, Edna."

She shook her head. "Do you have any idea how arrogant that sounds?" To say nothing of deranged, Edna thought.

He poked her in the ribs with the barrel of the revolver. "Man with the gun, remember? I'd like you to keep your mouth shut." He looked away and breathed deeply, starting to worry he could lose his composure. The *Times-Herald* office was only a few blocks away. Thankfully, Drake did as she was told. "I know the press believes all secrets deserve to be revealed, but I assure you there are many things people don't want to know, things that would make their lives a misery if they knew about them."

Edna couldn't help herself. "But that's the point, General. What's happening now is no secret, is it?"

"Who told you about the meeting?"

She said nothing.

"I'll find out anyway, I have a fair idea. Miss Drake, I'm going to tell you this calmly and clearly now before we go into your editor's office. I've killed many people, but never an American. I've never even had to think about killing an American. Until today. But I find myself in a position where I could be forced to stop you *at any cost*. Do you hear me? We're the same, you and me — we act without care of consequence. But it won't be you I hurt, it'll be someone close to you."

Edna Drake pulled up out the front of the offices on H Street, in a parking spot marked "EDITOR".

"I'm putting the gun away," he said. "If you try anything stupid, I'll club you over the head with it. Hear me?"

"Loud and clear." She hopped out of the car and started for the lobby. He holstered the weapon and had to step lively to keep up with her. She waved at the man on the door and pointed back at Donovan. "He's with me." She kept moving toward a bank of elevators.

The newsroom took up the entire fifth floor. The elevator opened right into the working area. A few reporters looked up from their desks; Edna could tell they recognized Donovan immediately.

Bazy Miller's office was in its own annex, walled off from the reporters at the head of the floor. Drake nodded to her secretary. "Dot, I think the boss is expecting us?"

Dot nodded. "Go right in."

Donovan curtly acknowledged the secretary and shut the door behind them.

Bazy was on her feet, looking concerned. "You OK?" she asked Edna.

"He had a gun to my chest all the way here."

"What are you playing at, General?" Bazy asked. She sounded perversely proper and old fashioned.

Donovan didn't answer right away. He took the nearest seat in front of Bazy's desk and slapped his pistol down on it, somewhat harder than he'd intended, making both women jump. "This is the gun she's talking about, just so we're all on the same page."

"I'm calling the police," Bazy declared.

Now Donovan slammed his hand down on the desk, making them jump a second time.

*Be calm. These women are no threat to you.*

His heart was pounding; he waited a moment. "Please," he breathed, "just give me what I came here for and I'll be on my way."

"What would that be?" asked Bazy.

"Don't play dumb. It's not becoming for a woman of your position," said Donovan. "I want the letter, as if you didn't know. Give it to me and I walk out of here, never to darken your door again."

*You want more than that. You need a guarantee.*

"It's not here," said Bazy. "I had it placed in a bank vault."

*She's lying.*

"The hell you did," said Donovan through gritted teeth. "I know who you bank with. I also know the law firm that represents your bankers. They know nothing about a letter."

For the longest time, Bazy had nothing more to say. Finally, she found her tongue. "I'm not in the habit of acceding to threats, General. I don't plan to do so now."

Donovan rose to his feet, picked up the gun, and pointed it at Bazy's head. Drake gasped in shock and muttered the Lord's name in vain. "I've killed people over matters far less important than this."

"No!" Edna yelled, stepping between the gun and her boss. A stupidly brave move. "For the love of God," she said, "put the gun away. Please, Bill. The war's over. You're not shooting anybody. We're unarmed. At least a dozen people saw you walk in here. Most of them know who you are. You'd get the electric chair, or at the very least you'd spend the rest of your life in jail."

*She's right about that.*

Donovan held his ground a few moments, reluctant to concede the point, but knowing his bluff had been called. He holstered the gun and smiled. "You're right. Nobody dies today. But this ends now. Whoever is feeding you information is trying to harm this country. And I'm not talking about saucer hysteria or Russian invasion. I'm talking about a nuclear holocaust."

"We know it was you who brought the saucer to America," Bazy said.

Donovan's eyes widened.

"I think that's very much something the public deserves to know about," Edna added.

Donovan looked at Edna. "It won't be you." He turned to face Bazy again. "Print that story and you do untold damage to your country."

The newspaper editor stared daggers at him. She was clearly rattled, but also incensed. "I think that's a gross exaggeration, General Donovan."

He wanted to explain how wrong they were, and how immensely important the saucer was to US weapons and aviation research, but that risked all of it ending up in print. "Come on, I'm not leaving without that letter."

Edna sighed. Donovan was turning purple. The man was coming apart. He was at the outer limits of keeping it together. "Bazy, maybe we should just give him the damn thing."

A look of betrayal flashed across Bazy Miller's face. "Like hell."

"Big mistake," he said.

"Is that so?"

"A risky move," Donovan reiterated. "And risky behavior can have unforeseen consequences. Terrible, deadly consequences. Tragedies."

"You hear that, Edna? This man just threatened us with deadly violence."

"I did nothing of the sort," said Donovan. "I stated a fact that you, as a newspaper publisher, must surely understand better than most. Miss Drake, you covered just such a tragedy yourself. The death of that poor liquor store owner."

"If you're saying you had a hand in that," said Edna, "the detective running the police inquiry would be very interested to hear it."

"Nothing to do with me, though you might want to ask your friend Lee Tavon the same question. And tell him his world is getting smaller by the day."

"Tavon. Doesn't ring any bells," said Edna.

"Tavon's a crook. He's playing both ends against the middle. Now come on, where's that letter?"

Bazy was still refusing to move.

"Boss, let it go. No story is worth this much trouble."

Bazy looked like Edna was asking her to strike a deal with the devil. "Did Truman put you up to this?" she asked Donovan.

"Like I said, you've stumbled into a situation of critical national importance."

"Then why not tell us more?" returned Bazy. "Help us understand your point of view."

Donovan laughed. "Nice try. But that would be breaking the law."

"As opposed to waving guns at unarmed civilians," said Edna.

"Suffice to say I am a loyal servant of my government. Now please, the letter."

Bazy Miller stood her ground a moment longer, pointlessly forestalling the inevitable. Eventually, she turned and removed a portrait behind her desk to reveal her wall safe. She withdrew the letter and handed it over.

Bill Donovan folded it up, shoved it in his coat pocket, and headed for the door. "None of this makes the paper. Remember those unforeseen consequences.

# FORTY
# THREE

July 22, 1952

From all angles, she was a thing of beauty. It was a perfect summer afternoon for a trip down the open road, and the first time Hoyt Vandenberg had put his new red Oldsmobile 88 coupe through its paces.

He had cancelled all his appointments for the day, offering no explanation nor emergency contact. All Air Force matters had been delegated to his deputy, General Twining, a member of Majestic who knew why Vandenberg was flying below the radar.

Vandenberg glanced over at Bill Donovan in the passenger seat. "If only you were my lovely lady wife, then my day would be complete."

"Hands on the wheel, buster. Don't get any ideas."

South of Washington, the highway took them through a green belt of trees, lining both sides of the road and obscuring their view of the way ahead. On any other day, Donovan would have been glad to spend time on the open road, but he was being pulled in too many directions at once. The confrontation in Bazy Miller's office kept playing out in his mind, over and over again. He could have handled it better. He got the letter, but had he succeeded in shutting them down?

"You think it's one of us talking to that reporter?" Vandenberg asked.

"I have no idea, Hoyt. But she turned up outside the hotel right when you arrived. Any chance she was tailing you?"

"What?" said Vandenberg. "You sure?"

"Silver Packard."

Vandenberg shrugged. "I got there ten minutes early like everyone else. She probably just knew the meeting time."

"Meaning you don't know whether or not you were tailed."

"I'm not in the habit of glancing over my shoulder from the back seat. I'll ask my driver, but he didn't mention seeing anything unusual."

"Don't worry. I think I know where the leak is coming from."

"So why the third degree?" Vandenberg asked.

"I told Truman I'd look into the leak. You're assisting with my inquiries."

"I'm starting to see why you get on his nerves."

"I don't know what gave you that idea," said Donovan, prompting an amused snort from Vandenberg. "Hoyt, there's something I've been keeping from the President." Vandenberg's expression remained neutral. "Lee Tavon got hold of a letter from Roscoe Hillenkoetter's personal files. The letter mentions FS-1. It has your name on it. Tavon leaked it to Edna Drake."

"Holy crap, Bill. What the hell are you thinking, not telling Truman about it?"

"I've dealt with it. I got the letter back. Destroyed it."

"You've got to tell him."

"Truman's a lame duck, Hoyt. In a few months, he'll be moving back to Missouri and we'll still be here carrying the can."

"There's a ways to go between now and then," Hoyt argued. "If you want to crash and burn in a blaze of glory, I'd rather you didn't take me with you."

"Let's get to Petersburg and take it from there."

They sat in silence for a long time. South of Thornburg, the tree line was broken up by rural townships. The further south they ventured, the faster Vandenberg pushed the car. The wind noise made talk nearly impossible. Every now and then, Donovan glanced at Vandenberg. He still had his movie star looks, like Clarke Gable or John Wayne. The car helped, but Hoyt Vandenberg had a presence that garnered admiration from men and women alike. Men wanted to be his friend. Women just wanted him. Donovan had given up counting the dames he'd seen falling at the man's feet. Yet despite the regular distractions, he and his wife remained close. Mrs Vandenberg knew who she'd married. They had the sort of connection that was sorely missing from Donovan's own marriage.

They slowed to a crawl through Petersburg, taking in the local attractions. It had a remarkably diverse range of services on offer for a small town, even its own three-level department store.

The main street was deserted. People were indoors, escaping the heat. They pulled in at a Conoco gas station on the southern end of town. A woman in an Audrey Hepburn scarf parked her red Corvette beside them. She noticed Hoyt immediately, lowering her sunglasses to check him out. Vandenberg was busy talking to the attendant and barely seemed to notice.

Back on the road, Donovan asked, "Did you get a look at that beautiful creature back there?"

"The car or the gal?" asked Vandenberg.

"Both."

"I almost bought a Corvette. Decided they were a bit extravagant. But I have a feeling I've met that gal before," Vandenberg admitted. "Didn't want to look too closely, just in case."

They arrived at their destination a few minutes further down the road. It was a large open property: a farm house and barn about half a mile in off the highway. Well maintained, yet no immediate signs of life.

Donovan double-checked the map. "This is definitely it."

"Tavon owns this?"

"So Stamford assures me. Officially, it's owned by a company called Guild Trading Incorporated, but that's a shell company set up by Tavon and linked to something called Bermuda Investments. Some sort of food transportation business."

Vandenberg drove up the trail to the farmhouse. The air around them filled with dust, making Donovan cough. "This is why farmers don't drive convertibles."

They knocked on the front door of the house. No answer. But through the front windows, they could see a remarkably clean and well-ordered interior. Someone lived here.

They made their way around to the rear. The back was open. They knocked loudly again, then entered a large eat-in kitchen. "Hello?" Donovan called. "Anyone home?" No response. They kept looking. A separate dining room, plates stacked up on an old colonial sideboard against the wall, an eight-seater table in the middle. Not a speck of dust anywhere.

Three bedrooms upstairs, all set out neat and tidy, like the cleaner had just been through. Nothing out of place, but at the same time curiously clinical. Like it was made to look perfect. There were no photographs, no clutter, no newspapers or books scattered about. None of the normal signs of life.

Under the stairs, a door led them down to an underground basement. Tools on the wall. A brand-new Bendix front-loader washing machine stood in one corner. The basement floor and walls were all concrete.

"It's a bomb shelter," Donovan realized.

"Yeah, looks like it," Vandenberg agreed.

They made their way across to the barn, which was likewise easy to access via a side door that had been left unlocked. Inside it too was strangely clean, devoid of the usual dirty objects and the mess of rural commerce you'd expect to find on a working farm. No animals, no obvious signs of activity, though the building itself was massive.

Vandenberg stomped his feet on the concrete floor. "That's thick." He found a spade, went back outside, and began to dig where the edge of the slab met the earth. For a solid ten minutes, he kept at it. Two feet down into the ground, he still couldn't find the bottom of the slab. "It costs a fortune to pour a slab this thick. But I can't see why they'd need it. You could land a B-29 on this."

"There's something screwy here," said Donovan.

"Could Tavon and Stamford be running some sort of off-book Lockheed project here?"

"Skunkworks is already off-book. This is something else."

"If Tavon's hiding something, it's probably under this slab. But we'd need bulldozers and jackhammers to get through it. That's gonna attract a lot of attention."

"Which is not what the President ordered. So, we wait."

"For what?"

"Damned if I know," said Donovan.

# FORTY FOUR

July 23, 1952

Edna let her boss yell. She knew what trauma looked like when she saw it in someone's eyes. She knew Bazy Miller was still imagining the barrel of Bill Donovan's revolver pointed at her head. She was screaming at Edna for making her hand over the FS-1 letter. Edna took it on the chin, knowing Bazy's frustration was really directed at Donovan. The editor was furious at the idea that Donovan might get away with a criminal act in the name of a president she now believed to be "morally bankrupt and illegitimate".

But Edna knew it was time to speak up when Bazy bitterly declared her determination to put the whole sordid tale on the front page of the following day's paper. Edna closed the door to the publisher's office then, and quietly went to great lengths to explain why that was precisely what they could not do. They had nothing to gain by writing a story about a top-secret operation when they no longer had the written evidence in their possession. It would put them in an indefensible legal mess if Truman or the Air Force came after them in the courts.

"Highly unlikely," Bazy argued, "because that would mean admitting to the conspiracy."

Edna conceded her boss might be right. "But what if Donovan's right too? What if we started a war? Is that a risk worth taking? He will swat us down like flies and make it look like an accident."

Meantime, they had another story to focus on. The sighting over Washington was big news around the world and remained a topic of intense public debate. More importantly, Edna could say with the confidence of her own firsthand observation that Truman himself had convened a secret high-level meeting on the matter, illustrating the extent of concern within government circles. She assured Bazy they weren't done on the FS-1 project, just that it now required a more thorough investigation. This wasn't something regularly undertaken by *Times-Herald* reporters; it needed careful consideration. *Life* magazine had spent a year on their saucer story.

None of this was welcome news to Bazy Miller, but she eventually agreed it was the best way forward.

That afternoon, Edna went to work on a front-page flying saucer exclusive. It felt like her first genuine foray into investigative reporting.

# CAPITOL SAUCER FLAP HAS PRESIDENT ASKING QUESTIONS

*By Edna Drake, staff reporter*

A SECRET high-level meeting involving the President and senior members of the military and intelligence service has been held in Washington to discuss the security implications of last weekend's flying saucer flap.

Capitol sources have told the *Times-Herald* serious concerns have been expressed in top echelons of the military about the squadron of strange lights that appeared over the White House and the Capitol building, objects spotted on radar as well as by numerous ground observers.

None of those concerns have been expressed publicly, with the Air Force only saying it would not comment while an investigation was underway.

There has been no comment of any sort from the White House.

Republican senate minority leader Styles Bridges condemned what he called "obsessive secrecy" and called on President Harry Truman to speak plainly to the people.

"This is another sign the Truman administration must be called to account by the people," Senator Bridges told the *Times-Herald*.

These strange objects were spotted making their way unimpeded into restricted air space, flying just hundreds of feet above the heart of this nation's government.

The incident was serious enough to prompt the Air Force to scramble two F-94 interceptors to pursue the lights, though by that time they had disappeared.

This newspaper can also confirm President Truman has taken a personal interest in the matter and yesterday met with senior members of the military and intelligence services, including CIA Director Walter Smith and Air Force Chief of Staff Hoyt Vandenberg.

The meeting was convened in an apartment suite at the Mayflower Hotel, four blocks from the White House.

President Harry Truman arrived in an unmarked car minutes before the meeting began, but refused to comment as he entered the Mayflower Hotel.

"I have nothing to say, I'm sorry," Mr Truman told the *Times-Herald*.

It is understood those attending the meeting are members of a top-level investigation team examining the Washington incident.

So far, that investigation remains firmly behind closed doors.

\*\*\*

It was Bazy's idea to add in a free kick for the Republican senate leader. Bridges was a McCarthy acolyte and a staunch supporter of all the anti-communist bile. Edna didn't think much of him, but he was one of the paper's go-to critics of the Truman administration.

Edna had read her own story at least five times when she eventually folded up the paper and laid it down on the bench beside her. She pulled a pack of cigarettes from her purse. Edna had never been a determined smoker, but sometimes it felt comforting to have something to do with her hands. She'd been on a park bench outside the National Geographic Society for almost twenty minutes, enjoying the tranquility of the early morning.

She couldn't exactly say what had stopped her from her destination. The University Club was right across the road, but her legs didn't seem to want to take her in there. Some sixth sense told her to stay put, and for the moment she was just going with it. Above her, a long flagpole held the stars and stripes proudly aloft. She listened to the flag rippling in the breeze and wondered what that flag meant now. Patriotic fervor must mean nothing to visitors from another planet. What would knowledge of their existence do to the American dream?

For all those poor young boys who'd died in her arms in the field hospitals of Europe, the American flag was the symbol of everything they were fighting for. It was the essence of liberty, and they'd given their lives in its name. There could be no doubt their blood was spilt for a just cause; history would always remember them for that. But it had never been a fight for truth, because who could say what that was? Edna Drake thought she'd known, but realized now that when people spoke of truth, liberty, and justice, it had been a concept she'd taken for granted.

She'd always believed justice was the most elusive of the three. She had become a journalist assuming it was her job in a free country to report the truth, and that even hidden truths could be revealed by those who cared to look. To Edna, it was up to the men and women of the "free" press to find the worst examples of injustice and corruption, to hold them up to the light of the law, and see them judged in the court of public opinion.

Now, Edna knew better.

Justice might never be meted out in equal measure to those who needed it, and money could always buy favor for those who didn't deserve it.

And Edna had come to see the truth as a different matter entirely. Even the definition of the word was open to interpretation: *that which is true; the true or actual facts; conformity with fact or reality*.

Actual facts. When were they ever beyond dispute or interpretation? To whose reality did said facts conform? Lately, her world had become a whole lot harder to define.

An old couple stumbled slowly past her along 16th Street on their early morning downtown constitutional. Edna gave them a wave. "Morning." They smiled and waved back. Would their reality crumble if they had to confront the truth that humanity was not the only intelligent species on this planet, that they were not alone in this galaxy and its billions of stars? Were they happier because they didn't have to think about it?

When governments told lies to their people and those people, through fear, ignorance, and apathy chose to believe it, did that lie then turn into truth?

A dark sedan pulled up in the driveway of the University Club. Edna immediately recognized Bill Donovan as he emerged from the back seat and made his way into the club's interior. She smiled, thankful she'd followed her instincts. It wasn't Donovan she'd come here to see and she had no interest in another confrontation with him. Edna hunched over and unfolded her newspaper, hoping her scarf and sunglasses were a good enough disguise.

Gordon Gray was in the habit of taking a room at the University Club during his times in Washington; he'd told her it was easier than keeping an apartment and cheaper than a hotel. The club was, of course, for men only.

He had revealed this much about himself presumably to persuade her he was telling her the truth. Gray certainly believed she would never dare set foot inside an exclusively male domain, where the masters of the universe came to pat one another on the back. Women were allowed only as guests in the club's dining rooms.

Donovan's arrival confirmed one thing: Gray was in there somewhere. One way or another, Edna would force Gray to speak to her. One way or another, she needed to learn the truth.

# FORTY FIVE

J uly 23, 1952

The cocktail bar off the Taft Dining Room was thankfully empty this early on a weekday morning. Gordon Gray directed Donovan toward two high-backed red leather chairs in the corner of the room, where they wouldn't be disturbed. Gray tapped a waiter on the arm, mentioned something about a quiet chat, and asked for two black coffees. The waiter returned with the beverages while Donovan was still removing his jacket; he deftly took the jacket from the general and hung it on a brass coat stand before disappearing.

"Excellent service," said Donovan, throwing a copy of the *Times-Herald* on Gray's lap as he took his seat. "Seen this morning's front page?"

Gray took one look and grimaced. "President's not too happy, I imagine."

"Correct." Donovan had been none too pleased himself, though it was at least no small consolation that the story mentioned nothing about the Hillenkoetter letter, nor anything relating to his heavy-handed retrieval of it. He knew there was no point trying to stop them reporting on the weekend sightings; it was a hot topic for every news organization in the country. "I wonder if it occurred to the person who tipped off Edna Drake about our meeting yesterday that he was breaching his oath of secrecy?"

Gray knew that was directed at him. "Is that what you came here to discuss?"

"Professor Menzel thinks maybe you're sleeping with her after all."

"Edna Drake is not my lover. She's a charming young woman who believes she's chasing the biggest story of her career, but I have done nothing to help her in that regard."

"Apart from introducing her to Lee Tavon?"

Gray sighed. "I had no idea who he was at the time. I told you that."

"Call yourself a CIA man," Donovan scoffed. "I saw you talking to her outside the Mayflower. Thoughts? Observations?"

"I thank you, Bill, for not mentioning that to the President. But if you're suggesting it was me who told Miss Drake about the meeting, you're wrong. She caught me completely unawares. If you saw me talking to her, you also saw we spoke no more than a few words. I gave her the brush-off."

"It was enough time to confirm she was in the right place, and that Mr Truman would be along directly."

"If that were the case, my presence alone would have confirmed that for her. Think about it. She's a smart woman. If I was her source, the smart choice would've been to ignore me completely."

"Except you knew I was watching. A chance meeting of two people who know one another? It looks strange if you don't at least say hello."

"Oh, for God's sake," said Gray. "You can't have it both ways. She leapt out of her car and ran across the street to meet me. She was as surprised to see me as I was to find her there. If that's all you came here to say, go away and let me have my breakfast in peace."

Donovan took a large sip on his coffee and stood up slowly. It was his only option these days. "Hear me now: keep your mouth shut around Edna Drake, or I might be forced to do something regrettable."

"I take it you still haven't mentioned any of this to the President. Maybe it's time I did that," Gray suggested.

"That," Donovan said, tapping Gray on the shoulder, "would be truly regrettable. For both of us. Besides, my gut still tells me the leak isn't in Truman's office."

"Your gut?" Gray rose to his feet.

Donovan smiled. "My instincts are never wrong."

Gray shook his head. "I'm not sure I'd bet the House on it."

# FORTY SIX

J uly 23, 1952

Edna had taken refuge behind a hedge by the time Donovan's black car returned to collect him. He wasn't in the club for long, which was a good thing for her. Anyone climbing the steps to the National Geographic front entrance was bound to see her lurking suspiciously.

She waited for Donovan's car to vanish into traffic before making her way across the street.

"Oh Jesus, Edna." Gordon Gray was standing in the entrance to a very expensive-looking bar, looking panicked. "Do you know who...?"

"Don't worry, he didn't see me," Edna assured.

"Did you follow him here?"

"No, but it's remarkable how our paths keep crossing. I was outside working up the courage to come in when he beat me to it."

"We don't encourage your type in here," Gray told her.

"Women?"

"Them too. But I meant reporters." He took her by the arm. "Let's take a walk." His expression told her that whatever she had to say, it was better said outside. Gordon Gray led Edna south down 16th Street and around the corner into M Street; it was lined with office blocks and still deserted this early in the morning. He kept moving, almost like he was trying to get away from her.

"Slow down, will you?"

Gray stopped dead in his tracks and turned to face her. "I just finished assuring Bill Donovan I wasn't your leak. It's almost like you're here to make me look like a liar."

He was angry; Edna hadn't expected that. She'd felt she was the one with a right to be annoyed. "I get it. You're one of the boys. Holding secret meetings with the heads of the CIA and the Air Force. Oh, and let's not forget the President. I saw them all, Gordon."

"That could have been coincidence."

"Oh, spare me," Edna spat.

"What's the matter? Don't want to let the facts get in the way of a good story?"

Edna Drake laughed in his face. "That's priceless. Did you know Donovan kidnapped me at gunpoint yesterday? He's damn lucky we didn't put that in the paper. You might also have noticed I kept your name out of print. You're welcome, by the way. Frankly, I don't know why I bothered. I won't be so inclined to keep your nose clean in future."

Gordon Gray looked away. "I can take care of myself."

"Look, you and I both know this thing between us has been a game from the beginning. But it's gotten seriously out of hand. Donovan is issuing none-too-subtle threats of deadly violence."

"What do you think he'd do to me if he saw us together?" Gray bit out. "I can't help you, Edna. I like you, maybe more than I should…"

"The feeling is mutual, more's the pity."

Gray touched her cheek with genuine affection. "But this is as far as this goes." Edna melted. At that moment, he could have said or done anything. "Go home," he said. "Give this away, it's not going to end well."

"He took it, Gordon. He took the letter. Pointed a gun at my editor's head and threatened to blow her away if we didn't give it to him. I stood in front of him and I swear he was ready to pull the trigger. He's out of control. Somebody needs to deal with him."

"You think I'm that person?"

"Go to the President," Edna insisted. "Tell him."

Gray shook his head. "Edna, you're kidding yourself if you think there's any chance Truman will take your side. A reporter for the newspaper that declared war on his administration? Bazy Miller and her uncle won't stop until they see Harry Truman hurled unceremoniously from office. Why on Earth would the man have any sympathy for you?"

"Donovan's a Republican too."

Gray scoffed. "Come on, you're not that naïve. You want to know why Truman trusts me? He knows I operate outside politics. You'll need to do better than that."

"All right, then do it because you know it's the right thing to do. Because sooner or later 'Wild' Bill Donovan is going to snap his flimsy leash and let his gun do the talking. He's gone way past wild — the man's a ticking time bomb. I could see it in his eyes. He's out to lunch, Gordon. A regular menace to society."

Gray's eyes narrowed. He took her by the shoulders. "Has it occurred to you Donovan is exactly the man Harry Truman wants him to be?"

Edna smiled, but she wanted to scream. She had found her way inside a world where normal rules didn't apply. Part of her wished she'd never seen that damn letter. "Just tell me this — where can I find Lee Tavon?"

Gray patted her lightly on the arms, nodded dismissively and smiled sadly. He took two steps, stopped, and turned his head ever so slightly in her direction. "Don't come here again."

Gordon Gray walked away and didn't look back.

# FORTY
# SEVEN

July 24, 1952

The sub-editors had put the late edition to bed, and the subs were on their second tumbler of liquid dinner at the bar across the road. Edna and Johnny Galbraith were the only ones in the newsroom when Galbraith took the call.

"I'm sorry, can you say that again, I can't hear you too good. Oh yeah, sure. Edna, it's for you."

She could hear jazz as she lifted the receiver to her ear. "Edna Drake."

"The Gerry Mulligan Quartet is playing at the Jewel Box. You better be quick. Set's about to end." It was Gordon Gray. He hung up before she had a chance to speak.

"Johnny, grab your coat."

Galbraith smiled. She didn't like the look in his eyes, but decided to ignore it. "Where we going?" he asked.

"To see a man about the thing."

"THE thing?"

Edna nodded. The kid caught on quick. "You're learning."

It was only half a mile from the paper to the Jewel Box and a pleasant night to walk, but according to Gray they had no time to waste. Edna hailed a taxi instead.

"Jewel Box," she told the driver.

"That joint's a dump," said Johnny.

"I think that's sort of the idea. Anyway, what would you know?"

"I could show you a much better time."

"You and daddy's money?"

Galbraith tried to make like he wasn't bothered by the jibe. "I got money."

"Sure, Johnny. It's called a trust account."

"You should be nice to me, Edna. Maybe one day I'll be your boss."

Edna tapped him on the cheek. "I don't doubt it for a minute. But tonight, you do as you're told."

His eyes lit up. "Yes ma'am." From the gleam in his eyes, the whiz kid thought he was still in with a chance. If Eldridge had been talking to him, she'd have Joe's balls for a coin purse.

The downtown streets were empty. Edna wound down the window. The night air was cool. Half a block from the Jewel Box, she was sure she heard Chet's trumpet calling to her in the breeze.

The joint was packed. Cool cats were swinging their heads to the sound of brush caressing cymbal. Chet began again, his mournful call pulling her to the stage like a fish on a hook. He held her in a trance right to the end. She moaned when Mulligan announced they were taking a break.

"Not bad," said Johnny, "not bad at all."

Edna had forgotten Galbraith was there. She spotted Beverley King behind the bar. He was staring right at her, and nodded as their eyes met. He had something to tell her. As she walked over to find out what it was, King placed a cocktail on the bar. "Tom Collins. I hear they're your favorite."

"Who told you that?" Like she didn't know. She picked up the glass and took a long sip, then nodded her approval. King closed his eyes and pursed his lips. He knew it was good.

"Boss is waiting for you. Wants to talk." He nodded in the direction of the band. Lee Tavon was chatting with Chet Baker like they were old buddies. The whole deal felt like a dream. She pushed the whiz kid down on a bar stool and told King to fix him a drink. "I'll pay."

King shook his head. "Boss says you on the house tonight."

No sign of Gordon Gray, which was disappointing but hardly a surprise.

When Tavon saw her coming, his face lit up. "You were right, Edna. These guys are wonderful." She didn't even remember telling him about the Mulligan Quartet. "Edna Drake, let me introduce you to Mr Chet Baker."

He was even more handsome in the flesh; she'd only seen his face on record covers. "Chet," he said, shaking her hand.

"Thank you," Edna said.

"What for?"

"For the music. You've helped me make it through some...long, lonely nights."

"Yeah." Like he knew.

"I only wish I could have gotten here earlier. Lee didn't tell me you were here."

"Last minute booking," said Tavon. "But it's the first night of many, and that's down to you, Edna."

"Guess I should thank *you*," said Baker. Edna felt her cheeks go red. "It's a pleasure to meet you Edna, but if you'll excuse me, I need to sort out the next set with the boys."

"Just tell me you'll do *My Funny Valentine.*"

"You got it." Baker smiled shyly as he vanished into the crowd.

Tavon took her by the arm while she was still glowing. "Come sit with me."

"That was...wow," she said. There were people all around. Nobody paid them any particular attention, but Tavon had his eye on the front door. Johnny Galbraith was still at the bar, watching attentively. She glanced over and nodded to tell him she was OK. "You did all this for me, Lee?"

"It wasn't exactly a selfless act. I know a good idea when I hear one."

"Miles Davis, that's another good idea."

"You never mentioned him before."

"I just bought his latest record. It's sublime. Call yourself a mind reader. And why didn't you call me about Chet?"

"You're here, aren't you?"

"Everyone's still looking for you, Lee. You're not safe here."

"Which is why I have to make this quick. I'll tell you what I told Gordon..."

She had questions, but she didn't want to slow him down.

"The moment they've been waiting for is almost upon us. The visitors have delivered an invitation. They'll be back again, this Saturday night."

"How could you possibly know that?"

"I'm well-connected."

"When you sent me that letter, you crossed a line," Edna stated. "Donovan came after me. But I think you might be at the top of his list."

"The General is on his way here now."

Edna shook her head in disbelief. "Why bother to go into hiding at all?"

"I needed to be ready."

"For what? What's going on here?"

"There are things in this world that defy explanation, Edna. They challenge everything we think we know about ourselves, our core beliefs. Science tells us belief is not enough, that we should always look for proof. Yet there are things we know to be real that can't be measured, just as there is evidence at hand of phenomena that many scientists don't want to accept. We're at a crossroads. The day is fast approaching when science itself will be compromised by belief. Its high priests are ready to declare that certain ideas are off limits."

"I write simple stories for simple people," Edna said. "Give me something I can work with. Who's behind all this? What's going on?"

"They will come again this Saturday night. To the skies over Washington. But you will need to be somewhere else. In Petersburg, Virginia. Go to the southern end of town and wait."

"Wait for what?" Edna asked.

"The passing parade. When you see them, join the procession, then all your questions will be answered." Tavon tapped her fondly on the arm. "Now if you'll excuse me, my limousine awaits."

Tavon walked purposefully toward the entrance to the bar. He reached it just in time to meet Bill Donovan as he walked through the door.

# FORTY EIGHT

July 24, 1952

They were on the riverfront in Old Town, Alexandria. Lee Tavon was tied to a chair, arms behind his back, feet bare and exposed to the dirty warehouse floor.

Clarence Paulson screwed up his nose. "Something died in here."

"Yes," Donovan agreed, "some time ago, judging from the smell. But the rats are still very much alive. I've always had a fondness for this place. It's so quiet at night. Nobody around for miles. The owner doesn't mind if I make a mess, which is another benefit."

Paulson had done the heavy work, dragging Tavon in here and tying him up, though the man had put up no fight.

"There's no need for the strong-arm routine, Bill," Tavon said. "Ask me what you want. I'll answer truthfully."

Donovan frowned. Straight answers were the last thing he expected from Tavon's mouth, but he was willing to roll the dice. "Are you CIA?"

Tavon laughed. "No, I'm something much more interesting."

"Do tell."

"I'm not just going to throw my cards down on the table," Tavon grinned. "That's not how we play this game."

Donovan sighed. "That night in the casino, how'd you pull off those wins on the roulette table? Did Paul D'Amato help you out?"

"I read minds. I see the future. Not much of the future, but sometimes it's just enough."

Donovan didn't believe that for a moment. "The two options are, you're a crook or a mind reader. I know which one is the more likely."

Tavon was nonplussed. "None of this is what you'd call 'likely', Bill."

"That guy in the liquor store. Was he some sort of business rival?" Donovan's voice was growing high-pitched. "Why did you have him killed?"

Tavon waited a moment before responding quietly and calmly. "I didn't play a role in the death of that poor man. I don't like guns. They're crude weapons. I don't need one to defend myself."

"I guess you'd probably prefer karate. Or mind control." Donovan paced up and down, like he was delivering a closing address in a courtroom. "What if I shoot you, how about then? Crude weapons can be effective. We didn't win the war in Europe with bows and arrows."

Tavon considered this a moment before once more responding quietly, this time with implied menace. "I wonder, did you happen to know there is a particular combination of sounds that will shatter every bone in your body?"

Donovan smiled, then shook his head. "No there's not."

"Don't be so quick to dismiss the idea. You who know the power of sound better than most. You saw it with your own eyes — the right combination of sounds opened your secret vault in Lebanon. The one containing your flying saucer."

Donovan's eyes widened. Nine notes, played in just the right sequence, had unlocked the vault. This discussion was not going the way he'd intended. "Did Garrick Stamford tell you that?"

Tavon shook his head. "Garrick doesn't retain that sort of fine detail on matters he doesn't understand. You play Garrick a song, and he's lucky if he can hum a few bars."

"Then how?"

"You told me," said Tavon.

"The hell I did."

Paolo Favaloro appeared beside Donovan, as if stepping from the darkness into the light.

*He does read minds.*

Donovan had to crane his neck to look Paolo in the eye; he had chosen to reveal himself at his full eleven-foot height.

"My," said Tavon, gazing up, "you're a big boy."

"Mind reading is just a gimmick," Donovan shouted.

"You might not want to believe it, but that doesn't make it untrue," Tavon argued. "Being a man of faith, I'd hoped you might have grasped that much by now. Though I understand your little escapade in Lebanon caused quite a deal of consternation amongst the Pope and his merry men." Donovan knew Tavon was trying to get under his skin; this was supposed to be working the other way around. "Yes, I can read your thoughts," said Tavon, "and yes, I can use sound as a weapon. The particular notes are different for every man, woman, and child, making it a very personalized method of killing. But I have the means at my disposal. I know all the right notes. Would you like to hear them?"

"What means?" asked Paulson.

"I am part of a network. There are more than a hundred of us. We work together in small groups, all of us closely interconnected."

Donovan had no response to this, mostly because he didn't know what the man was talking about.

"No doubt," said Tavon, "you're aware there are great advances being made in computing."

"Funny," said Donovan. "The last I spoke to Garrick, he said he was keen to talk to you about IBM."

"I'm talking about something that is like a computer, but better. In my network, we are always connected." Tavon tapped the side of his head. "Mentally connected. You have no idea of the potential, what we are capable of achieving. Together we are of one mind. We can solve the most complex of problems in an instant."

Donovan decided to fire questions more quickly, in a bid to knock Tavon off balance. "Is this a government project?"

"No. Purely private enterprise."

"Who are you working with?"

"I'm not yet ready to reveal my partners."

"Other than Garrick Stamford?"

"Mr Stamford knows nothing about this," Tavon assured.

"Are your partners linked to organized crime?"

"I'm not the man you think I am."

Donovan raised his hand and moved to slap Tavon across the face, stopping himself just in time.

Tavon didn't even flinch.

"Come on, don't be coy," said Donovan. "I have a pretty vivid imagination."

Tavon smiled. "You do. I know you do. But I am neither devil nor demon, Mr Donovan. Your religion is no good to you here."

Now Donovan felt like he was the one being slapped. "How did you...?" *Devil. Demon.* Donovan wasn't even fully conscious of the words, but they were there, hovering on the periphery of conscious thought. Tavon had said them aloud.

No. Impossible. It had to be sleight of hand.

"Not convinced I see. Go ahead then, ask me."

Donovan could almost feel Tavon inside his head now. "Ask you what?"

"About the farm, of course."

Now Tavon had his attention. "You don't deny it's yours," said Donovan.

"Mr Stamford kindly purchased it in name, but the interest in Virginia farmland is mine and mine alone."

"What's it for?" Donovan asked him.

Tavon just stared at him for the longest time, unmoved — or maybe unhinged — and utterly devoid of fear. "Produce, of course. Finest farmland in America. It's tobacco heartland, as I'm sure you know, but I've been working on something a little more useful."

Donovan took a breath, sensing his own angst was somehow being used against him. "Would you care to enlighten me?"

Tavon smiled. "A good businessman never gives away his secrets."

"Last Saturday's lights over Washington," said Donovan, "are they another one of your secrets?"

"Not so secret now," said Tavon.

"Let's stop beating around the bush. The visitors have pointed to your farm. You seem to have some advance knowledge of their arrival. How are you talking to them?" Donovan demanded.

Tavon smiled and just tapped his temple. "It's all in my head, General. I'm hearing voices." He glanced up at Paolo again. "You know how it is."

Donovan looked away; he was a hair's breadth away from punching Tavon in the mouth. He took a deep breath, allowing his anger to subside. "This knowledge of yours, this network of mind readers, if it's real, it's a wonderful scientific achievement. How does someone like you manage it without any help whatsoever from the scientific community?"

"I'd tell you," Tavon said coolly, letting the words hang in the air a moment like he was about to reveal all. "But then I'd have to kill you."

# FORTY NINE

July 26, 1952

Edna had to take it on trust that Lee Tavon was on the level with his tip about a second Saturday night flyby. She wished she'd had more time before Donovan had hauled him away. She wouldn't be at all surprised if she never saw him again. It was distinctly possible Donovan figured on making the bar owner vanish for good.

Knowing this had soured any thought of staying on to hear the Mulligan Quartet play their last set. Five minutes after Tavon's departure, Edna was on the pavement looking for a taxi, ignoring all of Johnny's questions. The highlight of the night was the doe-eyed look of disappointment on Johnny Galbraith's face when she put him into the taxi and told him to go home without her.

Edna took a walk to Lafayette Square; she made it all the way to the front gate of the White House on Pennsylvania Avenue before it dawned on her it might not be safe, being out alone so late at night. But somehow thugs and molesters no longer registered high on Edna's list of concerns. She was neither pleased nor quick with a comeback when a taxicab driver pulled up and told her she'd better get in, because he didn't want to be reading about her demise in the morning paper.

Bazy Miller was unavailable for most of Friday morning. According to Dot, she had Chicago on the phone. After that phone call, there was the daily editorial meeting, and it was lunchtime before Edna got in to see her. Edna started talking, but she noticed she didn't have the publisher's full attention.

Bazy was a tough customer, but for a moment Edna thought she might cry. The moment passed quickly. You didn't survive in this business by letting people see weakness.

"What's the matter?"

"The Colonel has told me I need to choose between Tank and the paper. He says I can't have both."

"Like hell."

Bazy smiled. "I'd suggested that might be the staff's reaction. But he won't budge. Won't hear a word about hypocrisy or double standards. It's his way, or the highway. I'm afraid I'm not going to be the boss for very much longer."

"Well, goddamn it. What if we went on strike?"

Bazy shook her head. "Wouldn't matter. He doesn't care about this newspaper anymore. I rather think he'll sell it when I'm gone."

It was desperately unfair. Edna felt like the rug was being pulled out from under her, when what she needed most was solid ground. "Is this Donovan's doing? Do you think he knew all along the trouble he could cause?"

"I think he had a pretty good idea. But by God, it would be nice to go out with a bang. You say we're to have a return visit?"

Edna knew the Petersburg tip was a long shot, but she said they had nothing to lose in checking it out. Bazy agreed. Her boss said Eldridge could cover the Washington end of the story, and that Edna should head south. "But I don't want you going down there on your own. Take Carl with you."

Edna shook her head. "I can take pictures. I'd rather have Johnny. He's more nimble, quick on his feet. I don't think Carl's much of a country boy. And I suspect Johnny will be easier to fool with a cover story."

"Why don't you just be up front with him?"

Edna laughed. "This could be a wild goose chase. I'm not having the whiz kid second-guessing me. Telling the truth means dealing with all the questions that come with it."

"If something really is going on down there, you'll have to bring him up to speed real quick so he has your back."

Edna and Johnny hit the road in a work car a little after lunchtime. Johnny insisted on driving. He felt it was a man's job. She had no interest in fighting him on it; the work cars had no power steering and they were a bitch to handle. Theirs was a Ford Super Deluxe Coupe. It was only four or five years old, but casual abuse and neglect had taken their toll on the interior. It took to the open road about as smoothly as the front carriage on the Atom Smasher at Rockaways'.

"You still haven't told me what we're doing," Johnny said.

"Get us to Petersburg. We'll talk when we get there."

"A woman of mystery. Am I supposed to be impressed?"

"Eyes on the road, buster."

The kid smiled. "One of my favorite funny men. Did you know Buster Keaton wrote gags for the Marx Brothers and Lucille Ball? I saw him do a piece on the Ed Sullivan show a couple of weeks ago. He's a big tickle."

She had to marvel at his exuberance. Johnny was still wide-eyed and confident enough to believe he could do anything he wanted. Since going to war, she'd forgotten what that was like. Edna had long learned to top and tail her emotions; it was the only way she knew how to survive the horror. But ever since then, she'd never found her way out of the safety zone. For Edna Drake, happy and sad clung tight to one another, one never allowing the other get the upper hand.

"Keaton always seems so miserable," she said. "For a comedian, I mean."

"I've never liked guys who laugh at their own jokes."

"You'd never do that, would you Johnny?"

"Me? Never. Forget about it."

Edna laughed. "That's the worst Brooklyn accent I've ever heard."

"You're from round there, aren't you?"

"Queens. Rockaway Beach."

"Get back there much?"

"Christmas. A few times a year I talk to my folks on the telephone, but it gets expensive."

"You miss home?"

"Not as much as I thought I would. I mean, I love my parents, but I'll never be the woman they wanted me to be." Why was she telling him this?

"I'm a major disappointment to my father," said Johnny, by way of consolation. "Which, of course, was my plan all along."

They reached Petersburg just before five in the afternoon and grabbed a burger at a diner on the southern end of town, on Highway 301.

"This is the part where you tell me what's going on," he said.

She had a lie at the ready, but decided Bazy was right; he deserved to hear the truth. Johnny Galbraith listened without comment, nodding and eating until she'd finished.

"You're taking it well, I must say. Any questions? Doubts?"

He shrugged. "I'm guessing you've got enough of those already. We'll either see something tonight or we won't. Either way, I've had a drive in the country and a fine meal with a beautiful woman, and I'm getting paid to do it." Edna pulled a face. "That came out wrong," Johnny said. "You know what I mean."

Four hours later, it was looking like the night wouldn't go the way they'd hoped. They hung about in the parking lot of the diner until it closed shortly after eight o'clock, then ventured further down the road, pulling up on the driveway of an auto mechanic workshop that was closed for the night.

"What sort of a procession are we looking for?" Johnny asked her. "I'm guessing it won't exactly be the Thanksgiving Day Parade."

"Official vehicles. A string of cars following one another closely. Tavon seemed pretty certain we'd know it when we saw it."

He yawned. "There are other ways to pass the time, you know."

"Don't even think about it. If it's past your bedtime, hop in the back and I'll drive."

To her surprise, he did exactly that. An hour later, Johnny was fast asleep as the trucks began to roll by. They looked like Army vehicles, but bore no markings. Two of them followed behind three black sedans — a definite procession. Edna started up the engine and pulled out behind the last truck. They were driving fast. She doubted the Ford had ever been driven flat-out, and hoped the engine was up to the task. Johnny woke up when she took a sharp bend that threw him off the backseat and into the footwell.

He sat up, rubbing his eyes and picking off a chewing gum wrapper that had stuck to his forehead. "Where are we?"

Edna was worried they'd be spotted, but the convoy was apparently more focused on what lay ahead. She pulled up on the side of the road as the trucks turned into a property, rumbling down a dirt road toward a farmhouse and a barn a few hundred yards away. There were several other vehicles already parked outside, and the front of a large barn was lit up by portable flood lights. Three men in suits exited the sedans and quickly made their way inside the barn. The two truck drivers remained outside, staring at the barn entrance like overeager witnesses at the scene of a car crash.

"What now?" Johnny asked.

"You stay here. First sign of trouble, you go back to town and call Bazy for help."

"What? No way, I'm coming with you."

"This is not a democracy, Johnny. These are big, scary men with guns. If we walk in there together and something goes wrong, we're both in hot water. I need you to be my witness. From out here. You get me?" He didn't like it, but he understood. Edna grabbed her camera from the trunk and headed up the dirt track.

Her every footfall sounded deafening. There were no sentries posted along the dirt drive leading to the property. She was hidden by darkness, watching and listening carefully for movement as she reached the truck at the rear of the line. Gently, ever so slowly, she lifted back the canvas cover on the back of the truck, and stuck her head inside. Empty. Rows of seats lined either side of the tray. A troop carrier, minus the troops.

Using the truck as cover, she crept forward slowly in the shadows between the trucks and the farmhouse. She crouched down by the front wheel and peered around slowly. The two drivers were deep in discussion, their backs turned as they closely watched the barn. That was where she needed to be, but there was no way in without those two men spotting her. She thought about it a moment, then doubled back to Johnny.

"How's it looking?" he asked.

"I need you to get up there and distract those men so I can get inside."

"The men with guns?"

She nodded sagely. "They're truck drivers. They won't kill you."

Johnny shrugged. "Let's hope not," he said, as they began walking in the direction of the farm.

He kept to the fringe of the dirt road and managed to remain remarkably quiet as they reached the first truck. "OK, so what's the plan?" he asked.

"You pretend to be a nosy local. Say you saw all the commotion and wondered what was going on."

Bold as brass, Johnny stepped out from the rear of the truck and began marching into the light toward the barn door. He was making noises like some kind of drunken yokel; it would have been funny if the situation didn't immediately take a turn for the worse. He caught the attention of one of the truck drivers, who pulled a pistol from out of his pocket and raised it at Johnny like he meant to shoot.

"Woah woah woah," said Johnny loudly. "Take it easy, pardner, I'm just wondering what all this commotion's about? I could see your lights from a mile away."

A nice touch, she thought.

The driver said nothing, but shoved the pistol right in Johnny's face and grabbed him by the collar to march him back the way he came.

Which still left Edna with a problem: the other driver remained right outside the barn.

She could hear Johnny's complaints disappearing back down the driveway and started to panic. Her plan hadn't worked.

When the front door of the farmhouse opened just a few feet from where she sat crouched, she nearly yelled out in fright, figuring at that moment the game was up. Someone inside the house had spotted her. The man who caught her eye was all too familiar.

Lee Tavon gave her a short nod, then began waving his hands. "Sergeant? Over here." He was calling out to the second driver. Knowing it was over, she stood up.

But Tavon signaled with his hand for her to stay crouched down.

"Who the hell are you?" the driver demanded, marching in Tavon's direction.

"My name is Lee Tavon and there's something in the house I believe you'll want to see."

The young soldier followed Tavon into the farmhouse like a dog on a leash without catching sight of her. Edna knew she wouldn't get another chance — she ran toward the barn.

# FIFTY

July 26, 1952

Edna could hear chatter on the two-way radio in the car nearest the barn door. The driver door was hanging open. *"There's at least a dozen of them this time. National has them. They're on the scope at Andrews as well. Air Defense Command scrambled more interceptors from Newcastle."*

Newcastle was the name of the Air Force base in Delaware.

*"We've got one F-94 here already. Pilot says he's got no closing speed. He can't get near them, they're too fast."*

The barn was lit up even more brightly on the inside. About twenty feet in, the concrete floor fell away. She moved a little closer. Men in uniform stood at the edge, peering down. At first, she tried not to be seen, but she needed to see what they were looking at, and eventually curiosity overpowered caution.

The men were too dumbstruck to even notice she was there. Then she saw why.

The space below them was like a vast cavern, or more precisely an atrium, revealing multiple levels of an underground facility. It looked to descend hundreds of feet into the Earth.

A light flashed above her head. She looked up; the barn roof was open to the stars. Hovering over them, directly above the atrium, were three silver flying saucers, each about twenty feet in diameter. They hung in the air independently of one another, as if suspended by wires.

But there were no wires.

One after another, they vanished. It happened so quickly. But they had been there, she wasn't imagining it. Edna stared, feeling like she was held in some sort of trance, knowing all the while she had just witnessed something miraculous.

At that moment, a familiar voice yelled behind her. "Somebody get her out of there."

Hoyt Vandenberg and two other military men she didn't recognize were just a few feet away. Like Edna, they were breathlessly taking it all in. They looked as shocked as she felt. They must know she was here, but they didn't move toward her. She was the least of their concerns.

She was both ecstatic and terrified; she didn't know which way to turn. It was like being stuck in the middle of a minefield. She stepped closer toward the opening in the floor, knowing whatever was down there was not of this world. She walked closer toward the other men, instinctively feeling like there might be strength in numbers. They were all strangers in this strange place. They turned to look at her, expressions of awe in their eyes that no one had the words to express, then turned back to the scene below their feet.

Edna turned her eyes slowly toward the floor, feeling like she was about to be confronted with something wild and unpredictable. Instinctively, she kept her movements to a minimum. She gazed down into the sub-floor space, and was immediately hit with the sensation that here, the normal laws of gravity no longer applied. The underground facility was some sort of Escher model. On the nearest subfloor, ten feet or so below them, there were children. The floor was perpendicular, so that they were staring right back at Edna and the other men. The children were in groups, but they all held exactly the same expression on their young faces as they stared back with an oddly profound sense of purpose. There were about fifty of them. But it wasn't the number that was most disturbing. Mirroring the uniformity of their expression, many of their faces were identical. She counted them in groups of seven, each child in a group indistinguishable from the next. Septuplets.

"It's Munchkinland," said Vandenberg.

While they looked human, something told Edna they weren't.

On a lower level of the underground facility, a group of adults emerged: six men and seven women. Edna had a feeling that they too were also identical; the women looked up first and confirmed her suspicions. The men followed, six look-alikes gazing back.

All of them had the face of Lee Tavon.

Finally, Edna felt the weight of the camera in her hands. She lifted the eyepiece and began snapping pictures of the faces below. In her head, she tried to find the words that she might later use to describe what she was seeing.

But what she was seeing was impossible. She stared at this underground labyrinthine world open-mouthed. She wondered how deep the tunnels might go, and how long they had been here. Years? Centuries?

From the corner of her eye, Edna noticed Hoyt Vandenberg finally begin to walk toward her. He took her gently by the arm and walked her back from the edge. "Miss Drake, I think we need to talk."

He knew her by name. How funny that this, of all things, surprised her. They emerged into the open air and at once the world felt like a different place. Edna breathed deeply. Somewhere nearby, an owl hooted, its call imbued with a different sort of knowing. It was a normal sound, yet somehow it was also oddly jarring, like nature itself was conspiring against them.

More trucks were pulling up outside the farmhouse. A platoon of soldiers in jet black fatigues jogged past them into the barn. Her camera was out of her hands before she had the chance to object. "No.

I need that," Edna heard herself say. Vandenberg handed it to one of the soldiers, who nodded and took it away.

From the far side of the nearest troop carrier, Johnny Galbraith stumbled toward them. He was bleeding from the temple. Bill Donovan was two paces behind him; he reached out and violently grabbed him by the collar, pushing Johnny to his knees. Donovan shoved a pistol in Johnny's mouth and he gagged on it.

The terror in Galbraith's eyes snapped Edna out of her trance. "No!" she screamed, dashing forward. "Leave him alone. He's just a kid. I'm the one you want."

Donovan ignored her. He was looking at Vandenberg. "Simplest solution," he said.

Vandenberg shook his head. "For God's sake Bill, we're not the Gestapo. Bring him with us."

"I'm sorry," Johnny whimpered. "I led them straight to you." Tears rolled down his cheeks.

Her heart just about broke. Edna touched him on the cheek. "You did what I asked you to do."

A soldier produced a hood from somewhere and threw it over Johnny's head. A moment later, they did the same to Edna. It smelled strangely sweet; she recognized that scent. They marched her down the drive, past the trucks. She was already feeling dizzy as they bundled her into the back of a car. The hood was making it hard to breathe. Then she remembered...ether.

When Edna came to, the hood had been removed. They were still driving. She sat wedged between two men. They were still somewhere in the country. Through the left passenger window, she saw a jet take off. The lights of Washington were visible on the horizon. She had to be looking at Andrews Air Force Base. They were somewhere around Upper Marlboro or Westphalia. The car pulled into the driveway of a farmhouse. There were no signs of life. The front door was open.

They marched her inside and down a set of basement stairs, locking her in a room with no windows.

"Feel free to scream," one of the soldiers told her. "Nobody will hear you."

There was no sign of Johnny. Her room had a single mattress on the floor and a bare lightbulb in the ceiling above that was too high to reach. The walls were bare, nothing to offer stimulation of any sort. The door to the room was made of steel; it had no handle.

Edna was left on her own for hours before anyone returned to check on her. By that time, she'd started to wonder if they had forgotten she was here. As horrific as the idea was, anything was possible given what they'd all seen under that barn roof.

Eventually, the door opened and she found herself facing an older man. No uniform, but he was military. "Edna, my name is General Nathan Twining. You are being held here by order of the President under the provisions of the Espionage Act."

Edna stared at him, incredulous. "You're accusing me of spying on my own country?"

"We're not accusing you of anything," said Twining. "I'm telling you we have the legal right to hold you here as long as we like. I'll try to get you something to eat. And a bucket. It'll have to suffice for a toilet, I'm afraid."

When General Twining locked the door behind him, it was the last sound she heard outside those four walls for what felt like an eternity.

# FIFTY ONE

July 27-30, 1952

She wouldn't have been surprised if it had been more than a day, but if Hoyt Vandenberg was to be believed, it was only four hours between Twining's departure and her eventual removal from the cell.

They let her use the toilet. She'd been busting for so long she had been close to wetting herself, but she was damned if she'd drop her pants and pee in a bucket when she was almost certainly being watched.

After that blessed relief, a man in a ski mask directed Edna to a bigger room devoid of all furniture that had once been a country kitchen. The sink was full of water. "Drink," the mask said. "Sorry, no glasses. And no food yet." Like it was no particular concern to him if she starved.

"Where's my friend? Where's Johnny?"

"Not here."

"I want to see him." She stuck her head into the water and sucked in a mouthful, but spat half of it out in a coughing fit because most of it went up her nose. She tried again, more slowly this time, angry at herself.

The mask left the room. Vandenberg reappeared, carrying two chairs. He was out of uniform. She realized he'd been dressed that way at the Tavon farmhouse. CIA chief Walter Smith was with him. Smith waved the mask back in to deliver another chair and to unfold a small card table. Vandenberg offered her a chair and urged her to sit. She was happy to get off her feet. The two men sat opposite.

"Tavon tipped you off?" Smith asked.

She smiled at the suggestion. "One of the Tavons, yeah." That night at the Jewel Box seemed like such a long time ago.

Vandenberg laughed incredulously. "It's a hell of a thing."

"You're in quite a spot of bother here, Miss Drake," said Smith.

"Is that right?" she replied bitterly. "Because I wasn't sure until you said it out loud."

"We could kill you." Vandenberg said it like he was talking about stepping on a roach. "It would solve all our problems, though it's not my preferred option."

"General Donovan will be sorry to hear that," she said.

"Let me be clear, Edna," said Vandenberg. "You're facing the prospect of military prison. We can lock you up on charges of treason and espionage and it might never even go to trial."

A few days ago, she'd have sworn that kind of thing could never happen in America. After what she'd seen, Edna couldn't be certain of anything. Vandenberg was still talking. "Your family won't even know where you are. Do you understand me? To the outside world, you'll be dead."

Edna Drake thought about her parents and tears rolled down her face. "You call it treason. I was just doing my job."

Smith asked, "Tell us about your relationship with Gordon Gray. Are you lovers?"

Edna laughed. "No."

"I'm not sure I believe you," said Vandenberg.

She wiped the tears from her cheeks defiantly. "He's a married man. Not that it would stop me, but Gordon is a man of honor. He wouldn't do that to his wife."

"A rare man indeed," said Vandenberg.

"One of a kind," Smith agreed.

Vandenberg smiled like an apex predator ready to devour its prey. "Your loyalty to him is admirable. He really doesn't deserve it. Gordon's happy to let you rot in here. Self-preservation trumps altruism, I find. And it'll beat lust any day of the week."

"You've seen something tonight," said Smith. "We can't let you talk about it. To anyone."

"Ever," added Vandenberg.

"You don't even know what it is yet," said Edna.

"Oh no, that's not true," said Vandenberg.

"All right then, tell me."

General Vandenberg rubbed his eyes and leant forward on the card table. "It's classified."

"OK fine. I promise never to write about this, never to talk about it. Just let me go. And for Christ's sake, let Johnny go. He hasn't seen anything."

Vandenberg stood up. "You promise. That's a good one. I'll be sure to take that to the President."

Smith got up and folded the card table. They left without saying another word. The ski mask had Edna back in her windowless cell a minute later.

Meals came and went. It was the only way she could estimate the passage of time. By the time fried chicken arrived, her fifth meal in captivity, she figured it had to be Monday night — more than two days since she and Johnny had set out for Petersburg from Washington. She wondered what Bazy was doing to find them. She hoped they hadn't hurt Johnny, that he hadn't done anything stupid to force their hand. They'd developed a system. She knocked when she needed the toilet. She didn't try to escape. She had neither the energy nor the inclination to bother. They weren't going to kill her. But neither, she felt sure, would they place her in any sort of official lockup. Wouldn't that require paperwork, lawyers, bureaucracy?

Too many uncomfortable questions.

But Edna also wondered if America had secret prisons. If so, was what they all might look like? Impossible was a word that no longer seemed to have any relevance to her situation. There was no normal. No comparison. No rules. As far as the outside world was concerned, she might already be presumed dead. Nobody was talking to her now. Ski Mask didn't respond to questions, and neither Vandenberg nor Smith had shown their faces again.

The light above her switched off, plunging her cell into pitch black. She felt her way to the mattress and lay down to sleep. It had been little more than two days, and already she was a lab rat dutifully responding to all commands. Lights out, sleep.

Eyes open. A glimmer of daylight. Another meal. She asked for a newspaper. Ski Mask shook his head. She asked for the toilet. He led the way. Tuesday now. Another meal... Lunch. Toilet break. After-noon nap. Glass of water, cocktail hour. Burger and fries for dinner. The fries were cold; nothing worse than cold fries. She ate them all, every last one. Her reward was an after-dinner stroll around the house, up and down a darkened hallway, a brief glimpse of the night outside. Then something new; a toothbrush. An Oral-B 60. Latest technology, soft bristles. Accepted gratefully. She thanked Ski Mask like it was the greatest gift she'd ever received. "Make sure you leave it in the bathroom," he said.

She did as she was told. She wanted to see that toothbrush again. Maybe next time there'd be toothpaste.

A newspaper arrived with breakfast. Wednesday's first edition *Times-Herald*. A front-page story by Joseph Eldridge. The weekend saucer sightings over D.C. were nothing to worry about, the Air Force declared. Details had emerged during an 80-minute press conference held by USAF head of intelligence Major General John Samford. At Samford's side, Director of Operations Major General Roger Ramey, Air Technical Intelligence Center radar expert Captain Roy James, and ATIC aerial phenomenon Branch Commander Captain Edward Ruppelt.

Radar anomalies seemed to be the official explanation. The so-called "Menzel theory of temperature inversion." That had to be Donald Menzel; another of life's rich ironies. She remembered air traffic controller Harry Barnes mentioning inversions. He'd been certain what they saw was no inversion. The Air Force apparently saw things differently.

An inversion, the newspaper explained, could cause anomalous radar reflections with hot air, a substance clearly familiar to General Samford. He was remarkably sure-footed in telling the press there was nothing of danger or consequence detected in the skies over Washington.

Yet on everything else, he sounded a little hazy. He admitted temperature inversion was at best a "50-50 proposition". Captain James said there was insufficient information to say it was definitely the cause.

Asked to give a personal view on what had occurred, General Samford offered nonsense: "I think that the highest probability is that these are phenomena associated with the intellectual and scientific interests that we are on the road to learn more about, but that there is nothing in them that is associated with material or vehicles or missiles that are directed against the United States."

He delivered another steaming pile of gibberish when asked how temperature inversion could explain the lights in the sky pursued by F-94 pilot Lieutenant William Patterson. "He had motive, he had direction, he had interest, he had opportunity," said Samford. "But he had no measuring devices to measure this thing, or these things, that need to have measurement before it can become anything other than a sighting."

Samford was mangling his sentences in a deliberate attempt to be as confusing as possible. He went on to offer a final explanation that made so little sense that Edna was amazed the quote made it to print.

"That very likely is one that sits apart and says insufficient measurement, insufficient association with other things, insufficient association with other probabilities for it to do any more than to join that group of sightings that we still hold in front of us as saying no."

What Samford was really suggesting was that they didn't trust the eyesight of their own fighter pilot. A remarkable admission from the head of Air Force intelligence, and one that apparently went unchallenged by the reporters present, who had been lulled into an intellectual stupor by his blathering bullshit. Samford had outflanked them with a bloated explanation that defied logic, but he'd done it with experts at his side backing him up. They talked the subject to death by burying it in scientific uncertainty. Yet somehow, Samford was adamant this curiously ill-defined phenomena posed no risk to America.

Edna threw the paper down on the floor in disgust.

# FIFTY TWO

July 31, 2019

Edna stared at the newspaper on the floor with the bitterness of a jilted lover for a full ten minutes, before she finally got over herself and picked it up again to read the rest of it. What else was she going to do, other than stare at the walls? She spent the next hour devouring every word from the news section, the women's section, even the sports page. She'd had nothing to occupy her thoughts for days. It was a gift to have something to read. Anything. Yesterday, she'd almost started scratching the paint off the door hinges so she could make out the name of the manufacturer underneath, simply because the name was partially obscured and it had been bugging the hell out of her.

She'd started to wonder if the rest of her life would be spent in this small abandoned farmhouse, shuffling from one room to another, never again to see the light of day. Edna wondered what her family had been told, or even worse, if they had been told anything at all. Bazy would have called them by now. What could she have told them? Edna wished she'd called home more often. She longed for the sound of her dad's voice down a telephone line.

The oddest thing about her captivity had been the fact that they didn't seem to want anything from her. The newspaper was a message, that much seemed clear. They were telling her the world was moving on. She'd been left behind. Hot air had won the day.

Edna wondered if that might mean she'd be set free. She was ready to play ball now; she would do whatever they wanted. She banged on the door to her cell, called out to Ski Mask. She figured it couldn't have been the same man out there all this time, but she had no way to know for sure. Sensory deprivation, that's what they called it. Solitary confinement. By Christ, it worked too. She was putty in their hands now. Compliant. Submissive.

Ski Mask opened the door. She stared at him a moment longer than she should have, just because he was the only other person here. "You could take that off, you know. I still wouldn't know who you are."

"What do you want?"

"Tell them I'm ready to talk."

He nodded and shut the door.

Nothing happened straight away. She read the paper again. Infuriated herself a second time with Joe Eldridge's story that gave so little away, and yet said so much about the men who ruled the world.

In time, Edna began to see it from their point of view. How could they be honest? What would it do to the nation if the chiefs of the greatest defense force in the world were compelled to admit the skies above were not under their control?

If she had to guess, she'd say it was around 11 o'clock when Ski Mask returned. Her stomach told her lunch wasn't far away. He opened the door. "You know the way."

She did. Second door on the left past the bathroom. The kitchen.

Vandenberg was waiting, the chairs and card table already set up. He smiled, told her to sit. There were four chairs, hers and three others facing her.

There was a coffee percolator on the draining board beside the sink. That was new. She could smell the coffee brewing. "Would you like a cup?" he asked.

"Very much," she said.

"It'll have to be black, I'm afraid. Nobody remembered to buy milk."

"Black's fine. And if you want to throw a little whiskey in it, I wouldn't say no."

"The coffee will have to do for now."

She heard a door open in the other room. "Who else is coming?"

"You're about to find out."

Two men walked in. Donovan. With Donald Menzel, the astrophysicist.

"Oh Jesus Christ," Edna muttered. She pointed at Donovan. "You want me to cooperate? Get him out of here."

Nobody moved. For an uncomfortably long time, nobody spoke. Finally, Donovan demurred. "I'll wait outside."

That was unexpected. Menzel had a folder in his hand. He put it down on the card table, took off his jacket, and placed it carefully around the back of the middle chair facing her.

"Donald Menzel, the hot air man," Edna said.

He smiled dimly, like it was a joke he'd heard many times before. "Any chance of a coffee for me?" Menzel asked.

"Of course," said Vandenberg. He poured a cup, placed it down on the table, then took a step back to let Menzel take the lead.

The scientist looked Edna up and down, his expression like that of a school principal trying to make his mind up about expulsion. "I take it you've read the paper."

"Yes. Quite the snow job."

"I thought so too," said Menzel. "General Samford excelled himself. It was a master class in media manipulation. He just stood there and talked and talked until they had no more questions left. He made no sense at all, but they still took him at his word."

"It's not hard to baffle reporters with science," said Edna. "Even pseudoscience."

"He didn't lie," said Menzel.

"Except for the bit about being certain there was no threat to America."

"No, he was telling the truth there too," said Vandenberg.

"If the visitors had nefarious intent, don't you think we'd know about it by now?" said Menzel. "They seem more interested in stopping us from killing each other. Anyway, enough of that. I hear you're ready to play ball."

She nodded. "Whatever that means, but yes. Tell me what you want."

"Actually, we want you," Menzel said. "More specifically, Lee Tavon wants you."

"Which one?"

"All of them," said Vandenberg. "They're all the same. They think and act like seven fingers on the one hand."

"That's good," said Menzel. "I like that analogy."

"Who is he? What is he?" she asked.

"First things first," said Menzel. "I have a proposition for you. Think carefully about it before you give me an answer." He looked over at Vandenberg, who took his seat at the table.

Vandenberg said, "Edna, we want you to work with us."

Edna Drake raised an eyebrow. "You want me to quote your lies and put them into print, and stop asking so many difficult questions."

Menzel smiled. "Not exactly. In fact, we'd like you to ask your questions. All of them. Tavon is agreeing to work with us. Not on technology, but on advanced development of human consciousness. But he says it's conditional upon working directly with you. If you say no, the deal is off the table."

She thought about that. "You've taken him and his little tribe into custody, yes?"

"We've taken control of their Virginia facility," said Vandenberg.

"Which is precisely what they knew we would do," said Menzel. "Fascinating people. Utterly enthralling. I feel like I could spend the rest of my life studying them. You have the unique opportunity to make that run a lot more smoothly for us all."

"But here's the thing," said Vandenberg. "It would have to be in secret. You'll have to give up your career as a journalist — and once you start working for us, there's no going back."

"If I say no, you bring your pit bull back in here so he can put a gun to my head again, is that it?" Edna asked.

"Bill Donovan works for me," said Menzel. "I can make sure you don't cross paths."

"But who do you work for, Dr Menzel? And please don't say Harvard University."

"I retain a chair at Harvard. As I think you may know, I'm also a member of the Majestic Twelve group of consultants that reports directly to the President. But today, I'm here in my capacity as the Director of the Verus Foundation."

"Never heard of it."

"I'd be concerned if you had."

"Verus...as in truth?"

Menzel looked impressed. "Very good."

"Is the irony intentional?" Edna jeered.

"It is the task of Verus to document the unpalatable truth. The facts that are kept hidden from people for their own peace of mind."

"You mean you hide the truth."

"One day, perhaps, our work will be revealed to the world. But not until the world is ready for it."

"Who gets to make that decision?"

Menzel smiled. "A very good question. One we must keep asking ourselves. I believe you to be someone who will always question our motives, challenge our beliefs. This is a good thing. I find myself all too often in the company of like-minded old men. To be honest, it scares me. Us scientists need to be challenged. I believe you're just the person for the job. Lee Tavon thinks so too. In fact, this was his idea."

Edna thought about that. "You'll be keeping him under wraps, I take it."

Menzel and Vandenberg exchanged a knowing glance. "Of course," said Menzel.

"How does a man of science rationalize hiding the truth? Aren't you supposed to be about advancing human knowledge?"

"Some knowledge is as powerful as an atomic bomb, and just as destructive," said Vandenberg. "We're guardians," said Menzel. "Protectors."

"More like high priests."

Tavon's words had come back to haunt her: *science itself will become compartmentalized by belief.*

"You're not leaving me with any choice," she said.

"Oh, you have a choice," said Vandenberg. "Work with us, or spend the rest of your life in places like this. You'd be what the Russians call a non-person. We'd probably have to move you offshore — Africa, India, Indochina. You'd never see friends or family again."

Edna shook her head. "A pack of bastards, the lot of you."

Menzel leant back on his chair. "Is that a yes?" She said nothing. "It's not nearly as bad as it sounds," he continued. "I'm offering you an incredible opportunity. I'll pay you a lot more than you could ever hope to make as a journalist. And you'll be on the inside. All your questions answered."

"What about Johnny Galbraith? What have you done to him?"

"He's fine," Vandenberg assured her. "Johnny doesn't remember much. As far as he's concerned, we released him and he went on a very long bender. He woke up in bed with some queer who showed him photos of their night together. He won't be saying anything to anyone."

"He's a bright kid," said Menzel.

"I hope you haven't broken him," she said.

"He's strong. He'll be fine," said Menzel. "He has his job back, at least for the moment. He got a rap over the knuckles for losing you, that's all."

Vandenberg added, "We considered killing him, but then we thought that might not be the best way to earn your respect."

Edna glared at him. "I thought you said you weren't the Gestapo."

"If it's any help, your old job won't exist much longer. Bazy Miller has resigned. We understand Colonel McCormick's selling the paper to the *Washington Post*."

Edna knew it was going to happen, and still she couldn't believe it. "They'll shut the place down."

"I think that's the idea, yes," Menzel agreed. "Swallow the competition."

She shook her head and tried to breathe. It was a lot to take in. "I spend four days locked in a room and the world goes to hell."

Both men were staring at her with an air of expectancy.

"One more thing," said Vandenberg. "You'd need to give us your source on the MJ-12 meeting. We can't have internal leaks. Who told you where to find us?"

The final test — a show of faith to prove she could be trusted. She imagined Fournet and Cabell being marched out in handcuffs. Good men. Loyal Americans who'd simply dared to question a culture of secrecy. Vandenberg was asking her to sell her soul by betraying the confidences she had made as a journalist. To blow up all the bridges. So, she'd give him a name; she didn't even have to lie. "You were my source, General Vandenberg. I tailed you all the way from the Pentagon."

Vandenberg's face went ashen. "That's impossible."

"It's entirely possible. Your name was on the Hillenkoetter letter. We guessed a Majestic meeting would be called after the first Washington sighting, so we set up a surveillance operation and waited. We played you at your own game."

Menzel shook his head and quietly chuckled to himself. "I think we owe Gordon Gray an apology."

Vandenberg stood up and pushed his chair back angrily. "Son of a bitch."

Menzel extracted a sheet of paper from his folder and swung it around so Edna could read it. He placed a pen beside the paper. "It's a security oath. Sign this and you leave journalism behind forever."

Edna Drake stared at the paper. "If I do this, I'd have a condition of my own. One that's non-negotiable."

# FIFTY THREE

July 31, 1952

Edna stepped through the front door of the farmhouse and found herself blinded by the bright morning light. She hadn't been outside in days, and the glare hit her like a spotlight. She held up her hand to shield her eyes, blinking away tears as she struggled to adjust. She could see Donovan in silhouette. She knew that figure anywhere; it had been haunting her dreams.

"You've either signed the non-disclosure agreement, or you've overpowered them all and you're making a daring escape." He was trying to sound witty. Edna thought it came off as awkward, but then she wasn't inclined to allow Donovan the privilege of wit.

"Last time we met, you were a hair's breadth away from shooting me. Was that really a bluff? Because it felt like you wanted to pull the trigger." She blinked a few more times and thought she saw a hint of self-doubt creep across his face.

"I don't know how much they've decided to tell you at this point," he said.

"Dr Menzel says to tell you the curtain is lifted and you should feel free to talk openly."

Donovan turned away. "Still doesn't feel right. I'm not much of a believer in 'Road to Damascus' conversions. Especially on matters as important as this."

"That's OK. I'm not much of a believer in Paul the Apostle."

Bill Donovan wheeled around to confront her. "You have no idea of the world you've entered. And I doubt you understand the severity of the commitment you've made. It will jar against every fiber of your personality. Do you realize that?"

"It's not like I had much of an alternative."

"You're a truth-seeker," said Donovan. "Believe it or not, I respect that. Chasing facts and committing them to print, it's a noble profession when it's done for the right reasons."

"Reasons people like you are always ready to define."

"That's all gone for you now. What you know, what you've seen, they'll never let you forget it and they'll never let you tell. For ever and ever, Amen."

She had to admit, it did weigh rather heavily when put in those terms.

"You're what...twenty-seven?"

"I'm twenty-nine actually, not that it's any of your business."

"By now you must have at least thought about getting married," said Donovan.

"Not really, to be honest." Where was he going with this? "I know that's a shock and a disappointment to men of your generation."

"Hoyt thinks you've missed the boat already."

"Spinsterhood, yes I get a lot of that." She kicked a rock and it ricocheted off the hubcap of a car parked nearby with a loud clang. "Of course, that's mainly from older women. Which puts you two in the same category, I suppose, though again it has nothing to do with either of you."

"No, you think you can sleep with whoever you like, and to hell with the consequences."

"If that's true, and I'm not saying it is, it is only because there is no shortage of men willing to do the same. Ever thought about that?"

"Men are wired differently. Maybe I'm old fashioned. I've always believed a woman's place was in the home. As God intended."

Where did he get off talking to her like this? "It'll be a cold day in hell when I start taking moral cues from you, old man."

"Strange as it might sound, I'm trying to help you."

*She doesn't want your help.* Paolo's thoughts were still encroaching upon his own.

Edna laughed mockingly. "Come on, admit it: you'd just as soon line me up against a wall and have me shot."

She expected anger. But his eyes displayed something resembling empathy. "I didn't want to. But you're right, I would've pulled that trigger if I thought I had no choice."

Donovan couldn't hold her gaze. She'd unnerved him. He didn't understand her anger, didn't think she had the right. The constant internal debate bounced around his skull, getting harder to manage. Each day, the debate grew louder. It was getting harder to pick one voice from another. *Tell her everything. No, she can't be trusted. She must be trusted; you have no choice.* She was the last person in whom he could confide. He sensed her staring. Donovan wouldn't tell her, wouldn't give her the ammunition.

"What's wrong with you?" she asked.

"Nothing," Donovan said. "Just a headache. I'm tired."

But it was clear to Edna his problems were more serious than he was willing to admit. "I was there at the Jewel Box when you took Lee Tavon into custody. What did you do that night? Did you kill him? Only to find you had six more to go?"

Donovan had his eyes closed; she knew she'd pushed him far enough. She'd seen this before on the front line, the moment it all became too much and a man's sanity began to unravel. He was right there now, on the precipice. She'd been ready to deliver the final blow, but couldn't bring herself to say the words. Was it compassion, or simply weakness?

She heard footsteps on the landing.

"Bill?" It was Menzel; he sounded concerned. "Come inside, I'll get you a coffee."

Edna knew they'd been inside eavesdropping.

Donovan opened his eyes. "Coffee. Good idea." He tailed Menzel indoors. Vandenberg took his place on the front stoop of the farmhouse.

"You let that man carry a gun?" she asked.

"He'll be fine," Vandenberg assured. "He just needs a rest. Did you tell him?"

She shook her head; Edna had walked out here to tell Bill Donovan she'd made his removal from Verus a condition of her employment. "Better he hears it from Dr Menzel."

Vandenberg stepped closer. "Bill's a warrior. Many people I respect say Bill and the OSS were the ones who really won us the war in Europe. He believed you would start a nuclear war if you went public with that FS-1 letter."

"I think you're greatly overestimating my influence."

"No, actually it's fair to say that up to now, the opposite has been true."

"Everyone's so terrified by the thought of reds under the bed, do you really think people have the energy to get that worked up about visitors from outer space?" Edna snapped. "Why not go out there and tell people the truth?"

Vandenberg let out an old man's groan as he gingerly lowered himself to sit on the porch step. "It's not just about that, though I do believe we'd see global panic on an unprecedented scale. I've seen where you live. You of all people must understand prejudice. People fear each other when they're different — racism is when that fear turns to hate. We fought a civil war over slavery, but ask the negroes in Alabama how that's been working for them lately. The Nazis killed Jews in the millions. We stopped them, but plenty of people in this country think we'd have been better to let them finish the job. How do you think those folks might react to news they're sharing this planet with a bunch of visitors from another world?"

Edna nodded. "I hear what you're saying. I'm still not sure that justifies keeping everyone in the dark."

"Have you given any thought to how it plays out? I mean in the days after the moment of great revelation, after the global headlines about aliens in our midst. What happens next? I'm assuming there's peace between our two peoples. Would they live openly among us? I wouldn't if I were them. Way too dangerous. Which means they'd have to live in enclaves, fenced off from the rest of the world. That's safer, but it's also guaranteed to engender fear and mistrust. People would start saying, 'What are they doing in there? What don't they want us to see?' Next thing you know, some God-fearing good ole boy from Texas starts quoting the First Amendment, gathers a bunch of his buddies together, and it's cowboys and Indians all over again. Except none of those knuckleheads have worked out that this time, they're the Indians."

Edna thought about that a while, and might have been willing to admit he had a point. But Vandenberg wasn't done.

"There's also another consideration," he said.

"What's that?"

"The alien tech itself. Right now, FS-1 is all ours. We're fairly certain no other nation on Earth has their own flying saucer. If we go public now, we'll be forced to share the knowledge. If we do that, I do believe we'll be fighting nuclear wars in space by 1960."

It was a somber note on which to finish, but she could see his point. She could also see the enormous peril of a small collective of men keeping powerful secrets, with so little governmental oversight.

Nothing about this was going to be easy. Edna sighed, and ran her fingers through her hair. She had no answers to the dilemmas

Vandenberg posed. "Donovan just tried to tell me I need to find myself a husband."

Vandenberg chuckled. "He comes across like he disapproves of you, but truth is you could be his granddaughter — you two are remarkably alike. Neither one willing to give an inch. But I know what he's getting at. You're about to dive into very deep water. It's no bad thing to have someone on shore, who can throw you a lifeline when you need it."

"In your experience?"

"My wife puts up with a lot. Bill's wife... You wouldn't believe what she's put up with. He's lucky she didn't divorce him years ago. Our women keep us sane. They keep things in perspective. From here on, your life will be all about hiding in plain sight. You'll have to appear normal to offset everything in your life that isn't."

"What about Bill Donovan? Does everything go back to normal for him?"

"He'll hit the campaign trail with Eisenhower. After that, who knows? Life hasn't held the same allure for him in recent years. He needs a new challenge. Something overseas, I'd suggest. Bill's like a caged bird if he stays too long in one place. Maybe a nice, juicy diplomatic posting somewhere in Southeast Asia. Somewhere he can still be a man of action."

Edna wondered if a bullet might be more humane.

"What I guess I'm saying here is that if you try to double-cross us, we will snuff you out, no questions asked. You breathe a word of our arrangement to anyone and you put them as well as yourself in grave danger. Do you hear me?"

"Loud and clear, General."

# FIFTY FOUR

A ugust 5, 1952

Edna Drake had an hour to pack up the most precious of her belongings from her old apartment on M Street. For the next few weeks, as she got up to speed, Edna would be eating and sleeping at the Verus Foundation offices in Church Street. Her idea. There was so much to take in, and Donald Menzel refused to let files leave the premises. The building had more rooms than they needed, so there seemed little point in living anywhere else for the foreseeable future.

In the end, there wasn't much she'd wanted to take with her. Two suitcases of clothes and makeup were all that would make the transition from the old Edna to the new. Neither her mangy furniture nor the chipped crockery was worth the effort of packing. The new Edna would have the money to surround herself with a better standard of creature comforts; they would provide her with a house as part of her deal.

She took a final look around the apartment and couldn't help feeling a pang of disappointment. As a journalist, she had failed. It was something she would have to learn to live with, but it would soon be the least of her concerns. Edna Drake was, at least, glad to have the chance to pull this door closed herself, so she could remind herself it had been her call.

She heard two knocks on her open door, and Bazy Miller threw open her arms like a long-lost friend. "I really did think you were dead."

"I'm terribly embarrassed," Edna told her. "It was such a lot of fuss over nothing in the end."

"Virginia seems terribly close by for an Army live-firing range," said Bazy.

"They have them all over the country, I'm told. I was livid when they arrested me, but I guess it was my own silly fault. I saw strange lights and put two and two together and got five. Meanwhile I missed the real action back here." It surprised Edna how easily the lie rolled off her tongue.

"Did you read the paper?" Bazy asked. "The Air Force seems keen to write the whole thing off as some sort of weather anomaly. Not sure I'm buying it, but there you go."

"Not your problem anymore, is it?" Edna reminded.

Bazy sighed. "I don't suppose it is. I'm sorry about that too. Part of me feels like I should have put up more of a fight."

Edna knew exactly how her former boss felt. "I hope you and Tank have a wonderful life together."

Bazy looked like she might cry, and gave Edna a hug. "You're sweet."

"Keep that to yourself, will you?"

Bazy walked toward the window. "I don't understand it, Edna. Are you really going to let them get away with this?"

"What do you mean?"

"Come on, cut the crap. It's me. I don't believe this firing range story for a minute. I don't know what they did to you, but you've been gagged. Poor Johnny is a gibbering mess. They did that too, right?"

Edna took a deep breath. She felt particularly bad about Johnny, but she dared not say so now. "They were going to kill us. They still could. You too. Even now, if I put a foot out of line, they'll make me disappear."

"So, what then? You're walking away from a promising career and the story of the century goes untold?"

Edna walked toward the window. She didn't want to get bogged down on this. "Yes, if that's what it takes to stay alive. Don't you see? We can't beat them. Besides, it's not 'we' anymore, it's just me. You've already walked away, haven't you?"

"Goddamn it, I had no choice."

Edna smiled. "Neither did I, Bazy." She understood her frustration all too well. "I'm making a tactical retreat."

"I put in a good word for you at the *Post*."

"That bridge is burnt," said Edna. "I told Phil Graham it was me or Joe Eldridge. He made his choice."

"Oh Edna..."

"I'd have done the same in his shoes." It was another lie, of sorts. The *Post* editor had wanted them both, but she'd made demands Edna knew he wouldn't meet. She needed to be free to leave town without anyone chasing her. "I'm happy to go home to Queens for a while, spend some time with the family. Who knows, maybe I'll find myself a nice young man and settle down."

Just as soon as hell received its first decent fall of snow.

Bazy looked around her apartment. "Well, can I just say anything will be an improvement on this dump. I long for the day they tear down this neighborhood. Urban renewal can't come fast enough."

As good a point as any to bring it to an end. She gave her old boss a hug. "Goodbye, Bazy."

"You'll come, won't you? To the wedding? There's every chance we'll be light-on for friends and family."

"Of course." Edna pulled the door closed on her old life, and they walked down the stairs together without looking back. Bazy's car was parked right outside.

They hugged again; it was awkward, but it came from the heart. "I feel like I failed you," Bazy said. "I'm sorry, Edna."

"You've got more guts than I ever gave you credit for," Edna told her. A tear rolled down Bazy's cheek as Edna picked up her suitcases and walked away.

Edna knew she wasn't going to be able to hold hers back much longer. She made for the fish markets, keen to lose herself in the crowd and the noise one last time.

This was how it would be from now on. No going back. In time, perhaps, there would be things to say to former friends. When enough water had washed away the remains of all the bridges she'd blown up behind her. When their shared past had become a footnote. Until then, Edna Drake just had to keep moving.

# FIFTY FIVE

October 17, 1952

They had talked about this many times. For the most part, their conversations had taken place deep inside the underground complex, beneath the Virginia farmhouse built by Tavon and his people. It had helped to contextualize the topics they'd covered. Edna felt she was beginning to develop an understanding of it all. It had absorbed her every waking moment, and that singular focus had helped her come to terms with this new reality, this strange new world into which she had stepped.

Today, she and Lee Tavon would talk in Donald Menzel's Verus Foundation study with a movie camera recording the conversation. She would be playing the role of the reporter, seeking answers to the greatest questions in human history. It would be a news reel for the ages, but it would only be seen and heard by a handful of people.

When her camera operator gave her the nod, she began. "First of all, could you please explain to us in very clear and precise terms who and what you are?"

"My name is Lee Tavon. I was born here on Earth. But I am more than that. I am also a member of an interplanetary race of beings known as the Outherians. We hail from a now extinct planet, in a galaxy thousands of light years from your own Milky Way. My mind is of Outheria, but my body is human. I am both."

"Can you please explain how and why this has occurred?"

"Our planet is, or was, about three million light years away from Earth. Outheria was engulfed when our sun Zarben exploded in a supernova. For fifty-five of our years — approximately sixty-seven Earth years — we knew this would happen. We had time to make plans to depart from our solar system before the cataclysm.

"Zarben was about fifty times bigger than your sun. We had been observing it closely for hundreds of years, just as we observed the universe around us. We had seen many stars end their lives as supernovae or gamma-ray bursts, and knew that because of its unusually large size this was the imminent fate of our own star."

"You believed your world would die in that explosion?" Edna asked.

"Some planets have been known to survive a supernova, but by then they are no more than orbiting chunks of molten rock. No living thing survives a blast of that magnitude. Our scientists estimated we had at best one hundred years, and possibly as little as twenty-five years, before Zarben ended its life. In galactic terms, we were at two seconds to midnight. What followed on Outheria was a frantic bid to preserve our civilization and our people by any means possible."

"Were there other inhabited planets in your galaxy?"

"We were in contact with several civilizations. But none were willing to accept a world's worth of refugees. We knew we were on our own, and so for several years, life was hard on our planet. We fought amongst ourselves — the rules of law and culture broke down as people pleased themselves, knowing the world was soon to end. But many of us persisted in our efforts to preserve our species. We sent ships into space with thousands of our people aboard, seeking a planet some twenty light years away we knew to be uninhabited, but with a life-sustaining climate.

"We had not mastered interdimensional travel. The fastest our ships could fly for prolonged periods was around one half the speed of light.

It was doubtful they would make it there alive, but many were still willing to take the chance."

Tavon paused to take a drink of water. He appeared calm and spoke slowly and deliberately, like an old person remembering events that happened a long time ago. "After they left, we made another discovery. This is the reason I am here speaking to you today. We developed a way to preserve ourselves in entirety. We distilled our essence — the sum total of our knowledge along with the imprint of a million different individuals — into the form of a virus. This we could attach to almost anything and simply fire it into deep space. We did so many thousands of times, attaching viral information banks to artificial asteroids, giant rocks, small rocks, sending them into the cosmos in all directions. More than one of these rocks has landed on Earth. One of them was found by Lee Tavon. By me. That was in the Earth year of 1938. We are still not certain how long the rock had been there awaiting retrieval, but when Lee picked it up the virus was immediately absorbed into his body. That day, his life, our lives, changed forever. Lee Tavon is the embodiment of all Outherian knowledge. We are also an individual in our own right."

"That's quite difficult to understand."

"I know. It's why we have kept it to ourselves." He paused a moment before continuing with his story. "The next person to absorb the Outherian viral code was Lee's wife, Patsy."

"By doing this," Edna asked, "did you kill them? Did Lee and Patsy die so you could live?"

He shook his head. "Lee and Patsy are still very much alive. Their minds, their spirits were not consumed, but rather augmented with the addition of the Outherian essence. This has been necessary for many reasons. Firstly, it is abhorrent to us that our galactic expansion would take lives. Secondly, it is essential to our survival in your world that we retain an understanding of Earth culture. Arriving here and knowing nothing would have left us lost and helpless. Thus, the essence of Lee Tavon, that part of him you would call his soul, is still within me. But there is another seed, or soul, wrapped around it."

"Like a strangler fig?" Edna suggested.

"Perhaps, except we do not kill our host. We conjoin to live together in mutual benefit."

"Yet isn't it also true to say your host had no choice in the matter to begin with?"

"Yes," he agreed, "this is the sacrifice we demand of our hosts."

"It's a pretty big sacrifice, wouldn't you say?"

"I remember all that I am, all that I was before the Outherians arrived. I can truthfully say I much prefer the new me... Though it's also true to say I would have run a mile, if I had been free to choose in the beginning."

"I heard you use the words 'essence' and 'soul' — do you believe in an afterlife?"

Tavon nodded. "These things we have experienced firsthand. Many of us who have died have maintained communication via the dark space dimension, which is like a sphere within a sphere."

"It sounds to me like you are in the early stages of colonizing Earth and taking over the minds of the human race. Is that what's happening here? Is your ultimate intention to wipe out humanity as we know it?" Edna asked.

"No," Tavon said firmly. "You must understand, this fear of subjugation by a technologically superior alien race is a human supposition. It is a kind of anthropomorphism. In seeking to imagine an intelligent race other than yourselves, you have unconsciously projected human traits upon that race. The growth of human civilization on Earth has always been about divide and conquer, the strongest killing or enslaving the weakest. You assume this trait to be universal. But it's not the Outherian intention. It's essential to our peaceful spread through the galaxy that we become members of the host race on our adopted planets. We become like you, and in so doing we *want* to walk among you. We are Outherian, but we are also human. We are not better than you — we ARE you. Another type of you. And we value both as separate entities."

"Yet as you point out," she said, "we humans are very good at hating one another. What's to stop you deciding the Outherian-humans are the master race and that all others must be extinguished — as the Nazis tried with the Jews?"

"It isn't only the Nazis who've sought to do this. Right here in America, you tried to wipe Indian tribes out of existence. In Australia, Aboriginal people are classed as part of the country's native fauna. In both instances, these assertions of cultural and technological superiority stem from humanity's learned tendency for the strong to subjugate the weak, and to fear all that is foreign. I can't say anything to convince you Outherians won't follow suit. But if this was our intention, it would be far more easily accomplished by remaining hidden. Yet we have chosen to reveal ourselves."

"Are you responsible for the murder of Jimmy Peterson?"

"No. Though it's true we knew it would happen and did not stop it."

"How did you know?"

"We can read the currents of human emotion around us. It became my habit to walk at night to read those currents, to get a better sense of what people are thinking. Sometimes those currents reveal events that are about to occur."

"Would you call that mental telepathy?"

"There is more to it than mere mind reading."

Edna paused a minute, trying to collect her thoughts and not disappear down tangential paths. "I want to talk to you about the unidentified objects that appeared over Washington. Were they yours?"

Tavon nodded. "Built and flown remotely by us. When we saw so many craft appearing, we thought this would get your attention."

"You're saying not all the saucers have been yours?"

"No. Just the ones over the capital."

"Why did you want our attention?"

"We'd hoped to force your hand. To make it plain the people of Earth are not alone. We underestimated how easily you'd dismiss something that had been right in front of you."

"It surprised you the Air Force lied to people about it?"

Tavon laughed lightly. "It surprised us people believed the lie. We see now humanity's capacity for self-delusion is the way in which you maintain the illusion of sovereignty."

"What do you mean?"

"You want to believe everything in this world is under your control."

"What do you know of the other visitors?" Edna asked.

"It is clear there are many others here. We want to help you find them. But our strange arrival in your world necessitated getting your attention in a strange way."

"Why do you think they haven't made themselves known to us?"

"I think they fear your capacity for destruction."

"Which brings me to another important question: are you willing to share Outherian technology with us?"

"We will share what that cannot be weaponized, so long as you treat us with honor, respect and trust. We will not be birds in a cage."

Edna paused a moment to collect herself. "Lee, I'd like to ask you now to bring your other selves into the room."

Tavon beckoned toward people who until this moment had been standing just outside the frame of the camera. Tavon was joined by six identical versions of himself. They joined arms like brothers and smiled as if they were one person, at precisely the same moment. Edna had been around them for months, and still she found it genuinely disturbing. "There are seven of you. But you're not septuplets in the normal sense of the word, are you?"

"No," they said together. Seven versions of the same voice, like Lee Tavon through a loudhailer.

"Perhaps it's best if only one of you speaks," she suggested.

The Tavon who was began the interview nodded and resumed the role of speaker. "You're right. We're not brothers. We are identical versions of the same person. We are all Lee Tavon."

"But you also said you were human. How is this possible?"

"It is via a method we call genetic synthesis. This is an Outherian technology far in advance of Earth sciences. A little bit like the embryo splitting proposed by Aldous Huxley in his novel, *Brave New World*. In our case, we are not splitting embryos to create different people — we are recreating the same person over and again. We use the blueprint of Lee Tavon, his code, and graft it into six identical bodies bred to maturity at an accelerated pace."

"You grew six new versions of yourself?"

"That's right."

"How long did that take?"

"A little over one Earth year."

"I guess the question most people would ask is, why?"

"The viral seed that carries Outheria can also perform other wonders. The part of the virus that pulses in the veins of the original Lee Tavon — me — was transplanted to the repeat versions we generated. In so doing, we not only transferred Outherian knowledge, but the essence of Lee Tavon himself. That soul, or living essence, now exists undiluted across seven separate beings, all of whom are mentally and psychically connected. We are as one.

"In so doing, we have increased our mental capacities exponentially. We are not just seven times as clever, but many times more than that."

"Why seven?"

"We experimented and determined that seven is the ideal."

"Seven being God's number."

The Tavons smiled as one. "Yes," they said.

As if on cue, six of them turned and walked out of shot, leaving the single original Lee Tavon behind.

"You speak to one another via mental telepathy?"

"We are of one mind. Our powers of extrasensory perception are greatly enhanced. In the right circumstances, we also see into the thoughts and intentions of others. At certain times, as I mentioned, we also see the future."

"Are you saying our future is predetermined?"

"Not always. But there are moments in time where events reach a point, making a particular outcome inevitable. In measuring and foreseeing these probabilities, we are able to prepare. Where possible, we act to encourage or discourage predicted outcomes."

"You've sought to change the future?"

"For the better, yes."

# FIFTY SIX

Wednesday November 5, 1952

For weeks before Election Day, Tavon had assured Edna the outcome was beyond doubt. He told her he'd been certain of it since before Dwight Eisenhower had secured the nomination to be the Republican candidate. Ike's election victory was an outcome the Outherians had been happily doing their part to help bring about. Tavon had insisted their actions were honest and beyond reproach. He'd said they'd done no more than use money and influence to sway opinion. That no strange Outherian science had been brought to bear to rig the outcome.

She had no way of knowing if this was true. But he'd told her the seven Tavons had spent weeks touring Republican districts across the nation, singing Ike's praises to men and women of influence. They'd raised concerns about the caustic temperament of Douglas MacArthur. When Robert Taft became Ike's greatest rival, the Tavons went to work at the Republican convention, accusing Taft's forces of unfairly stacking the delegations of southern states with their own supporters.

It worked. The delegations shifted their position, and Texas voted for Ike by thirty-three to five.

All this and much more, Lee Tavon had explained to Edna Drake ahead of polling day. It meant she felt an odd sense of inevitability come election night. Finding herself in the unusual position of know-ing the outcome of a presidential election ahead of time, Edna decided to amuse herself by watching the live television coverage, while pen-ning the story she might have written for the *Times-Herald,* if things had turned out different:

# IKE WINS PRESIDENCY

By Edna Drake

General Dwight D. Eisenhower has swept to victory for the Re-publican Party in the election for the presidency, claiming a landslide win over his Democratic opponent, the Governor of Illinois, Adlai Stevenson.

General Eisenhower won the national popular vote 55-45 percent and left his opponent reeling in the Electoral College vote, which he secured by 442 to 89.

Stevenson only carried nine states and fared poorly outside the southern Democratic bloc.

In conceding defeat, Stevenson congratulated his opponent on his overwhelming win.

"Someone asked me how I felt, and I was reminded of a story that a fellow townsman of ours used to tell — Abraham Lincoln. He said he felt like the little boy who had stubbed his toe in the dark. He said he was too old to cry, but it hurt too much to laugh," Mr Stevenson said.

It took some time for General Eisenhower to officially claim victory, and when he faced his supporters at party headquarters, his words were continually drowned out by the cheering.

However, his first words were intermingled with those of his oppo-nent.

"I am not certain, my friends, whether or not you have read or heard the telegram that Mr Stevenson has sent to me. It read: 'The people have made their choice and I congratulate you, that you may be the servant and guardian of peace and make the day of truth a door of hope is my earnest prayer. Best wishes, Adlai Stevenson."

\*\*\*

Edna was not entirely certain what Mr Stevenson might have meant by making "the day of truth a door of hope". It might simply have been a platitude offered by one politician to another, the sort of remark tossed out like confetti on a bittersweet occasion.

But it might have been something more. Edna couldn't help thinking that, via Harry Truman, Mr Stephenson was delivering a coded message, urging the new President to be ready for a day of truth to arrive sooner than Ike might have expected.

Either way, the Verus Foundation and Majestic-12 must now decide how much to reveal to the new Commander in Chief. As far as Edna was concerned, Eisenhower must see and hear it all. Then again, she'd been at it for months now, and she'd barely scratched the surface. From inside the circle, she'd seen the complexities that compelled the keepers of secrets to guard such knowledge so jealously.

She quietly longed to find a way to bring their wall of silence crashing to the ground.

# What's next:

Caught in a lie on the President's behalf, Edna Drake is accused
of betraying the American people.
*Pagan's Spy* takes the cover-up to a whole new level.

Made in United States
Troutdale, OR
07/07/2023

R00177